FORCE OF NATURE ANTHOLOGY

Seth & Casey, All The Kings Men, Alpha, Delta

RJ SCOTT

Janet,
Love, hugs & kisses
Hope you enjoy
Hugs
RJScott ♡

Love Lane Books

Breckinghamshire
22 Sep '21
xx

Copyright

All The Kings Men - Copyright 2011 RJ Scott

Seth & Casey - Copyright 2015 RJ Scott

Alpha, Delta - Copyright 2015 RJ Scott

Cover design RJ Scott

ISBN - 9781793930323

This literary work may not be reproduced or transmitted in any form or by any means, including electronic or photographic reproduction, in whole or in part, without express written permission. This book cannot be copied in any format, sold, or otherwise transferred from your computer to another through upload to a file sharing peer-to-peer program, for free or for a fee. Such action is illegal and in violation of Copyright Law.

All characters and events in this book are fictitious. Any resemblance to actual persons living or dead is strictly coincidental.

All trademarks are the property of their respective owners.

Dedication

Thank you to Tanja Ongkiehong, Helena Stone, Jessica Matos, Amy Cain & Chris Lamb, who all suggested something along the lines of *Force of Nature* for this anthology title. Kisses, Rj xx

And, always for my family.

SETH & Casey

RJ SCOTT

Love Lane Books

Chapter One

"...New York's LaGuardia and JFK International airports officially closed on Thursday afternoon due to the storm, according to the FAA. Both airports had been open earlier despite significant flight cancellations. LaGuardia resumed operations around 7 p.m. ET, while JFK said it planned to reopen sometime during the course of the night."

Casey McGuire rinsed the last of the mugs and placed it on the drainer with the rest. For some reason, it was always mugs they ran out of in this house. Seth had this idea that the dishwasher ate them but Casey was convinced that they just needed a system to make sure they brought all the mugs back to the kitchen when they were done. Last week he'd found a mug in the bathroom, inside the cabinet, full of cold coffee.

Seth had sworn it wasn't him, but Casey knew it had been.

He didn't make a fuss. After all, what was one full

coffee mug teetering on the edge of a glass shelf? In the grand scheme of things, it meant nothing.

The TV droned on behind him as he took a dishcloth and wiped the first of the mugs.

"...states from South Carolina to Maine are under a winter storm warning and the governors of Georgia, North Carolina, Virginia, New Jersey and New York have declared states of emergency. Forecasters say the northeast states can expect hurricane-force wind gusts and blinding snow..."

The news channels had been warning about this storm for a week, a huge dump of snow that would cripple the eastern seaboard, but that as yet hadn't caused much concern here in Vermont. Casey glanced out of the window at the yard and wished for more snow. That way maybe Seth wouldn't be able to leave the house, and possibly the two of them could have a rational conversation that didn't end with Seth leaving and Casey wondering where the hell he was going wrong.

"...the situation is "ugly" and "dangerous," and people should stay indoors..."

Last night, all Casey had said was that Seth shouldn't forget about his appointment next morning. Seth left the house, clambering back into bed at some ungodly hour, reeking of beer or worse. In his sleep, Seth tried to pull Casey close, but Casey had deliberately scooted up and away, and left his husband in the bed.

Today, at ten, Seth had exploded, accusing Casey of meddling in things he didn't understand, telling Casey he was fine and didn't need a shrink.

Yet another night when one of them ended up on the couch.

"Hey."

Casey stiffened at Seth's soft, gravelly voice. His chest was tight, he didn't want to argue. He wanted Seth to admit there was a problem, because he couldn't handle it anymore. Six months of this had taken its toll. Maybe if Seth had seen the specialists when he should've, maybe if he'd seen a counselor, then Casey would see he was trying.

Seth was in denial, and it was destroying their marriage.

He didn't turn to face Seth; he'd made a decision in the early morning, packed a bag with what he could get without waking Seth, and decided they needed space. If Seth had space he might face up to himself instead of taking it out on Casey.

Seth slid his hands around Casey's waist, resting his chin on Casey's shoulder and sighed. He'd brushed his teeth so the only scent was peppermint, which at least was a step up from yesterday when he'd attempted a clumsy kiss with beer still on his breath.

"I'm sorry," he murmured near Casey's ear.

Casey could turn now, accept the apology, even offer one of his own for pushing Seth, and everything would be normal for a while. Seth could go back to pretending he was okay, and Casey could go back to walking on eggshells and avoiding conflict.

But what kind of a marriage was that?

What kind of a man did that make Casey?

"I know you are," he said. Then he tensed because that wasn't the answer Seth wanted, and Casey knew what would happen next. Seth would go straight onto defensive mode, give some bullshit about how he was a firefighter and didn't need a counselor.

Meanwhile, Seth not accepting any of what he needed was tearing their marriage apart. Casey had been careful with him for a long time, after all, Seth had nearly died. But when months had passed and he was still refusing to listen to reason, that was when Casey realized he'd been wrong in accepting Seth's view on what kind of healing he needed.

"I think we need some time apart," Casey said, and placed the dried mug onto the counter. He eased away from Seth's hold and moved to the other side of the kitchen table. Somehow, having it between them gave Casey the strength to do what he'd decided was the right thing. Seth had this way of holding him, with a near desperation that never failed to have Casey crumbling.

Seth didn't answer at first. Casey stopped himself from repeating the words and hoped that Seth was just thinking. The only noise in the kitchen was the news, focusing on Greyhound buses and the routes being cancelled.

"Why?"

Casey held back his instinctive disappointment when Seth used that word.

"Last night, when I reminded you about your counseling you told me you didn't need it and that you resented you had to go."

Seth crossed his arms over his wide chest and stared at Casey belligerently. He looked so much like some of the teenagers Casey taught that if this hadn't been serious shit Casey would have laughed.

"I know I have to go. Hell, they won't let me back if I don't go. Doesn't mean I *want* to go."

And therein lay the rub. Seth was adamant he was going back to being a firefighter, despite doctors telling him it was unlikely, despite the fact that the damage done to his body was extensive and that his eyesight had been affected.

"And I said that if you didn't get counseling, whether or not you get to go back to work, then our marriage wouldn't survive."

"I don't do ultimatums," Seth growled.

"Please, Seth, you have to see the bigger picture here." Casey pleaded.

Seth stepped closer to him, temper in his eyes, his hands clenched into fists.

"All I see is my fucking husband telling me I'm done, that I'm used up and useless."

"I never said that."

"Every time you tell me I need help you tell me I'm broken."

"You're not getting this, Seth. What about your nightmares?"

"I was trapped in a burning building watching people die in front of me. You'd have nightmares if that happened to you. I'm well enough to get back to work."

"But you have headaches—"

"You can pull someone out of a fire with a fucking headache!" Seth shouted in his face — so angry that Casey took a step back.

When Seth moved closer yet, his hands still curled into fists, his words angry, his temper so close to the surface, something snapped inside Casey. "You're scaring me, Seth!"

Holding Seth through the nightmares, listening to the man he loved as he railed at everything being someone else's fault. Moment by moment, he was becoming someone who scared Casey.

"Get out!" Seth shouted. "I don't care about your shit, or anyone else's shit. I don't need a counselor, so take your bag and get out. I don't need you up in my space, telling me that my career is over. It wasn't you who nearly died and I can make my own damn decisions."

"And I don't need a husband in denial who refuses to admit he needs any help, that he won't ever be a firefighter again, with a hair-trigger temper who scares the hell out of me," Casey snapped and then clapped his hand over his mouth.

Something got through to Seth. It wasn't the statement about his career because, as usual, Seth was avoiding that part.

"I would never hurt anyone," he said, horror in his expression. "I would never hurt you."

"But you do," Casey insisted. "Every day you tell me you're okay, every memory slip, every tablet you take, every headache, every time you shout at me for no fucking reason, you're hurting me."

Casey looked down at his hands, the way they were clenched into fists over his heart. He felt this in his soul.

"You're being stupid," Seth said, and that arrogance was back. The part where all of this was Casey's fault, somehow. "You don't understand what I went through and my process for dealing with it. It's important that I get back to work."

"Your career doesn't define you."

"Not that again." Seth shook his head and disappointment marked his expression. He showed this all the time, that sadness that somehow Casey was letting him down.

Casey didn't want to hear any of this. He might be acting like a coward, but he was done. He needed a time-out, space to get his head around what Seth was doing. Maybe they were done, maybe Seth's career meant more to him than his husband.

He picked up the bag at the door and Seth uncrossed his arms.

"You're leaving?"

"You wanted me to go. You said so."

"Don't lay this on me. Your bag was already packed."

"I need some air, I'm staying for a while at Jessie's."

Seth snorted. "Well, that's one way of not facing our problems."

Temper spiraled in Casey. "You think I'm the one not facing our problems?" he said, his voice louder with each word. "I'm not the one coming back from the bar at two in the morning smelling of beer, avoiding talking, and crying in the fucking bathroom!"

Seth rocked back on his heels, opened his mouth to say something, and for a second, Casey thought he saw the old Seth, the man he'd loved for so long that he didn't know what it was like *not* to love him. Then Seth shut down.

"I'm going to the fucking counseling," he shouted back. "Okay?"

Hope swelled inside Casey. "Good."

"For what good it will do. Whatever it takes, I *am* going back to work."

And there it was. Seth's determination to push his way through pain and mental grief and have being a firefighter his whole reason for living.

"Go and talk to the counselor," Casey began, keeping his voice level, "And then, if you want to talk to me rationally you can find me at Jessie's."

"Wait, I'm doing what you asked for fuck's sake, why are you still going?"

"If I have to answer that question, then that is why!" Casey opened the front door and, as he closed it, Seth roared.

"Fuck you, Casey! You're making no fucking sense!"

CASEY'S SISTER lived five minutes from their house, and he almost jogged it, fear that Seth might come after him making him fly. One hug from Seth, one more empty promise from Seth, and Casey might crumble. Back down. Enable his husband's denials. He couldn't do this anymore. He was tired, grieving, and he had to cut ties so that Seth could work things out for himself.

Jamie, his nephew, opened the door on the second knock, grinning at first, and then his smile fell.

"I'll get Mom."

Casey followed him into the house, straight through to the kitchen and took a seat before his sister said a word. She made him coffee and put it in front of him, then looked pointedly at the bag.

"I'll make up the back bedroom for you," she murmured. She placed a hand on his, squeezing it gently. She'd been Casey's sounding board since the day they'd pulled Seth from what was left of a destroyed office block. Held his hand when he cried, as they waited to see if Seth was even alive under the rubble, hugged him with relief when they found him.

Then three months later, when she'd realized Casey was holding back on her, she'd prodded and poked about how Seth really was. She understood Seth needed help, that the pressure on her brother and his husband was unending, and was totally encouraging.

Casey needed unconditional love and support from someone.

Sadness consumed Casey, and for a while he thought about what he'd just lost.

No. That wasn't right.

Actually, he'd lost everything the day the man he loved had responded to a call about a kitchen fire in an office building and had chosen to go inside against every order. He'd lost Seth the moment the walls had collapsed around him and the people trapped inside.

"What happened?" she asked finally, and Casey knew he owed her something.

"He said…" the words wouldn't come, his throat tight, tears not far off. "Said he doesn't need the counseling. Said he's fine…and I didn't…I couldn't…"

"It's okay, little brother, this will work out, Seth and Casey are forever. Right?"

Everyone said that.

They'd been together continually, friends as kids, met in college, fell in love. They were solid as a rock, and so in love. They were Seth/Casey.

"What if that isn't true anymore?"

Chapter Two

ANNETTE WILD, SETH'S DEPARTMENT-MANDATED counselor, had counseled people after much worse than what he'd been through; first responders whose entire lives had been destroyed by disaster. He admired her experience, and the concept of her being there for first responders in their time of need.

"How are you feeling?" she asked as soon as they'd finished with introductions.

"Can we start with an easier question?"

She inclined her head, the tiny crystals hanging from her ears swaying with the movement. He'd thought she'd be grim and focused, if anything she smiled just a little bit too much.

"Are you sleeping?"

"You call that easier?" Seth joked, although it wasn't really a joke. He *was* sleeping, but not enough, and when he did sleep he would wake from dreams he didn't recall with panic and fear flooding him. "I sleep," he finally admitted.

"How long?"

He could lie now, but he'd looked at himself in the mirror after Casey left, after the temper had receded and he saw what others must see. Bags under his eyes, exhaustion bracketing his mouth. Tension.

"Couple hours a night, some in the day."

She made some notes.

"Specifically, how much in the day?"

"Depends on the day."

"Okay, how much yesterday."

"An hour in the afternoon."

"Are you having nightmares?"

"Not that I remember."

She nodded, scribbled some more notes, and then looked up. She had the warmest brown eyes, but they weren't flooded with compassion or understanding. He'd expected her to be all touchy-feely, but so far, she'd stayed on her side of the room. He sunk deeper into the sofa after the first few minutes, feeling more relaxed than he'd thought he'd be. Hell, if all she was asking was these simple questions then he could get this checked off the list, show Casey he was wrong and that he just needed to mend physically and then he'd be done.

"When can I get back to work?" That was all that he cared about.

"You say you don't recall the nightmares."

What? "No, I said I don't remember—" he stopped.

"Which implies you think you might be having them."

Fuck. I need to be more careful.

"We all dream," he defended.

Questions became more generic. He talked about his mom, his dad, Casey, but he kept the answers on the surface, nothing she could dig into. Then, abruptly, she changed direction with her questions.

"I had a note you attend your medical appointments regularly."

"I'm ready to go back to work. You're the last box I need to get checked"

"Yet, it's taken you six months to see me."

"No disrespect, but you're not as important as me getting my fitness back."

She didn't disagree, just made notes. Then she tapped the folder on her lap, "I see here that your medical team is considering opportunities for you."

"Yes, they are. Timescales for returning to work."

"I must admit I read it differently. I see there is an option for medical discharge on the table."

Seth shook his head. "Not my option. I'm getting better every day. Are we done here now?"

They had to be done. Seth was hot and irritable and he needed this to be *done*. Screw the department and their mandated shit. He was over this poking and prodding of his brain.

He'd said as much to Casey last night, and he'd expected his husband to hug him and tell him it was all okay and that he didn't have to do anything he didn't want to do.

But in actual fact, Casey had guilted him. He'd listened to Seth explaining how the counselor wouldn't help, and all Casey had done was tell him that the counseling was an important part of Seth's healing and that Casey wanted him to go. Actually, that he was desperate for Seth to get *help*. Then Casey had smiled at him; that sad, small smile which never seemed to leave his face these days.

Seth tried his hardest to argue with his conscience, but if he wanted back on truck twenty-three out of Poultney, then he had to get the all clear from Annette. Of course, he needed the doctors to agree he was okay as well, but they were taking their sweet-ass time.

So here he was, *guilted* into talking, pushed, kicking and screaming, into having to discuss things that no sane man wanted to.

"Tell me about the last few days, quite apart from sleeping."

"It's been okay," Seth lied. Everything had been far from okay.

Three shouted arguments with Casey.

Four cold disappointed silences.

One night on the sofa.

And that was just in the last two days.

And this morning when Casey had looked at him steadily and said that Seth scared him.

"Define okay," she prompted and then waited.

"I'm bored." Not that this was an answer, but he really wanted to get back to work of some sort. Okay, so his injuries would have him on desk duty for the longest time but structure would be good. He needed it because he would die without it.

"Tell me more about your husband? Casey, right? "

"I already told you about Casey."

"You told me his name," she corrected quickly. "How long have you been married?"

"Five years."

"And does he support your wish to return to work?"

"That's not his decision. It's mine. We have our own

lives and Casey's married to a first responder, of course he supports me."

"I would just like to get a better idea of how things are with him, specifically in relation to you."

Things? Things were fine. Casey was fine. Apart from the arguments and the separate beds, and the fact that this morning Casey had packed a bag to stay at his sister's.

And what the hell was wrong with that? Every couple needed space at times and he and Casey had been together since college.

Relationships changed, that was life. Maybe they couldn't be Seth/Casey forever. No partnership lasted eternally.

"He's okay." Seth lied. Actually, Casey looked sad all the time and didn't want to talk to him, but that didn't matter here in this room. He'd work things out with Casey eventually. Or not. Either way he was getting back on the job where he belonged.

"Often partners, family, they suffer along with the person sent to see me. A client's mood swings, anger, grief, it affects everyone. My job is to look at the bigger picture."

What did Casey's mental health have to do with getting Annette and the department off his back? Seth had an idea of what these people were like. Sneakily, they would circumvent the words he used and end up making out that things were a million times worse than they had ever been. Look at his mom, years on antidepressants, diagnoses that contradicted each other. No one had actually known what was wrong with her until a brain tumor had taken her, and all that time spent with shrinks had been proven to be a waste.

"Tell me more about your family."

"Jesus Christ, define 'family'." Seth snapped, and then sat back in his seat, forcing himself to relax. "What do you want me to say that gets a check in the box to allow me back to work?"

"There are no boxes here," Annette said. "You said both your parents are deceased."

Seth held back the need to yank the notebook from her hands. Why were his parents relevant to his job, or the accident, or getting the hell back to where he belonged? He shifted in his chair and his muscles tensed. He was ready to leave and he wasn't going to talk about his family with someone he didn't know. They were both dead. End of story.

"Can you tell me a bit more about them?"

No.

Seth hesitated. What was there to tell? Carefully, he considered his options.

"Mom died when she was thirty-seven, brain tumor, I was twelve, in school." Seth added the details he knew Annette would ask for, before she could even open her mouth. "Dad lasted for another ten without her, didn't make it out of a car accident when he was forty-six. I was twenty-two, in college, and no, I don't miss my mom and no, I wasn't close to my dad."

There. He had summarized his family life in a couple of sentences and she couldn't ask him anything else. If anything, he felt a little smug that he'd forestalled the kind of crap he didn't need right now.

"You say your dad *lasted* for another ten, what do you mean by that?"

Oh fuck.

Seth wanted to leave right then. He nearly did. The muscles in his legs bunched, but of course the snap of pain reminded him why the hell he had to stay where he was.

"It was just a turn of phrase."

"Was he ill?"

Jesus, she isn't leaving this alone.

"Easy, my mom and him were close. He was devastated when she died and never got over it."

"How did your dad's grief make you feel?"

Stupid question. "My mom died, how do you think I felt? I never even noticed his grief, I had my own to deal with."

"Did your dad turn to you for comfort in that time?"

Seth snorted a laugh. "Dad didn't need me, he just needed Jack, José, and his career."

"He was a firefighter the same as you?"

"Yes." He really didn't want to admit that. Why, he didn't know, but just from that question, he guessed his dad's choice of career was important. Clearly, some major fucking milestone in the 'fix-Seth' horror was happening here.

"Is that why you wanted to become a first responder?"

"Partly."

He wasn't good at these one word answers. He should have just said yes and be done with it.

"And the other part?"

"I think you're born into the job—that it's in your genes."

Like all kinds of other things, drinking for instance. What I wouldn't give for a whiskey right now.

"Tell me a memory you have of your dad when you were younger."

"Crying and drinking aside you mean?" He didn't give her the chance to answer that rhetorical question with further probing. "I remember him coming home smelling of smoke and I'd stand with him in the kitchen making dinner and we'd talk about the call he'd gone to."

"But one specific event?"

Jeez. One event out of all of his dad's stories? Some of the stories had been given to him after his dad had died, from friends and colleagues who had kept an eye on him. Strong tales of heroism and fighting the demon that was fire. Then there were the stories that made him laugh.

"How about the one where he nearly pissed himself?" Seth began. "They were clearing a post-fire building, working with forensics, and it's eerie in a building that's been burned. None of the shapes make sense, like, a wall comes down on top of a desk and you think there's no room there but it's still under this weird melted shape. It is dark and wet everywhere, and the smell of burning and smoke is acrid in your throat. So, my dad is scouting the top floor, and his buddies hear a yelp, and they go running to find out what's wrong, fearing the worst, and it's a cat. Way my dad tells it the cat, who decided a burned-out building was a good place to explore, was under what was left of this wastepaper basket, and when it moved so did the basket. Scared the shit out of my dad."

"Why is that a special memory?"

"It's funny, and hell, it made my mom smile, and not much made her smile."

"Why?"

"No," Seth said. "We're not here to talk about my mom, or my dad, or some memory that probably wasn't even true. Sign the letter to clear me. I'm fine."

She countered. "Not yet."

He stood then, even though there was fifteen minutes left on the torture clock and headed for the door.

"I'm done," he announced.

"Call the office to make another appointment."

She didn't call him back, or chastise him for leaving, but it was only when he was on the street inhaling lungsfull of icy-cold air that it hit him just how rude he'd been. She had a job to do, as much as he had, and he'd been brought up better than this. He turned to go back in, but a tall, skinny woman got to the door first. He recognized her from school, a paramedic he recalled, married with kids. She had the same haunted expression in her eyes that he saw in his.

What kind of horrors had she seen?

He let her in first and then changed his mind about following her inside.

Really. Right Now. All he wanted was a drink.

Chapter Three

Casey hated that there had been no sign of Seth. It was as if he'd gone off to the counseling and then vanished off the face of the earth. Casey had rung the bar, the gym, even gone home to check, but somehow Seth was avoiding everyone.

And he hadn't come to see Casey, which didn't bode well at all. Had he even gone to see the counselor? Fear was Casey's constant companion; Seth had been focused on getting back to work so much and the only thing he did outside of worrying about getting back to work was drinking.

"Uncle Casey?" Jamie asked from his side. "Are you staying with us for a long time?"

Casey roughed his hair; there was no way he was dragging his nephew into this. He was mature for fourteen but it was Casey's job to hold it together.

"Uncle Seth just needs some space to think, and I wanted to spend some time with my favorite nephew."

"I'm your only nephew and you see me at school every day."

Casey grabbed him and gave him a thorough and dramatic noogie which had Jamie laughing so hard that Casey couldn't help but smile.

"Is he still coming to Shorefields with us?" Jamie asked when they separated and fell back onto the sofa with game controls in their hands. Casey hadn't even considered some of the things the two of them were supposed to be doing together. As the school visit to Shorefields, the dinner at a fellow teacher's house, or the awards ceremony at the station for local heroes. Everything was up in the air now that Casey had officially walked out on Seth.

Maybe he should have held his fears back and pretended just a little longer?

I hate that I even think that.

"Of course. He said he would."

Surely the last thing Seth would do was let down his nephew. He adored Jamie and the two of them had this whole relationship based around football teams that went right over Casey's head. Or at least Casey allowed it to go over his head and let Seth and Jamie have their Uncle/Nephew time.

"Cool. Because Andy says he can build the biggest snowman, but he won't, not if we have Seth on our team. Remember last year's trip? We so beat everyone."

They carried on playing but Casey was lost in memories of what last year had been like. Before the accident. Before he'd nearly lost Seth.

"What about the Snownado?"

Casey snapped back to the here and now right about

the time his controller vibrated to show him he was dead. "The what now?"

"Like Sharknado only with snow. I saw it on the news, a monster storm heading for New York. They've been warning us about it."

Casey had already checked the advisory service and cleared the visit with the parents of the kids he was taking. This was Vermont, they knew snow, and none of the warnings covered the state, so he doubted it would head this far inland. This town was used to snow, they could handle anything thrown at them. They were using the van Casey had bought a while back, with snow tires, serviced regularly, and which comfortably held the kids and him. He wasn't stupid. He had shovels, and blankets, and all the other gear that a well-prepared Vermonter would have. Anyway, if it snowed heavily while they were up there, then they could go to the education buildings on the land and drink cocoa and play games.

"It's all good."

Casey sat on the sofa half watching the television and half lost in his own thoughts when Jamie vanished to take a call from one his friends. Jamie bouncing back into the room startled him.

"Uncle Seth is here."

Casey stood immediately and there in the doorway, looking exhausted was Seth. They stared at each other for a long time. Jamie got the hint, vanishing with a murmured, *later.*

"I went," Seth announced.

Casey wanted to be pleased, hopeful even, but Seth's tone was clipped and forbidding. He didn't sound like a man who was coming to terms with his demons, and

Casey's chest tightened in worry. What should he ask? Should he question methods, or poke at what Seth had talked about? His own counselor had suggested Seth work at this in his own way and that Casey should give him time. But, time was breaking them apart.

"Was it okay?" he asked, cautiously.

Seth shrugged. "I'm not going back."

Right there and then Casey's world crumbled. The counselor was his last hope in an increasingly bleak landscape at home. It was stupid how he'd put so much optimism into that one huge thing.

"Did they…did it make you see…?"

"I don't need that shit. Casey, this is stupid. Come home."

"You need help." *I need help.*

"Fuck's sake," Seth cursed and stepped fully into the room, pulling the door shut behind him. "Casey, you're supposed to love me, and this is not what I need from you."

"I do love you."

"Then I need you to understand what kind of a man I am, and that I don't need a shrink messing with my head." His tone was pleading, and there was still affection in the tone. This wasn't angry-Seth, this was cajoling Seth, the one who could get around Casey and leave him feeling as if he was in the wrong. "I just need to get back to work, and I can do that on my own."

Casey closed his eyes briefly, and shook his head. "You can't do this on your own."

Seth smiled, and moved closer, placed his hands on Casey's biceps and held him. "That is why I have you."

Horror and shame in equal quantities flooded Casey.

He should be the one helping Seth, he had to be the person who was there for him. Then the horror won out.

"I can't," he blurted, and pulled away from Seth. "You're angry all the time, and when you're not angry you're judgmental, and oblivious, and you're drinking way too much, and you won't listen to me, so why would it change now."

Seth's cajoling expression dropped and in its place was cold calculation. "If you loved me…" Seth left the words hanging. Casey shoved Seth, causing him to stumble back, wincing and cursing as his knee took his weight.

"Don't do that, don't you fucking dare tell me that if I loved you I would be happy being your emotional punching bag, because I'm not, okay!"

Seth's eyes brightened with emotion.

"Then we're done," he said, and yanked open the door. Casey heard the slam, and he froze in place.

Jamie's voice snapped him out of his stupor.

"Uncle Casey? Are you okay?"

Casey turned to face his nephew, careful to keep his expression neutral. "I'm fine, Uncle Seth is tired is all."

"He was fucking angry."

"Language," Casey said automatically.

"I'm not sorry," Jamie murmured. "He's made you sad and angry and I don't get it."

Casey hugged his nephew, and by unspoken agreement they went back to playing games.

An hour into mindless zombie killing Jamie called a halt to the game.

"I'm sorry Uncle Seth is making you sad," he offered.

"We'll be okay," Casey lied.

Jamie leaned into him. "He's not coming with us to Shorefields is he?"

"I don't know," Casey murmured into his nephew's hair.

"Doesn't matter, we'll still have the best snowman just me and you."

Casey pressed a kiss to his nephew's head and tried not to think about his heart breaking.

THE NEXT MORNING Casey tried his hardest to be the best uncle and the greatest teacher in the entire world. His act was flawless, and the veneer of happiness was enough to cover the broken heart he was nursing. He hadn't slept much. He had spent a lot of time staring at the ceiling of his room wondering what to do. He'd tried the hard approach, stopped enabling Seth's behavior, got him to talk to someone, everything his own counselor had said he should do.

And he'd fucked it all up.

Because none of that had worked and now Seth had said they were done.

What did he mean by that? Was he done with this relationship, or would they find their way back? They'd been married five years, and Casey couldn't imagine loving someone the way he loved Seth. How could they be done? How could something so right fall apart so badly?

Despite feeling heavy with anger and grief, he was determined not to ruin things for his small group of kids. He played his part and he hoped that not one of them would know he was anything but excited about the trip.

Except for Jamie who kept looking at him sadly, and every so often patted Casey's arm.

Shorefields was a birthday trip for Jamie but also a reward to these kids for hard work. They were all friends, and the ten of them were a fun group.

The Shorefields complex had once been a large house set in extensive grounds, now used as an education center, with activities and classrooms, and a big adult playground with zip lines and large climbing frames in the area.

The caretaker, Owen, met them in the parking lot. "You sure it's okay if I leave?"

Casey shook his hand, "No worries, I can take it from here."

"Keys for the main house," Owen explained and handed them to Casey. Then he gave a grateful smile. "Better you than me," he said, as a snowball hit Casey in the back of the head.

The snowball fight had been intense, and fun. The snowman building as hard-fought a competition as the Super Bowl. All in all, when the playing stopped and it was time for food and hot chocolate, everyone was tired out from all the activity. The sky was blue but clouds threatened snow.

"Snownado is coming!" one kid called out, and then all of them ran around like headless chickens laughing and rolling around. Casey reminded himself that his van had chains, the storm was still west of them, and in half an hour he'd have the kids home.

Then he could hunt down Seth and face this head on.

If Seth/Casey was over then Casey wanted to be part of the decision-making process. He wasn't taking Seth's *we're done* as the end of everything.

Only, after ten minutes drinking cocoa and sharing the storylines of horror movies, the quality of light changed radically. The sky had become black with snow clouds, grey and dirty and heavy.

"Time to go, kids," Casey announced and received a chorus of groans.

They pulled on coats and boots and grouped around the door, but when Casey checked out of the window he could see the snow was heavier than he'd expected.

They made it to the van but the snow stung on bare skin, and the sucking heaviness of it was enough to knock one of the smaller kids off his feet. When the snow worsened, it happened fast, more severe than any blizzard he'd seen before, and Casey had to think on his feet. They were twenty minutes from town. He could drive them back to their homes and family, or they could wait this out in the house.

Five miles to town. Then everyone would be back okay. It was an easy decision to make.

He herded the excitable kids into a group and ushered them into the van, closing the door on the weather and slapping his hands together. Not only was it snowing but the temperature had dropped.

"Told ya! Snownado!" Jamie informed everyone excitedly.

Casey shot his nephew a warning look. "Let's get home, belts on."

The kids all settled, oohing and aahing at the snowstorm. Nothing this exciting happened in Rutland County, Vermont. The van was covered in snow, the windshield wipers not enough to clear the depth and weight of it on each pass, but he could see where he was going. He put the van in reverse and edged out of the space.

The engine made a gasping, groaning noise, and died.

"No, no," Casey muttered under his breath, then tried to restart it.

Nothing. The damn thing was dead.

"What's wrong Uncle Casey?"

"Yeah, Mr. McGuire, what's wrong?"

"Are we going to die?" That last one was from Paul who was known for his dramatics.

Casey thought fast and held up a hand. "Nothing to worry about, we'll call 911 and someone will come and dig us out us."

"Are we going back to the house?"

Casey looked out of the window, couldn't see a thing past the white, and swallowed the small poke of fear.

"Nah, we'll stay here. Wrap up guys."

That caused a ripple of excitement, a group of fourteen-year-olds were in the middle of a huge, exciting adventure.

All Casey could think was that he wished they'd gone back to the house.

CASEY POCKETED THE CELL. He'd not even been able to leave a message at this point, could not even connect to 911. He'd sent a message to the school and one to Seth when he couldn't start the damn van, but he couldn't even be sure it had gone through.

"What do we do, Mr. McGuire?" one of the students asked.

Casey located the source of the question, Kathy in the

pink jacket. She didn't look scared, in fact none of the kids were scared—they were all kind of excited. It seemed that being fourteen and stuck in a blizzard was enough to have them all talking eagerly about worst case scenarios.

I heard about this couple once, they ended up eating dog food...

I can't phone my mom, you think she'll be so scared she'll forget about the fact I'm grounded next weekend?

We might never get out. They'll find our frozen bodies in a year.

"Guys," Casey said using his best teacher voice. The firm one that had the chattering dying down and every one of the ten kids turning to listen to him. They had expectant expressions and Casey wished he could just tell everyone not to worry, but he'd tried turning over the engine and there had been no response. Ten pupils plus himself were effectively trapped inside the van. He considered all the options. The main buildings of Shorefields were a short distance in good weather but in the maelstrom of white outside the van they seemed impossibly far from the parking lot.

He'd heard of people freezing to death trying to reach shelter when they should have stayed where they were.

"We're going to ride this one out," he announced. "Now, can everyone check their cells, does anyone have a signal?"

That was the cue for ten cell phones to be waved in the air, with Jamie climbing into the front of the van and doing the same. Casey tried his again.

"Nothing," the first kid said. Soon, they were all saying the same thing.

"I have one bar," Jamie called over. "But nothing's connecting."

"Okay, come sit with the rest of us now," Casey said calmly. When he'd parked the van, he'd avoided the stand of trees, but reversing out of the space had put them under the boughs. Part of him hoped to hell that was enough to keep off the worst of this, the other part of him knew the dangers of being under trees in a heavy snowstorm. The weight of the snow could break boughs. "We'll ride this out. Settle down, and reserve phone batteries for when the storm eases up."

"What will we do while we wait?" Kathy asked, confused. She was staring at her phone and despite the concern in Casey's head he couldn't help but smile. Take away the cell phones and a fourteen-year-old girl was wondering what the hell she could do.

"Let's sing songs," Matty said from the back row.

Everyone groaned, Casey included, and they all teased Matty good-naturedly. The kid was an *American Idol* hopeful and spent his entire life singing.

"I spy with my little eye," Jamie interjected loudly, "Something beginning with S."

"SNOW!" Everyone chorused and then laughed.

Casey smiled along with them. Yes, they were caught in a snowstorm the likes of which he'd never seen before, in a broken-down van, in the middle of freaking nowhere, but everyone was calm.

"It won't be long. Emergency Services will be here soon. We just need to ride out the storm."

The kids talked among themselves, about music and exams. Casey sat in his seat and faced front. He hadn't gotten through to 911, but the facilities manager knew they were here, and the parents of the kids with him.

Then the snow had increased. Instead of dancing flakes and cute snowmen the sky had turned in an instant from blue with scattered snow clouds, to the most ominous slate grey.

The van not starting is a shitty cliché.

So, the parents knew where they were, and his family knew where they were.

So, no connection to 911 on first go, but he had managed to leave a message on Seth's phone before trying 911 again and realizing he had no bars on his phone.

Jamie slipped into the seat next to him. "Did you manage to get through to Uncle Seth?"

"I did. He'll pass it on to the station."

"Think he'll be worried about you?" Jamie asked with perception way beyond his years.

Casey tried for diplomatic. "He'll be worried about all of us."

Ten kids and a teacher trapped in a van in a snowstorm that was showing no sign of letting up? Yeah, Seth would be worried. It didn't matter what state his and Seth's marriage was in, Seth'd do his damndest to get help to them.

Casey watched Jamie move away and sit opposite Chloe. Jamie was sweet on the girl but he'd yet to pluck up the courage to ask her out. Maybe there would be a side benefit from the whole trapped in the snow thing. Maybe Jamie would finally ask Chloe for a date.

Chuckling internally at the thought, Casey turned around to face front. All they needed to do was wait. He pulled out his Kindle and thanked the heavens that he had almost one hundred percent battery life. He'd attempt to read to pass the time. That had to be a good thing. The digital clock at the top changed from 3:05 to 3:06. He'd left the messages a while back now.

And hell, he couldn't concentrate to read.

How long would it take for first responders to get here? Or at least a freaking mechanic to fix the engine.

Maybe Seth would come himself? But Casey dismissed the thought. Seth wasn't fit for duty yet, not physically or mentally

"Mr. McGuire?" Kathy was at his side. "What happens if we need to use the bathroom?"

Chapter Four

"Is that your phone?"

Seth counted down his reps quietly and disregarded the question. Just like he'd been ignoring the cell phone with its annoyingly insistent ring itself for the last hour.

He knew it would be one of two people trying to get hold of him.

Either it was Jamie calling his Uncle Seth out for not going to Shorefields. Or it was Casey wanting to know what the fuck Seth meant by *it's over*.

Seth had regretted the words as soon as he left Jessie's house, but it was too late to call them back and he was angry and emotional and no good to anyone.

He'd needed whiskey. It took the edge off things.

He wasn't ready to talk to anyone right now, and exercise was what he, and his bum leg, needed. There were reasons why he hadn't gone with Casey, but he would tell Jamie that he was busy. Busy exercising, busy filling in health forms, busy just being busy. Jamie would back off with that hurt expression he seemed to be perpetually wearing these days, but he wouldn't force the subject.

No one pushed a hero too hard.

Worse than Jamie though, it could be Casey. Likely saying something dramatic like *fuck this Seth, I'm not letting you destroy us. Come with me.*

Casey would shove and cajole and use every heart-tugging reason he could to get Seth away with him and the kids in Casey's class to the adventure center. It didn't matter that Seth had called time on their marriage, as if he had control over that at all. As far as Casey was concerned, Seth had made a commitment last Christmas to definitely go to Shorefields this year. It was a birthday trip for Jamie and a reward for the kids from the Christmas show that Casey had directed. Casey did it every year; treated the singers to a day of sledding and snowball fights and hot chocolate. And Seth usually accompanied him.

But this year?

Fuck commitment. A building fire, people dying on his watch, his own injuries leaving him on medical leave for *way-the-fuck-too-long-and-counting* was what he had to focus on now.

"Seriously dude, is that your phone?"

Very deliberately Seth counted out his reps loudly, enough so that whoever was talking at him backed the fuck off. "You want *me* to get it?" the guy asked.

"Two… One…"

Seth lifted the weights and laid them into the cradle. Tensing his muscles, he ignored the twinge in his upper back. Every muscle and tendon, hip and lower, had been torn, or bruised, his femur had snapped like kindling, his spleen gone, burns from ankle to hip, but he was over that now. *I have to be over that now.*

"Here." The guy with the annoying voice handed him his bag. "Nearly tripped over it."

Seth grunted. He wanted to point out that he'd placed the bag on the bench and there was no possible way that this guy could have tripped over it, but he didn't. That could open a can of worms that didn't need opening.

There were no two ways about this; Seth had trouble keeping a lid on his anger with annoying people.

So, he needed to be careful because if he spoke to Mr. Stupid, then he might end up hitting him, which would lead nicely to Seth getting another black checkmark in the permanently unemployable column.

There were jobs out there for former firefighters, his chief had said. Security, fire risk assessment, health and safety, teaching, the list was long. People wanted to hire heroes who could control situations.

None of the options filled him with the same passion as being a firefighter.

What would he do if Annette didn't sign him as okay to work? What if the doctors told him he wasn't fit for duty? Hell, what if the chief didn't want him back?

Grunting again, which was his way of explaining the matter in detail, he grabbed his bag and shoved it back onto the bench. His cell sounded as bag met wood but he ignored it. He wanted to reach in and turn down the volume, or switch off notifications, but if he did that then there was a chance he'd know who was trying to contact him and that was something he *did not* want to see.

He finished his workout, watching not-so-helpful-guy in his peripheral vision in case the idiot started talking to him again. Then it was the showers, letting hot water stream over his shoulders in a steady pummeling action as he went through his stretches.

It seemed like yesterday since he'd nearly died, since he'd been happy with Casey, in their small house on Main. The two-bedroom house was two minutes from the fire station and only a five-minute walk from the school.

But it hadn't been yesterday, it had been half a goddamned year and the accident had taken everything. If Casey didn't come home then Seth would live on his own in the house, now. Completely and utterly alone.

Casey had given up on him.

I've given up on myself.

He knew Casey had a point, that maybe he wouldn't be a firefighter again, but accepting that as an option meant he would give up fighting.

Facing that will destroy me.

Dressed, he left the gym, and stopped at Tammy's for coffee, the shop was next door and piled high with a selection of cakes and cookies. It seemed to Seth this was counterintuitive for anyone who used the gym seriously, like him, but he was grateful for the caffeine hitting his system. Added to which, Tammy, owner and barista, didn't talk to him, simply served him coffee. At least she was bright enough to know to leave him alone and not bombard him with the shit some people did.

You're a hero, Seth. You nearly died, Seth. You're lucky to be here. How do you feel? Can I see your medal?

He imagined the conversation changing a few months down the road.

I'm so sorry about Casey leaving you. What a bastard, leaving you when you were fucked as bad as you are.

They would assume it was Casey who had given up, Casey who didn't want to be with an injured man, a fucking hero for god's sake. When the rumor mill hit them, Seth would put everyone right about exactly who was the bastard in this relationship.

Ex-relationship.

There can be nothing left of that now.

He didn't need a shrink to let him know it was him fucking this up. All he needed was Casey's support and he'd get his life back on track. And what he needed was a shrink to help him come to terms with having to see a shrink. That much was obvious.

He pulled out his notebook, the one in which he detailed recovery, and fears, and turned to a clean page. He'd begun making lists of pros and cons when he was a teenager. It helped him rationalize his mom dying, the fact his dad had become a shell of what he used to be. He even had a list, somewhere, from when he was ten, of how important it was to have a friend like Casey.

Carefully, he drew a line down the middle. Pros at the top of one side, cons on the other. Then he needed a title. What was he trying to assess?

Being a firefighter, he finally wrote.

Pros were easy at first. Money. Security. Camaraderie. Pension. The cons were a little more difficult to assess. After all, he was a firefighter and he couldn't see a downside. Money went on the cons side, it wasn't as if being a firefighter paid as well as some big city financier. Then he crossed it out, because money wasn't what drove him, any more than money drove Casey being a teacher. So, the cons column was empty.

Was that because there were none?

Or because he was just what Casey said he was, a man in denial?

Aha! Paperwork. He hated that, and added it to the cons side. Then he added "bad food" and "night shifts".

Done. See, there was no really bad side to his career. Why did no one else see that?

Grimacing, Seth swallowed the bitter brew and stared at the light, dancing snowflakes hitting the window. The town was pretty when it was covered in white, a blanket of snow that hid the empty shops or the graffiti on the walls of the mini-mart. Snow was good at that, covering all the shit and leaving everything so perfect. Pity it couldn't make his life pretty and cover all the dark miserable parts inside him.

Feeling fortified with the black stuff, he finally reached into his bag, past his gym clothes and his wallet and pulled out his cell. Seven missed calls. Resignation flooded him and he scrolled to the list. Five from Jamie, two from Casey.

He listened to Casey's message, because hell, he was clearly a masochist.

"Today is Shorefields," Casey snapped. "You get your sorry ass out here for Jamie. He needs you here, Seth." There was a heavy sigh on the message, and Seth could picture the defeat in Casey's posture. "Look, Jamie might be my nephew by blood but he's yours because of what we have together. The kid looks up to you. Fucking hell Seth, just do something for Jamie. That's all I wanted to say." Then there was another sigh, and a rushed addition. "For God's sake, Seth, call me."

Pain stabbed Seth in the heart. Hell, he and Casey had met in school, kept in touch in college, had fallen in love, married five years ago and lived together ever since in the house Seth had inherited from his parents.

Wait. The house?

Seth hadn't even thought about what was going to happen to the house, if they were over. It might be Seth's house in name, but not really, because he and Casey were married and at some point, Casey deserved his cut. They didn't have much else to split, not really. Just things. Boxes of clothes and *things*. The posters from Casey's small office, the CDs they'd chosen together but Casey had paid for.

He thumbed to the second message and looked at the timestamp. This morning at ten. Casey and the kids would have made it to Shorefields by now. Filled with trepidation he pressed play.

"You're missed here, you asshole."

That was all Casey said in the second message. No explanations. No whys and wherefores. Only that Seth was missed with a small amount of added attitude.

Yeah right. Who missed a miserable fucker like himself on a fun day out in the snow?

He listened to Jamie's messages all in one go. They ranged from asking if Seth was going to Shorefields, to wanting to know if Seth would take Jamie to exchange Christmas gifts. Nothing about how he *wished* Seth was at Shorefields. Nothing at all. Seth had always been close to Casey's family, not really having one of his own, and Casey's nephew Jamie was a good kid.

For a second, Seth felt he wasn't needed, as if Jamie didn't care anymore, then he realized he was being an idiot and shook off the melancholy.

"Didja see the news?" Tammy asked as she refilled his mug.

"Hmmm?" Distracted Seth wasn't even really listening to Tammy, let alone the TV in the corner of the café.

"Said we're getting that storm," she summarized. "The one they've been warning about."

"Thought that was stopping before it got here?" Seth immediately regretted opening his mouth. Saying anything meant that Tammy would take it as a sign he wanted to talk. He had to smother his irritation when she plonked herself into the next chair.

"Turns out there's been this whole debate, I even heard it on Fox that there's this guy near Philadelphia who says we're getting the storm of the century."

Seth stared out of the window at the snow falling on his town. Nothing out there indicated a storm of the century. Out there was like a Christmas card, not a death threat.

"They're always saying shit like that," he finally answered because it looked as if Tammy was expecting one. It wasn't as if he trusted Fox. They were likely saying it was the storm of the century that would kill thousands, backed up by bright charts rating deaths in order of horror. He didn't say that though, because Tammy was frowning at him.

"Yeah, guess so," she said. Clearly him not rising to the news was enough to stop her in her tracks. "So how you doing?"

And there it was. That question people asked. For a brief, fiery moment, he considered being totally honest—about the headaches, and the pain, and the physical therapy and the nightmares of fire snaking toward him, or the scars that twisted up to his leg. The thought left him as quickly as it had come. No one actually wanted to hear that. They wanted the cleaned-up version.

"I'm fine," he said. That's what he always said. Safer that way.

"Saw you're back at the station," Tammy pointed out.

"Desk duty until I'm cleared, probably a week," he lied. The doc had said no such thing about clearing him for duty but he wasn't going to say that. Being honest only opened him up to more questions.

"Anyway, gotta go, cleaning tables ain't doin' itself." She left him and Seth thanked heaven that she'd gone. He'd trotted out the standard replies and he was done with socializing.

Chapter Five

Leaving the shop, he walked into icy cold air, colder than he recalled from a few hours earlier, and the sky was heavy with snow.

His walk home took him past the station, and as he rounded the corner he saw the engine leaving. No sirens or lights, just the graceful, beautiful, scarlet against the pristine snow.

"What's up?" he asked the young guy in uniform standing at the main doors with his hands around his middle. This was Jeff the new probationer, or Probie, as he was called, brought in to replace Seth. This was a two-ladder station and only one of the trucks had gone out. They covered the eastern part of the county and, even though they were based in Poultney, they were one of the busiest stations in Rutland County.

"Pileup on the highway," Jeff, answered quickly. "Snow's pretty heavy out there."

"Idiots driving too fast in bad conditions." Seth and the probie exchanged nods. The way a car could slide in a few inches of snow in Vermont was something that astounded Seth. Hell, drivers should have been used to it by now. He walked on, past the station, and to their house. *His* house. The clock on the wall inside the door showed it was two p.m. He was done for the day and he didn't know what to do with himself.

He grabbed his iPad, then sat in the chair by the window and looked out at the snow again. The dance was mesmerizing, and he had to admit to himself there was beauty in the flakes. Tiredness stole over him as he relaxed into the cushions.

Casey's chair.

He'll want this—it's his chair.

Casey had sat there and graded papers; had said something about natural light. Seth could picture him there. He recalled the way he'd push his glasses up his nose and frown and smile when he was reading what his students had sent him. When he worked with the kids he had such utter devotion.

As Seth watched the snow he felt more than tired. He'd pushed himself today, and his muscles ached. He imagined each muscle and attempted to relax and he didn't fight when sleep stole him away.

When he opened his eyes, it was dark and he glanced at his watch. He'd only managed a nap.

Hell, I can't even fall asleep when I'm exhausted.

It was only two thirty, it shouldn't have been dark. Outside the window was a white sheet, the quality of the light the dark grey of heavy snow.

Seems like they were right about a storm. His first thought was that Casey was out in this, but then, he remembered how modern Shorefields was. Brick-built building, heating, they'd be fine. Then the blinking of his cell caught his eye. Two messages.

Both from Casey.

WE'RE STUCK, van broken down, it's snowing hard. We're okay, can you get a message to the station to get someone to tow us out?

THE SECOND WAS SHORTER and cut off to static halfway through.

DID YOU GET MY MESSAGE, I wanted—

SETH TRIED CALLING Casey back but all he got was dead noise. He tried the station but then realized he only had one bar of connection. Fear gripped him and for a moment he was paralyzed. How was he going to contact anyone?

What could he do?

His chest tightened.

Oh fuck! What do I do? I have to help him.

He closed his eyes and concentrated on his breathing. When his thoughts were clearer his instincts kicked in.

He needed to talk to the guys at the station face-to-face. He pulled on boots, layered his cold weather gear, shrugged into his jacket. He opened the front door and walked out into an icy hell. Winds so strong they yanked him sideways and had him cursing at the shooting pains in his leg and back. Head down, tucked as much as he could into his thick coat, he stumbled in the direction of the station. He couldn't see the way but he could visualize the path, even if he slid off the curb a couple of times. When he reached the station, he shoved open the main door, nearly falling inside as he tripped over the entrance step. He'd never experienced anything this cold before.

He pushed the door shut against the howling wind and snow and stamped off his feet, coming face-to-face with a terrified looking Jeff.

"We have school kids and a teacher trapped up at Shorefields," Seth snapped out. Jeff blinked at him and it seemed as if the kid was in complete panic mode and meltdown. He glanced worriedly from side to side.

"There's no one here," Jeff said.

Seth waited for a second, then exasperated that there wasn't more of an immediate reaction, he pushed past Jeff and into the main area. Both trucks were gone.

Jeff hurried after him. "I said, they're not here, ladder one didn't come back in from the interstate, and engine two went out to Middleton Springs. There's been a building collapse from the weight of the snow. It's just me."

Seth rounded on the guy and was so close he could see the panic in blue eyes.

"Get on to other stations and call this in—"

"I can't. Sir, we have nothing. No comms, no Internet, nothing."

"Give me a sitrep." Seth ordered.

The probie blinked at him then visibly pulled himself together. He'd had training, but this was probably his first real situation.

"Uhmmm... Both engines out, reports of major

incidents, last said the storm has taken out power. I'm alone here…" He paused. "And sir, I'm not sure what to do."

Seth considered what he'd been told. Ten kids, Casey, Shorefields, trapped in the van, which meant they had maybe managed to get away from Shorefields itself and had no way of getting back. He doubted they were prepared for sudden and extreme weather.

As if a switch flipped inside him, he knew what he had to do.

"Okay. I want you here. You're not to leave and you're to keep your eyes on comms, see if we can get more intel. I need supplies in a bag from the kitchen, water, energy bars."

"What are you going to do?"

Seth looked directly at him. Jeff needed to know where he was going. "There's a vanload of kids trapped up at Shorefields and I'm going to help. I'm taking the Land Rover."

He didn't leave room for discussion, simply presented the facts as a done deal. He should wait for a team, for backup, but there was nothing stopping him from getting to Casey and the kids.

"I don't know… I should wait for… Yes, sir." Seth watched Jeff struggle with the fact that Seth wasn't technically a firefighter right at this moment in time, and then finally accept it.

They split, Seth checking the truck he was going to use, a modified vehicle capable of getting through most of the shit life could throw at it. It was equipped with most of the things he could need. As an afterthought, he grabbed coats from the supply room. He knew the kids would be dressed warmly but it never hurt to have extra insulation if this storm kept up.

He was supposed to have been there with Casey. He'd said he was staying at home.

Time is not right to start thinking I've fucked up.

But he *had* fucked up. Whatever their issues, he should have been there with Casey and the kids today. He was on the road in minutes, the vehicle slipping as it hit the loose snow on the road, then gripping as the snow chains cut into it. He knew his town well and made it to the outskirts quickly. It was only as he hit the open road beyond town that things started to go wrong. The Land Rover could handle it and there weren't any other cars that he could see, but that was the point. He couldn't see. He gripped the wheel so hard his fingers began to cramp and he had to consciously loosen them. He couldn't fight the weight of the snow and the buffeting wind, he had to work with it. The windshield wipers couldn't keep up and the way it was falling right at him was mesmerizing and frightening. He felt dizzy from focusing and blinked, then eased off the gas a little more. The car dipped to the right and he prayed to any god that would listen that he didn't end up in a ditch. Somehow, he managed to straighten, only using the tree line that would loom every so often through the snow, to keep himself level and on the road.

I'm coming. Hold on.

Shorefields was maybe five miles from town, the back roads were blocking up as he drove through, and it seemed to take forever. He didn't even look in his rear-view mirror. It was going to be hard, if not impossible to get back to town.

The ferocious wind from Lake Saint Catherine rocked

the car when he reached the outskirts of Shorefields. A sudden push, too powerful to be a gust of wind, shoved the car off the road. The tires slipped and slid, then finally gripped at the last minute.

Fuck! His chest was so tight, his hands locked on the wheel, but one more gust like that and it might take his car off the road entirely.

He thought about the kids trapped in the van. Would that sudden gust have pushed the van over? Where had Casey parked it? Was it sheltered? Was it under trees? Were they all okay?

The snow eased for a short time, enough for Seth to push faster, but he nearly missed the turnoff for Shorefields. The sign was hidden in the snow, the road barely there through the trees.

Please let there be no fallen trees.

Someone was listening to him; the going was slow, but finally he managed to get the Land Rover to the parking lot, or what he assumed was the parking lot. The headlights weren't cutting through the snow and he turned everything off including the heating—no point in wasting power. The cold permeated immediately. Christ knew how cold it was out there with the wind chill. He kept trying the radio as and when he could manage but he'd lost any connection to the station as soon as he'd left. He was just as stranded as Casey and the kids were.

He pulled on every layer he could then he grabbed everything he could carry, bags, ropes, and his knives. Bracing himself, he climbed out of the car and inhaled nothing but ice. The snow burned as it slammed into him. He closed his eyes and pulled on the goggles he'd found among the supplies. They were enough for him to be able to protect his eyes. He spun three-sixty in a clumsy wind-buffeted dance, and there, about ten feet away, Casey's scarlet van. He assessed the situation as best he could, alarmed to see the back end of the van under trees weighed down with snow. As if he needed confirmation of the clear and present danger, he heard an ominous cracking sound from one of the largest boughs. That tree was going to disintegrate under the weight of the white stuff.

He pushed against the force of the snow until he was as close to the van as he could get. There was nothing he could see except the snow-flecked scarlet while he attempted to make out which end was which. He failed miserably. The wind drove the snow against the vehicle. He had to scrape through the depth of it, blind in the whiteout, until he found something like a door. Then he thumped hard, harder, attempted to shout, but the storm stole his words. Cold forced its way under his jacket, around his neck, took every ounce of energy from him. Then arms yanked at him and, with muffled curses, he was pulled into the van, the storm following him until shouting and pushing had the door shut and he was face down on a metal floor.

"Jesus fucking Christ," he swore loudly. Then he turned onto his back, looking up into the faces of ten school kids and one shocked teacher.

Chapter Six

"Uncle Seth!" Jamie clambered toward him and hugged him before letting out a muffled 'shit' and releasing him.

"Hey Jamie, you all okay in here?"

His training kicked in. Yes, he'd sworn in front of Casey's kids but Casey wouldn't call him on it. Speaking of him, Seth turned his head to look directly at Casey, meeting Casey's worried stare with one of his own. He felt guilty about swearing but he'd be fucked if he was going to apologize for swearing in front of ten teenagers.

"We're all okay," Casey finally said. He appeared confused and glanced the way Seth had come, probably hoping to see more firefighters out there.

"Just me," he explained quickly. "How many've we got here?"

Casey blinked at him and then visibly pulled himself together. "Ten pupils, myself. Owen Foster was here as well, the new caretaker at the center, but he left soon after we arrived." Casey lifted some keys. "He left me keys for the building but I decided to try and get us home."

"Okay. Actually, a good call, but we need to get you over there." Seth imagined the distance from here to the center but was distracted with Casey talking and as he talked, Seth managed to maneuver himself into an upright position. Casey was explaining how they'd ended up in the van and why he thought they should stay here, then he stopped and tilted his head in that cute way he did when he was confused. He glanced at the closed door and at the wall of white outside.

"So, when is everyone else getting here to help us?"

"I'm all you've got, both rigs are out and roads are a mess."

Casey digested the information for a while, then nodded. That was one thing about Casey, he didn't panic, probably part and parcel of being a teacher, and the husband of a firefighter. Ex-husband? Ex-firefighter?

Casey nodded. "Okay, so what do you need us to do? You don't want us to stay here and ride this out?"

Seth's head rang from the force of the storm and he struggled to thread words together.

"No," he said finally. "This isn't safe here under the trees. The snow is a heavy weight on the old oaks. We need to get to the house."

Casey glanced at the kids, who stared at the two adults expectantly. They were all in winter coats, scarves, blankets, but one step outside the van and they wouldn't know which way to go. This was the proverbial rock and a hard place.

"Could this pass over?" Casey asked with way too much hope in his voice.

Seth knew how to filter information to stop panic. He'd been well trained in the ability to hold things back, but what he wanted to say to Casey was that they needed to get the fuck away from the van and get to where there were four walls, heat and food.

"Bad storm," was all he said. But Casey must have read everything else in his eyes because he nodded as he understood the enormity of it all.

"The house is maybe thirty feet from here," Casey said.

"We could all hold hands," Jamie offered.

"The wind is too bad," Seth said. "First off, I need everyone on the front of the van, away from the back." He didn't explain why and was gratified when everyone moved. "I'll go, find the house, tie off an anchor rope, and we use that to guide us to the house. I'll accompany each one."

"We can switch that up," Casey interjected. "Take turns with the kids."

Seth didn't argue; he wasn't going to turn away reasonable help, but this was his show. He rid himself of all the extra weight and took the length of rope. Quickly, he secured it to the steering wheel and hoisted the rest over his head and across his chest, testing the play. Then using his sharpest knife, he cut a length from the end.

"You need to make something that ties around your wrist that you can loop on the guide rope."

"I can do that," Jamie said immediately. "I did knots in Scouts."

Seth passed his knife to Casey. "I'll be back."

Casey took the knife and placed a hand on Seth's glove as he was about to move. "Stay safe."

Seth deliberately tied the end of the long rope to his belt. "I'll always find my way back," he said firmly.

Only when he was fighting through the storm in the direction of where he imagined the house to be did he think back to those words.

I wish it was that easy to fight my way back to everything I want.

He reached the house after god knew how long, uncoiling the rope as he went, watching to make sure that it didn't snag on anything that could cause it to fail. Only when he got to the door did he realize he had no fucking way of getting inside the place. Not caring if he'd regret the action later, he elbowed in the small upper pane of glass and fumbled for the handle and lock. His fingers felt wrong and he tensed and relaxed them, aware his extremities were not handling well the cold. Finally, he managed to grab the handle and yanked it down to open the door, stumbling into the old house.

He stopped for a second to catch his breath and to rub at the pain in his lower back. The doc had cleared him for light duty but the warning words about returning to work on calls rung in his ears. He was going to seriously set his recovery back, but fuck if that mattered. Eleven people depended on him so he pushed through the pain. Forcing past the clumsiness caused by the snow and ice, he tied the rope to an upright post on some steps and hoped to hell that it was secure enough. Then, inhaling one last breath of indoor air that didn't burn his lungs, he followed the rope back to the van. It didn't take as long to get back but when he fell through the door he was pleased to see that Casey and the kids had pretty much done as he'd asked.

Everyone had a loop for the rope, everyone was as heavily covered as they could be and all waited expectantly for the returning firefighter who was going to make things right.

Another thunderous gust of wind rocked the van.

"I reckon this is the snownado," a voice said from the back.

No one answered, and Seth couldn't find it in himself to even lie and reassure. He'd never experienced a snowstorm like this one. It felt as if it was going to pick up his six-four frame and throw it face-first into the snow. He needed to speed this up, they couldn't go with an adult each time.

"Okay, change of plan. We go in twos, stay close, leave a little room before the next two. Casey, Mr. McGuire, you go first with one of the students, I'll go last. We'll split the supplies to a little each, okay? We need to move out now. Is everybody ready?"

The group all looked at him and there were no words of agreement, just grim nods, and hell, one of the girls was crying. That was who he was taking first. He gestured. She came forward and, as she did, she stumbled. Seth couldn't fail to notice Jamie steadying her. The girl cast Jamie a grateful and adoring look.

"Remember our date," Jamie said quietly.

"Hurry after us," the girl answered.

Seth smiled despite his fears. That there was hella cute. "Okay sweetheart. What's your name?"

"Chloe."

"Okay Chloe, attach your rope like this." Seth demonstrated the loop, attaching then closing the rope over her wrist before repeating it on Casey. He tried not to focus on Casey's brown eyes, or the questions in them. He was here doing his job and he didn't have time to think about the worry in that expression, or the fear. Casey wouldn't let his kids see the fear. He was a good guy and a fucking awesome teacher.

Finally, poised to open the door, Seth addressed Casey, and Jamie, and the rest of the kids. "Stay close, if you feel lost, stop, hold the rope and the next person will find you. I'm last and I will scoop up anyone who's scared. Do *not* let go of the rope. Does everyone understand?"

He opened the door enough to let Casey clamber out, watching as he pulled his scarf up and over to cover most of his face. They helped Chloe down, and in seconds, with one last glance at Seth, Casey was lost in the whiteout. The rope moved to indicate they were walking and Seth counted to twenty before ushering the next pair out. Consciously, he paired them depending on different factors, size, weight. He knew he was doing it, but he never said it out loud.

Two by two, they vanished into the white and Seth pushed aside the feeling that he was sending these kids and Casey, out to die.

Not happening.

Finally, it was just him and the smallest of the boys who Seth recognized from the school.

"What's your name?"

"Andy," the kid said with a tremulous voice.

"Okay Andy, this is the easy bit, let's get out of here."

With a smile of reassurance, he climbed out first then held out his hand to help Andy. The ominous crack of the tree boughs above the van had him grabbing Andy and yanking him down as a large part of the tree crashed onto the back of the van. The van jerked and the rope tightened, yanking at his shoulder and pulling his hand up against the door. The pain was sharp and agonizing but he pushed through it. He could worry about pain later.

Andy screamed but Seth simply pulled him to the rope and, half carrying Andy, he felt his way along the guide. He caught up with the two kids in front but they were going at a nice speed and soon the side of the house was visible, the light intermittently visible through the swirling mass of white. He used his body to shelter Andy as much as he could, and at last, with every ounce of remaining energy he was through the front door.

Casey was at his side in an instant, helping set Andy loose and sending him through a side door. He couldn't see any of the other kids and, even though Casey was there, for a second dread filled him.

"I put everyone in the main room," Casey explained as he attempted to free Seth from the rope loop they had used on the main guide. Seth tried to help him but the cold had finally taken every ounce of energy. He had so many questions— was the inner room safe? Did Casey remember how many trees were over the house? Was there food? Was there any heat? Instead, all Seth could focus on was Casey's lithe fingers dealing with the knot on his wrist.

He'd loved watching Casey's fingers, when he was studying, or just watching TV, when the two of them would curl on the big grey sofa. That big old monstrosity had been the most comfortable thing ever. They'd spent hours close together and Seth's favorite thing was to hold hands and trace Casey's fingers with his own.

"Y—y—you 'member tha' sofa?" he managed to force out through chattering teeth.

Casey winced as a blast of cold air forced its way through the broken glass of the front door.

"What?" he replied, then added a curse when the knots refused to release easily.

"T—the grey'un."

"Fucking hell," Casey cursed again. He didn't do that a lot. He was the calm one, the quiet one, the one who was responsible for two classes of thirty kids at the local junior high school. "Come loose, you fucker."

"We—we—used to sit."

The knot loosened and Casey muttered under his breath before looking directly into Seth's eyes. "Stop talking," he ordered. "And relax your goddamned arm."

Seth closed his eyes and concentrated on relaxing his tense muscles. Finally, Casey removed the rope before grabbing Seth and pulling him toward the door he'd indicated before. They really needed to board the broken glass. *We'll do it later.*

Once through the main door, Casey helped him to sit against the wall and carefully stripped off his larger outer coat, then yanked off his boots. He was still shivering but at least he could focus enough on the faces of the kids all looking at him. He counted them, lingering on Jamie and exchanging smiles with him. All ten kids were here. Casey was here. And this room was warmer than the ice hell outside.

"Whadwehave?" he slurred then shook his head. He wasn't going to be giving the best impression if he was freaking slurring.

Andy crouched by him. "You saved my life," he said with no small amount of awe in his voice.

"You'da been okay," Seth managed.

"No, the tree came down, right where I was, you saved my life."

"What tree?" Casey interrupted.

"One of the old oaks," Andy said. "Cracked and fell. Bang!" Andy made a dramatic clap with his hands and grinned.

"It was nothing." Seth sent a warning glance to Andy who appeared to take the hint.

"Go sit with the others, Andy," Casey said gently. "Stay warm."

Andy moved back to sit with the rest of the class who had taken up residence on chairs around a large table piled high with books.

"What happened?" Casey said low and urgent.

Seth ignored the question. "We have heat?"

"No electric, some residual heat, but I know there's a generator. Don't change the subject. What happened?"

"Tree came down on the van," Seth managed. At least the cold inside him was easing off and he could actually form a full, non-shivering sentence.

Casey managed to peel off his right glove but Seth couldn't help the low curse when he went to pull off the left. It was stuck to his hand with frozen blood. "You hurt yourself."

"Caught my hand on the van, it's nothing. Leave it alone."

Casey pressed his lips into a thin line as if he was holding back the words, but then they spilled out anyway, hissed and low and full of anger.

"God forbid I show concern. Were you actually going to tell me? What the fuck, Seth? What if you'd fucking bled to death, you think the kids need to see that?"

Seth opened his mouth to answer, then stopped. What exactly could he say? Casey never lost his temper with Seth. Was he going to say that he wasn't going to mention the injury because hell, what the fuck could Casey do about it? As it was, when Casey managed to ease away the material of the glove, the wound wasn't as bad as Seth had imagined and certainly nowhere near as painful as his shoulder. The burning was intense there and he knew what he'd done.

Casey was poking at his hand, talking under his breath about idiots.

"Casey?"

Casey looked up at Seth and shook his head. "You need to get a bandage on that," he said firmly.

Seth gripped Casey wincing at the stretch in whatever the hell he'd done with his hand.

"Listen to me Casey, we need to block that glass up." That was the most convenient lie he could think of. He just needed Casey back in the other room out of sight of the kids who were all freaking, staring at the two men anyway.

"After I fix your hand—"

"Casey. Now."

Casey frowned and Seth hoped to hell his silent communication was working.

Finally, it seemed as though Casey got with the plan. He stood and extended a hand to Seth.

"Stay here kids, we'll be back in five."

"You need my help, Uncle Seth?" Jamie asked.

"We'll be okay," Seth reassured, even though standing

upright meant every breath he took was like fire shooting through his body.

Only when the door closed behind them separating them from the kids did Seth allow himself to fall to his knees and hang his head.

Chapter Seven

CASEY CROUCHED NEXT TO SETH, HIS HEART IN HIS throat. What was wrong? Was Seth hurt worse than he was showing? Fear curled inside him and he regretted deciding to call the man and put him in danger.

"Seth?" he asked fearful of what Seth was going to say to him.

"Shoulder is out," Seth managed. "Need your help."

Casey sat back on his heels. He didn't know whether to laugh or cry. Seth was hurt and asking for his help? Of course, a dislocated shoulder was very different from headaches and muscle spasms, or even the mental shit that circled in his head, but still, Seth wanted Casey's help.

"I'm going to lie down," Seth said, breathing hard, his face locked in a grimace. Casey held out his hand but Seth ignored it and climbed gingerly on the display table, pushing aside leaflets and souvenirs. Then he lay flat and positioned his body so that his arm and shoulder were hanging over the edge, while the rest of him was supported. He was pale, nearly white and he closed his eyes tight.

"Now what?" Casey asked. He stepped closer to the table.

"You need to hold tight," Seth instructed. He held out the affected arm and Casey took his husband's hand without conscious thought. He nearly pulled away when Seth laced his fingers through his, the touch seemed too intimate, too much of a reminder of what they seemed to be losing.

"Seth?" Casey asked, unsure.

"Don't let go, don't pull too hard. Fuck's sake, hold tight."

"When do I start to pull?" Even though his eyes were adjusting to the dark it was still difficult to focus. He switched on the flashlight on his phone and angled it for a better view.

"Now," Seth screwed his eyes tighter and began some kind of breathing exercise. Casey pulled. Seth's expression changed, his mouth falling open in a silent curse and Casey still pulled. He knew the mechanics of this, the ball joint and socket. He knew the bone needed to slip back in…

"You need leverage," Seth said through gritted teeth.

Casey forced a foot against the table leg and leaned back a little more. Providing constant tension on the arm would stretch the shoulder muscles, and after a few minutes the joint should pop into place.

Please move. He didn't want to hurt Seth like this. Yes, he wanted to punch the guy, and when he'd finished that, punch him again, but real hurt like this…

Slowly, after the tension released, Seth released the

entwined fingers and pulled his hand away. For the longest time, he lay with his eyes still closed, then just when Casey thought Seth had passed out, he opened his eyes. At least they were focused.

"Now we just have to decide what the hell to do next," Seth said. He rolled upright, his legs dangling over the table.

"How's your leg and back?" Casey asked.

"The rope took my arm."

"And you pushed through snow, so I'm asking you, how is your leg and back?"

Seth frowned. "They're fine. I'm fine."

"And your head? Any pain?" Casey stepped closer with his hand extended to touch Seth's head and Seth shrank back a little. Exasperated, Casey moved away.

"Fuck's sake Casey, I'm fine," Seth said quickly.

Casey opened the door to the kids and looked back at Seth. "Far from it Seth, far from it." Then he closed the door. He didn't slam it but he wanted to. If the fucking idiot didn't want Casey anywhere near him, Casey could live with that. Hell, he'd had years of living with Seth and his need to keep everything inside, then through the last few months when Seth had literally shut Casey out. Why would he think there was any connection left?

He crossed to the kids, all ranged in a circle around a large table. A few of them had their cell phones out for light, the rest holding onto theirs as if it was their lifeline.

"Any signal?"

A chorus of noes answered that one. But then, who would they phone? If what Seth said was true, there was no help coming anytime soon. He just wished they could get messages out to worried parents. He glanced at his watch—4:30.

"Okay, everyone, let's turn the lights out on the phones, conserve the battery. And here's what we're doing. Everyone out to the kitchen, we'll get an idea of what food there is. It looks like we're stuck here tonight, so see what we can find to sleep on."

Seth interjected from behind him. "We don't have anything but emergency low lights so I'm guessing the electric is out. I'm going to go kick-start the generator, then everything will be fine."

"Like an adventure," Jamie piped up.

"And I covered the window," Seth said to no one in particular.

Casey turned back to the kids. "We're all safe in here, so, kitchen first."

Casey ignored Seth, although he could feel Seth's gaze burning into his back.

He and the kids bundled through the other door that led to several rooms—two offices, a kitchen, bathrooms, and the back door. Beyond that, Casey knew there was a generator. He'd spent enough time volunteering here as a teenager at summer camps to know the setup. Seth pulled on his heavy coat and disappeared into the hallway.

The actual accommodation blocks were a good couple of hundred feet away, which was a bastard—they could have done with mattresses, as it was likely they would be there overnight, but at the least the generator shed was closer. Still, Casey knew there were supplies here, the laundry was part of this building and two large store rooms held bedding and towels. Looking back at the group that followed closely he held up a hand and they all piled to a stop.

"Okay I'm going to split us up. I need five working on making places for people to sleep, and five in the kitchen."

"I'll organize the beds," Jamie said. He and Casey he exchanged smiles.

"Okay Jamie, can you make up separate rooms in the offices, one for the girls, one for the boys."

"I'll help," Chloe said.

Andy and two others volunteered, and they parted ways, with the remaining teenagers following Casey into the kitchens.

Next to the kitchen was a large dining room but Casey couldn't see an easy way to keep everyone warm in such a large space. They had heating at the moment but no guarantee that the generator was fully fueled for the long term. What he could also see, in the snow-dark beyond, was the wall of white that was piling at a scarily rapid rate against the glass sliding doors between the dining room and the outside. This was not letting up and he had the very serious thought that he and Seth should ascertain whether the roof could handle the weight of so much snow falling so damn quickly. After all, look what'd happened with the damned tree.

"Mr. McGuire?"

Casey blinked back to the here and now and rounded on the five kids left in the group. All of them looked at him expectantly, which was as much as he could make out in the semi-darkness. He found a flashlight through touch alone and switched it on, filling the kitchen with enough light to see what was happening. He opened the nearest cupboard, systematically checking each one and finding a ton of pasta, soups, a lot of canned goods, and the fridge contained milk which smelled okay. He even found instant coffee, which was a godsend, and hot chocolate powder which he pulled out and put onto the work surface.

The lights flickered overhead. Seth had clearly figured out the generator.

The kids cheered and Casey turned off the flashlight.

"Hot chocolate," he announced. "Two of you on that, and the rest with me." Between themselves they organized everything while three remaining kids followed Casey into the walk-in larder. There wasn't a lot of fresh stuff but there was certainly more than enough food to keep twelve people from starving for a good week or so. Unless they froze to death because the generator ran out of fuel.

Casey ignored the inner voice of doom and, instead, pushed through the whole negative mind-set to focus on food. "Soup, bread," he announced. Between them, they pulled everything they needed from the shelves and brought it back into the kitchen. The scent of chocolate hit him as he walked in and the thought made him smile. He hadn't had hot chocolate in a long time. The kids had even found marshmallows and had put them in a bowl next to the steaming mugs.

"Someone call the rest," he said. Then with all ten of them sitting at the large dining room table Casey laid out what he imagined would happen. There was no sign of Seth to disagree, or to tell him he was wrong. These kids needed Casey to be honest with them.

So here goes.

"The firefighter who came for us, Seth, has informed me that he has made the emergency services very aware of where we are. It's only a matter of time before someone comes for us. Meanwhile we have plenty of food, so this will be just like camping." Casey paused and allowed everything to sink in with the kids. One by one they nodded.

"What Mr. McGuire hasn't told you is that this place has a generator, but we don't know how long it is going to last. Also, the storm out there is a bad one and we could be here for days in possibly freezing temperatures, so be prepared. People have been known to die in blizzards, not by being in snow but by being trapped inside somewhere with absolutely no way out."

Casey tensed at the sound of Seth's voice behind him, and even more so at the words. A couple of sentences that had the kids talking to each other with more of that dramatic "we're all gonna die" vibe. He thought he even saw tears in Chloe's eyes, along with naked fear.

"Nothing quite so dramatic," Casey reassured them. "Now, drink your hot chocolate, then we'll sort out who's sleeping where and make sure beds are all cozy and ready. Mr. Wild, if I could borrow you a moment?"

Casey smiled at everyone and, shoulders back, he left the kitchen, sensing that Seth was right on his ass. As soon as they were out of the kitchen and the fire door shut between them and the kids, he rounded on Seth.

"What the hell did you say that for?"

To his credit Seth just looked confused, as if he had no idea what Casey was talking about. Casey could read Seth's expression well and saw the moment realization hit Seth.

"They needed to know," he said.

"They needed to know? No, they didn't. Not all in one go like that. They're kids, Seth. You can't lay all that shit on them when they're still trying to process what's happening."

Casey had grown used to controlling his temper around Seth. There was no point in getting angry with him when any kind of real emotion seemed to bounce off him. But now, at this moment, anger coiled inside Casey and threatened to be blurted out in one long vomit fest of rage.

Seth fisted his hands. "Jamie is old enough to understand."

Casey stepped right up into Seth's space, but all Seth did was look at him with an implacable mask on his face. There was no warmth in his eyes, no sense that he'd crossed a line. Forcefully, Casey poked a finger in the center of Seth's chest.

"What happened to that?" he snapped.

"What?" Seth looked down with confusion in his expression.

"Your fucking heart is ice. It's just ice, Seth. These are kids, not your colleagues, not adults, not me, so don't treat them as if they need to know they could die. Not just yet."

Seth leaned against the pointing finger, his face very close to Casey's. "When you're a firefighter with eight years of experience in keeping people alive, you can stand here and tell me I'm doing things wrong."

Somehow that touched a nerve. "Well, you don't save everyone, do you?"

Seth inhaled sharply. "Fuck, Casey."

Casey wished he'd never spoken those words. That wasn't him. Seth had saved so many people.

What the fuck is wrong with me?

Seth tried to move past him but Casey stopped him

with a hand on Seth's arm. "I didn't mean to say that," Casey said.

Seth shrugged off the touch and his eyes were bleak. He said nothing, just let himself back into the room with the kids.

Chapter Eight

The door shut between them, leaving Casey on his own and feeling like shit. Only after a few minutes did he finally feel he could go back in and face Seth and the kids. He wanted to apologize but Seth wasn't there, nor were half the kids.

"If you're looking for Mr. Wild, he's showing them how to make the dens," Chloe piped up.

Casey followed the sound of voices until he reached the first office where he stood in silence and watched. Seth was dishing out instructions as if he was conducting a military operation. Andy and Jamie were up on a desk, pinning sheets to the office windows, another pushing the furniture to one side. The remaining two were laying out piles of blankets.

"Make sure you get any possible gaps," Seth ordered from the base of the table which he gripped with one hand, while he pointed at the window with the other. Seemed superhero Seth wasn't feeling any side effects from the dislocated shoulder incident.

"Uncle Seth? Is this okay?"

Seth examined the work then nodded. "Very good."

Jamie visibly preened before he and Andy climbed off the table.

"Hey, Mr. McGuire," Andy said. "This is the boys' room," he said.

Casey glanced at the floor space, wondering how were the kids going to fit in, let alone him and his muscle-bound ex.

"Girls next door, and Uncle Seth said you and him would be in the sitting room on the sofas to start."

"Awesome job," Casey said. Even though, inside, all he wanted to do was arrange things so he never had to spend the night alone with Seth and his emotionless crap. But he wasn't going to argue with the kids for an audience.

He'd just suck it up until his feelings slowly slid away to join all the other recent times in which Casey had kept his mouth shut.

He left the boys' room and checked in on the girls' room. The window was covered. The light on low and temporary beds laid out side by side. He checked all was okay then turned off the light and closed the door.

"It makes sense to save the generator where we can. We should turn the heat down when we're asleep," Seth said from right behind him. Casey couldn't help it; he jumped a foot in the air. He'd forgotten that stealthy Seth was something very real.

Casey quickly checked the corridor. "The heat?"

"And no powering of cell phones, just to eke out what we have."

"The generator may be fully fueled."

"We don't know how long we're stuck here."

Casey had no answer to that. "I'm doing dinner," he said. He glanced at his watch, it was dark, deep snow covering the windows. The face showed it was 5:30 and he couldn't believe how time was speeding past. He had so many questions about when the hell emergency services were likely to pull them out but he asked none of them. Instead, he went into the kitchen and made enough pasta to feed them all.

Only when all the kids were in their respective rooms post-dinner, could he finally relax and do a walkthrough. The fix to the front door had held, the wooden sign stuck over the hole was sturdy enough to withstand most of what Mother Nature threw at them. The room was cold and it made sense to keep this part of the whole complex out of bounds. He turned off the small heaters in there and closed the door. He checked the bedrooms, making sure the doors were tightly shut and finally moved to the kitchen. He was too wired to attempt to sleep, despite having had no coffee at all.

Just... He was in charge and there were ten kids depending on him. Should they even have gone to Shorefields? Fox News had made this big fuss about a killer storm and some of the other stations had backed them up. Was it possible that Fox had got something right? Was this a killer storm?

"You're doing that thing," Seth observed.

Casey jumped. "Stop creeping up on me," he snapped. Seth shrugged and moved to the kettle, testing for hot water to make coffee.

"I wasn't creeping."

"And what thing?" Casey said when he realized what Seth had said.

"Where you stare into space and you have these frown marks." Seth touched his own forehead to indicate where Casey was holding frown lines. "Then I come into the room and you hit the ceiling when I talk."

Casey ignored the more personal observation and instead focused on the frowning and worry. "I'm in charge of ten teenagers, one of whom is my nephew, and we're stranded in the middle of nowhere. Of course, I'm frowning."

"I was just saying—"

"Have you checked on the snow?"

"I opened the front door. It's a wall of white. No way out."

Deflated, Casey slumped onto one of the breakfast table stools and clenched his hands into fists. "Okay, so we rely on emergency services knowing we have kids here."

Seth nodded. "The snow may not be as bad elsewhere."

He was so clearly lying that it made Casey snort a laugh. "Is that you trying to make me feel better?"

"I was trying to…" Seth paused. "Yes, I suppose it was."

"Well don't. I'm not a child," Casey snapped.

"You're being irrational," Seth said exactly what Casey was thinking.

"Pot, kettle, black." Casey was tired and past the point of even bothering to fight anymore.

They subsided into silence. Seth pushed a coffee cup toward Casey and all Casey did was nod his thanks. He couldn't look Seth in the eyes anymore.

"I'm going to get some sleep," he announced. The snow had made this house a bunker and the only direction

Casey could go was to the couches in the front room. There was a huge pile of blankets on each of the two sofas, and by the time Casey had finished with his, he'd made a bed good enough for winter hibernation. Of course, being five-ten meant he actually fit on the couch, but Seth would struggle. And his leg…

For a few seconds Casey considered asking Seth if he needed help, then he bit his tongue. Help was the last thing Seth Wild wanted. He turned onto his side and snuggled under the blankets and towels and everything else he'd piled on. He wasn't facing out to the room but he knew when Seth came in. He heard Seth make his own nest to sleep in, heard movement, wondered if Seth had taken any of his clothes off, or if he was sleeping fully clothed like Casey.

Casey decided he was not going to consider Seth in clothes or out of them. That was his last thought as sleep pulled him under.

Chapter Nine

SETH MANAGED A COUPLE OF HOURS OF STARING AT THE ceiling before the pain in his shoulder and his leg drove him up and out to the kitchen. Casey was fast asleep, or at least Seth assumed he was, from the rhythmic breathing and the fact that all that was visible was short, spiky dark hair above the blankets.

What Seth needed was painkillers and he knew there had to be some somewhere. The kitchen was the best place to start, in search of a medical kit, so that was the first place he headed for. He found the box easily, but stared at it stupidly for the longest time when he saw it had been secured.

Of course, it was a locked box. This was a place where groups of kids stayed, everything would be childproofed. He pulled it down from the shelf and tested it anyway, in case someone had forgotten to lock it. The lid didn't move.

"Shit," Seth murmured. The key could well be in one of the offices, but it was five in the morning and the kids should sleep as long as they could. Considering the box from all sides, he could see it had pretty flimsy hinges. If he could lever them apart maybe there would be something inside he could use. Probably children's Tylenol or something equally useless, but hell, there might be something stronger. He rummaged in the drawers and came out with the sturdiest cooking tool, a knife sharpener, and set about levering the hinges. The first came apart easily, the second took longer, but finally it eased and Seth managed to lever off the lid. Inside was the standard stuff, a few rolled bandages, some Band-Aids, creams, including an antihistamine. And there, at the bottom, one bottle of Extra-strength Tylenol.

Gratefully, Seth took four from the bottle and hoped to hell they were enough to take the edge off. He had been due for physical therapy yesterday, and not only had he missed that but he'd put his leg through so much in the last twenty-four hours.

He'd argued so hard with the powers that be that he was physically fit enough to return to duty but this showed him how washed-up and pathetic he was. No wonder Casey left him to sleep at his sister's house.

He left you because you are so fucking angry all the time.

Seth didn't want to listen to that insistent voice of his subconscious. The one that wouldn't leave him alone and had got louder the longer he stared at the ceiling.

He'd chased Casey away and hadn't been able to stop himself from doing it. But, shit, Casey had fallen in love with a guy who could run a two-twenty marathon, not a cripple.

"Couldn't sleep?" Casey's voice came from the doorway and Seth slowly turned to face his husband. He knew what he'd see. Casey was so damn gorgeous first thing in the morning, his brown eyes sleepy before his requisite two cups of coffee, his hair all mussed. He was right. Casey ran a hand through his hair and yawned, before zipping up his coat "Coffee?" he asked hopefully.

"You should go back to bed, it's only five or so."

Casey ignored him and padded past him to the large water boiler. There was no coffee machine there but Seth knew Casey wasn't a snob about coffee; he would drink any old caffeine.

Casey's eyes widened and Seth knew what he'd seen. The broken medical box.

"What happened?" Casey asked.

Seth could lie, but there was no point. Survival was built on honesty. "I needed painkillers."

Casey poked at the box and picked up the bottle of Tylenol, shaking it. "Were these enough?"

Seth shook his head.

"How bad is it?"

"I'm—"

"If you say you're fine, or okay, I swear I will find the closest carving knife and stab you in the throat."

Seth opened his mouth to respond. He'd never heard this side of Casey, normally he was quiet and just let Seth carry on with whatever he was doing.

"You need coffee," Seth said. He waited until Casey made a cup and wondered what the hell to say. Casey had always been happy to back off with the questions, had spent the last six months asking Seth if he was okay and accepting what Seth said.

Only he didn't accept it, did he?

"I can see your brain working," Casey commented.

"I just don't know what to say," Seth said. The admission was hard to make. He was trapped in a hell of his own making and he knew it.

"Your shoulder. Is that painful? Give it to me on a one to ten."

Seth could understand that concept, it was what he asked people who were trapped to tell him how they were. "It's nothing. Sore." He tested the motion by rolling his shoulder and didn't wince. "A two maybe." Perhaps the meds were kicking in on that, or the bruised muscles and tendons had loosened since he'd walked around.

"And your leg?" Casey leaned on the work surface and sipped his coffee. He wasn't pushing for a response but Seth felt the pressure nonetheless.

"An eight. I hurt it when I yanked Andy out of the van, and the cold, it's not good in the cold."

He'd been trapped under masonry during the call that had ended his career, pinned with fire crawling closer. He hadn't cared. He'd been holding the hand of the mother of two he'd gone in to save when the whole building came down around them, trying to stop her crying. The fire had reached her, and she was dead. He could see her from where he was trapped. Eye to eye with her vacant gaze for over three hours. He'd never told Casey that. No point in giving him nightmares.

"Can I help?" Casey asked.

Seth closed his eyes and dropped his head a little. "I wish you could."

Seth heard Casey move, felt him close by, then the touch of a hand on his arm. "I saw the X-rays, I've seen where the metal pins are, but I need you to tell me."

Tell him?

Seth balked. He wouldn't have burdened Casey with the pain before when they were together, why would he do it now? "Nothing to tell."

Casey shoved Seth and turned him, before trapping him against the counter. Casey wasn't a tall guy, nor as strong as Seth, but anger snapped in his brown eyes and Seth had seen firsthand how that emotion could give strength.

"What the hell?" He managed before nearly doubling over in pain when Casey poked his leg.

"Does that hurt?" Casey asked.

"Jesus, fuck, Casey."

"Drop your pants and sit on the counter," Casey ordered.

"I'm not—"

"Do. It. The. Fuck. Now."

They stared at each other until Seth backed down. There was no arguing with Casey when he was like this. Seth could have pushed him out the way if he'd felt better, but his leg was weak and his head hurt and hell, he was fucked.

Finally, he pushed his pants to his hips and sat on the counter, which was cold against his ass. Casey yanked them lower still, causing Seth to curse before wriggling to help. Seth was mortified that Casey was examining his leg. He'd never wanted Casey to see it before, not the twisted skin and raised scars, nor the wrong feel of the muscle, but that was before, when they'd still shared a bed.

Casey and Seth were heading for being over now, and showing Casey his scars was nothing.

He just wished it actually *felt* like nothing.

Casey's touch became more, a firm press against knots in his muscles. A few of the peripheral aches lessened.

"Better?" Casey had his head bowed in concentration and Seth had a flashback to Casey kissing him there when he first came home, before he'd made sure to cover up. His treacherous cock filled a little and he didn't even recognize the feeling at first. He hadn't had any kind of erection in six months. Trauma, a few experts said; psychological, others said.

The feeling passed as Casey pressed a particularly tight knot and the agony carved through him for what seemed like forever but what was probably only a few moments until the knot eased.

"How d—do y—you know how to…?" Seth attempted to talk through his measured breathing.

"I talked to your PT in the hospital and she showed me what to do if you…" Casey looked up and Seth nearly groaned at the naked emotion in his beautiful eyes. Sadness and despair colored them and Seth hated it.

"You spoke to the therapist?"

"And your doctor. I learned enough to know what to do. But do you want to hear something funny?"

Seth wasn't sure. The tone of Casey's voice suggested whatever he was going to say wasn't funny at all. "Okay."

"Your captain was allowed in to see you as if he was more important than me, when you were unconscious. When you first came around, he was your boss and they just waved him through when they realized you didn't have family. Until the captain explained we were married. But me? I had to fight at first to even hold your hand. It's a fucked-up world."

"I remember you holding my hand."

"You were unconscious—"

"I felt you there." Seth was adamant.

Casey gazed directly into Seth's eyes and the sadness in Casey's was almost too much to bear. "Then I'm glad I was there for you."

Seth wriggled a little more as Casey worked the muscles, and nearly sighed as each part of him relaxed. The fingers were moving higher, but there was no chance of getting an erection, so Seth was cool with the path of pain, followed by warmth.

"Why did you go in?" Casey asked soft and low, as if he was almost hoping Seth wouldn't hear the question. They'd had this conversation before. Casey had asked him so many times, sometimes he had cried, or shouted, and others he'd spoken quietly. And every time, Seth had given the same answer. "It's my job, it's what I do. You live with a fireman then you gotta understand what we do".

Somehow that answer meant nothing since Casey had walked away. There was no point in being the strong silent one who could handle anything life threw at them.

"There's this kid, maybe the same age as the ones you teach, he's lying on the gurney with burns on his arm. He lived in one of the apartments on top of the offices. He said he'd tried to go back for his mom and sister, and asked where they were. I couldn't tell him they'd already pulled the sister out and she'd been rushed to the hospital because the paramedics had given us the look."

"The look?"

"The one that says a patient's chances are low. She'd had blunt force trauma to her chest." Seth pressed a hand to his own heart. "So, this kid is lying there and I ask his name, to get that connection, right? And he says it's Jamie and I imagine our Jamie trapped inside, or any kid, and how I would run straight into hell to get him out of a building."

"So that's what made you run inside?"

"I promised him I would find her. And I did. She had been in the laundry room one floor down, trapped, and hell, I even managed to get through to her and a group of others that were trapped. Then everything shifted and, in one breath, the building fell on us, with the fire coming closer. You know she didn't make it. No one else made it and I watched them die. I was trapped and thought I was next."

"I'm sorry." Casey's his voice hitched.

"You must have known most of it."

"I didn't know you saw the people die. You were unconscious when they brought you out. They said so."

Seth shrugged and winced at the movement.

"You're the bravest man I know, and running into that building? That was my Seth, helping others, wanting to save lives." Casey backed away and pushed his hands into the pockets of his jeans.

"I think that is the first time you've said that," Seth said. He spoke cautiously. There was something here, a spark of understanding, of talking, and it wasn't as painful as he'd expected it to be.

"That you're brave? Goes without saying. Any first responder is brave above all else."

"You said I was stupid, that I should have listened to the Chief, that you hated what I'd done to us, but you didn't once say I was brave."

Something passed over Casey's expression, remorse

maybe? It vanished as quickly as it had appeared. He appeared to struggle with what to say next.

"They told me you were going to lose your leg, that you'd disobeyed orders, that you'd willingly gone in there to die. You'd chosen someone else over me, and I lashed out."

"I'm sorry, C." There was so much in the apology, so many things unsaid and he was aware he'd slipped into using the familiar name he'd had for Casey.

Casey nodded. "I'm sorry too." Then he backed away and moved to the kettle to make more coffee.

Seth slipped off the counter and tested putting weight on his leg. Familiar pain stabbed at him, but it was localized, and not the nightmare of a cramping spasm. He pulled up his pants. "Is that it?" he asked, aware he was poking the bear.

Casey shrugged. "What else do you want me to say?"

"We should talk more."

"Now you want to talk? After six months of stoic silence, now, trapped in a building with ten kids to look out for, you want to talk?"

Seth couldn't make sense of what was in his head. They could feasibly die in this place, even though Seth would work his damndest to make sure they didn't. Didn't Casey see that? He didn't really want to talk, he didn't do that, but surely, they had stuff unsaid in case the generator failed, in case they were trapped indefinitely, in case emergency services couldn't get to them.

"Uncle Seth, can you come see this?"

Jamie stood at the main door into the hall, wrapped in a blanket and looking worried.

It seemed like the door that opened for talking had shut.

Seth side-hugged Casey's nephew and followed him out, only to return a few moments later with the rest of the boys in tow.

"Glass has cracked," he announced. "Boys' room is of no use."

"Cracked from the cold?" Casey asked. "Should we get the girls up?"

Seth considered the question. "Cracked from the weight of snow building there. The girls have an internal room, they should be okay, but it may be a good idea to get everyone out for breakfast now." He zipped up his bulky parka.

The boys gathered around the kitchen island, sleepy and quiet. Seth decided to get the girls up.

He knocked on the door, and a voice from inside replied "Hello".

"Everyone up now," he said firmly. "Grab all the blankets and put them with the sofas."

The door opened and one by the one the girls trailed out, carrying blankets and towels and all looking like they'd slept for shit. *Bit like me then.*

When the room was clear he checked the structure. There was no window and the walls were sturdy. He then rechecked the boys' place. The weight of snow against the window appeared to be the problem. It was a solid wall of white and even though the window hadn't given way there was no way the boys could sleep in there. He gathered as many blankets as he could carry and dumped them in the corridor, then did the same thing twice more until the room was empty of everything from the impromptu sleepover, including shoes and bags. Before he left, he checked the drawers and found a half bottle of Tylenol and a near empty bottle of Advil. He pocketed both, then scooped up pens and paper and sticky notes. All of which he added to the blanket pile.

Then he wrote a Post-it note with the words "no-entry" and shut the door.

Checking on the front entrance hall had him condemning that. It was clearly an addition to the main house and wasn't as sturdy. The weight of snow was a concern on the flimsy roof of this single-story extension. He added a Post-it to that area as well. A walk around each room showed that, to the north, the side with the boys' room, the wall of snow was taller than the building they were in. Which meant that this whole side was vulnerable to collapse. He'd seen it happen before and it wasn't pretty. He repeated emptying everything in the girls' room and posted a similar "no-entry" note on that door.

He'd need to get outside and see if he could clear some of the snow from pressing on the building, although he was one man and he didn't have a shovel, or anything like it. Maybe there was something in the shed with the generator; at least he'd be able to see now it was morning. Last night he'd started the generator by touch alone.

This left the bathrooms, which were still in working order and off the central kitchen, the sitting room where he and Casey had slept, and the dining area. The snow had walled up against the glass doors in the dining area but there was daylight above the snow so this side of the building was clearly more sheltered.

The snow had stopped falling, apart from the odd fat flake that was being shaken from the trees, but he couldn't see the outside generator shed, nor any way of getting out there to check on fuel, or to get a shovel.

For the longest time, he stood at the window looking at the crystal clear blue sky and considering the options.

If this much snow had been dumped in one night across the whole of the state, then the emergency services would be seriously overwhelmed. Roads would be blocked, accidents, snow drifts, people trapped in houses. Vermont knew snow, but snow like this was verging on the improbable.

"Well?" Casey asked from his side.

"I've closed off the offices and the main entrance. We really only have this side now. The kitchen and dining room, the bathrooms, and the sitting room."

"And no way out?"

Seth glanced at Casey and shook his head. "No."

"What do you think the ETA on first response will be?"

Seth had forgotten how much jargon Casey had picked up in the years they'd been together. After all, it had been Casey who had helped him study for his exams.

"I wish I knew. Contingency will have teams coming in from unaffected states, but cities will be priority, transit." Seth cracked his neck. "We're on the list. They know we're here."

"Twenty-four hours?"

"Maybe. Maybe more."

Seth saw Casey close his eyes then visibly inhale and exhale, settling his thoughts. The act was so familiar that it hurt Seth to watch. Then Casey turned to face the kids.

"Okay. Breakfast, then I think we'll get some schoolwork done while we're waiting for help."

All the kids talked at once in protest. The concept of

being in the middle of an emergency seemed to have had them all thinking that school work was off the agenda. But, today was Monday, and Casey was in full-on teacher mode.

Seth had never seen Casey in action.

This will be interesting.

Chapter Ten

Breakfast cleared, the kids took seats in the dining area with paper and pens in front of them. They were different groups, different levels, and Casey was wondering where to start. Math would send them all running, and English wasn't his strong point. History was his thing. He knew half of them here were studying The Cold War, the others Ancient Civ.

"Okay guys," he began, to get them all looking at him. "Let's talk about how disasters, both natural and man-made, have shaped the world we know today."

Casey was pleased with how it went. They broke for lunch, they debated disaster and how even the snow they were stuck in would be responsible for many different things. He tried not to feel self-conscious that Seth hovered around them. Yes, he went on his frequent perimeter walks, which didn't last long, but mostly he stood and stared. A couple of times, Casey nearly met his gaze, but always at the last minute he would pretend to be focused somewhere else, and it seemed Seth was doing the same thing. Seth was writing things down on paper, then staring thoughtfully at the class and Casey, then back to the paper, as if he was working on the hardest essay of his life. He would stare again and Casey felt the weight of the stare the entire time he was trying to lead a class.

As soon as it got close to three he stopped the lesson and the kids descended like locusts on the kitchen. By four, everyone was sitting down to soup and bread. The kids may well have been afraid, but they weren't showing it.

They decided on games and made cards for a loud and funny game of, what seemed to be, shouting out strings of words. Casey sat it out, watching them from the sofa as he flicked through books on his Kindle, unable to concentrate on even one. He didn't have to decide on a bedtime for them. They gravitated to the sitting room around ten and Casey moved to the kitchen where Seth had been for much of the day. They were out of sight of the kids, and more importantly out of hearing.

Casey made two hot chocolates and placed one in front of Seth.

"You said you wanted to talk."

Seth glanced at the wall between them and the kids, then nodded. He pushed a cap on the pen he'd been using and tapped it on the pad .

"I did pros and cons," he said. "Want to see?" That was more real conversation than they'd had in a long time. A whole two, albeit short, sentences that had no hint of recrimination or argument.

Casey couldn't help it, he was intrigued and cautious at the same time. "Pros and cons of what?"

Seth turned the pad around and pushed it over to

Casey. Along with the pen. Casey read the pros. *Friends, lovers, security, laughter, cuddles, bacon.* Then the cons. *Stupidity, reliance, forever.* The forever had a question mark next to it. The list terrified him. At the back of his head he always imagined one day he and Seth would somehow find their way back to each other, but this list, if it was to do with their relationship, looked pretty final.

"As much as I think bacon is a pro in any argument, I don't understand."

"Us," Seth said. "When I write down what I loved about you, it was easy. I had a list of thirty things, the way we were friends, and lovers, and that when I was with you, when I came home to you, I felt safe and wanted and secure. I loved how we laugh over stupid stuff, and that sometimes when I came home from a bad day you would just know, and you'd hug me and we would cuddle on the sofa and you made everything right. Then bacon, because yeah, I think your love of bacon is epic."

"Us?" Casey asked. He didn't know whether to be shocked or horrified that yes, this list was about them. Seth was attempting to distill an entire life to a table of negatives and positives? How was that even possible? The very fact he was doing this was like a knife to Casey's heart.

"You don't look like you think it's a good idea." Seth sounded hurt and that instinct Casey had inside him to make things better for Seth nearly won over the anger in his head.

Casey opened his mouth, then closed it again as anger curled in his chest and he was this close to letting it all out. "A good idea?" he said in a loud whisper. "You can't write down on paper what breaks a person's heart." He pushed himself up but Seth grabbed at his hand.

"I wanted to know exactly what to talk about, that's all."

Casey struggled to tug away from Seth's hold and Seth let him go, but Casey didn't move. Instead he stabbed a finger at the first item in the Con column.

"Stupidity. Talk to me about that then. Because all I can think at the moment is how stupid I am to even think you wanted to have a real talk."

Seth looked back at the wall as if he expected all the kids next door to suddenly appear in the kitchen. "Me," he said. "I'm the stupid one."

That took the wind out of Casey's sails and he sat back down with a thump, the stool rocking a little, meaning he had to settle himself by grabbing the breakfast bar.

"Sorry?" he said. Maybe he had misheard.

"At first, I thought I was stupid because I expected you to always be there, then you weren't and you were stupid to give up on us—"

"What the hell—?"

"No, let me finish, okay? Then, when I was thinking, because that is what I've been doing all day, just thinking. You were stupid to take me on." Seth stopped and looked at Casey expectantly, but Casey had no idea what he was supposed to say at this point. He had never thought he was wrong to be with Seth. As far as he was concerned Seth was the other half of him. "I was wrong," Seth finished.

"So, wait. You weren't stupid and I wasn't. I'm not following this."

"No, it was me. You tried to help, with my studying, my exams, my work schedule, my nerves, my fears, and each time I told myself that I could allow that, because…" He bowed his head.

"Because…"

"It didn't make me less of a man or anything," Seth mumbled.

Casey sat back on the stool and stared at Seth's bent head. "What?"

"It's hard being a firefighter, okay. Everyone I work with is all 'little women this' and 'my girl that', and they razzed me for having you, but it didn't matter as long as you were the one who…"

"Who was the girlfriend."

Seth looked up and his expression was hopeful. "See? That is what I mean."

"That's bullshit. Is that what you think? That I'm not a man?" Casey was way past confused and heading for walking right out into the snow and saying to hell with it.

"Fuck. No. God… C, no. They all came to the hospital, I got my reprimand but I had their respect somehow, all telling me what a hero I was and that they expected me back ASAP. Do you understand? Am I making any sense?"

"Not much, no."

"Then you're there, holding my hand and telling me you'd help me get better and I didn't want your help, or your pity, because I could do it on my own. Real men are strong." He used his finger to add quote marks to that simple and incredibly stupid statement. "Particularly when they said I could lose my leg, or not be a fireman again. How would you ever see me as a man again? If I couldn't work, or walk?"

Casey couldn't believe what he was hearing. "Because…wait… You mean you think I would look at you like less of a man because you needed help, or you were physically changed, or that you wouldn't be working as a firefighter?" Casey summarized everything in the vain hope he had finally clued in to what Seth had listed.

"Yes," Seth said immediately.

"That's fucking stupid, you asshole. Is that all you think of me? That I was only there for the good times? And what am I if I'm not a man? Chopped liver?"

Seth snapped his fingers then tapped the list. "See, I told you. Stupid."

Casey stopped for a second and Seth, to his credit, said nothing. It seemed it was Casey's job to ask the questions. He chose to focus on the list. "And the 'reliance' you have added to the list? Is that you hating that you might have had to rely on me?"

This time it was Seth who huffed a laugh. "Other way around. You relying on me when I can't even hold down a job. Because, how can you?"

"I don't get... We'd rely on each other... Shit Seth, this isn't making any sense. And 'forever'? Why is that in the con list?"

Seth worried his lip with his teeth. This appeared to be an answer that he really wasn't sure about. "It's there because if you tie your forever to mine, then what do you get?"

"What do you mean? I'd have you."

Seth jabbed a finger into his own chest. "A broken me, with constant physical therapy and metal in my leg and maybe not a job, not to mention I can't seem to even maintain a freaking erection."

"Our relationship is not defined by sex," Casey snapped.

"No, but we were good at it."

Casey knew Seth was in pain, that he'd been injured in his upper thigh, that he'd nearly died. Casey hadn't wanted anything that would hurt Seth. Did it really matter about the sex when the bigger picture was so much more?

"You suffered so much trauma," Casey said, refusing to address the sex issue. "But you couldn't talk. I understood."

Seth flushed and wouldn't meet Casey's eyes, again. "I pushed you away. The doctor said it could be because of the way the concrete fell and the stanchion pierced near my groin, but my doctor says it might just all be in my head. That my masculinity is tied up with my job, or some shit."

Seth looked devastated. He was a man of action, wanted to control situations, and suddenly he'd been told that he was unable to get his brain to let him control things. No wonder he was so damn lost all the time.

Silence. Casey didn't know what to say, but trapped here behind the wall of snow, he really had nowhere to go.

He used his most cautious tone. "You turned away from touching me, or hugging me, and all I wanted to do was be there for you."

"I didn't want to chase you away, but I know that is exactly what I did do, and I turned into this person I didn't recognize anymore." Seth's shoulders slumped and he winced. "No wonder you went to your sister's."

"I only left because… You were angry all the time, at everything," Casey said. "And you didn't even want to be in the same house as me, let alone talk to me."

"I'll go back to Annette, I'll see someone, talk it through. I promise I'll try." Seth met Casey's gaze instead of hiding his face. He ran a hand through his dark hair and gripped it. It was such a familiar gesture that Casey's heart broke there and then.

"Okay."

"But I'll need help to try, and I don't know if what I've done has made everything too much for you to come back home."

"I'll come home."

Seth hunched in on himself, "Just know that you're coming back to half a man."

"Fuck your self-pity, Seth Wild!" Casey snapped. "You say that again and I will knock you out."

"You can't find a way to love me again, not like you used to, I get that, not with the extra baggage."

"I never stopped loving you."

Casey couldn't believe what he was shouting. The words he'd held in for so long because he didn't think Seth wanted them.

"Casey, please."

But Casey wasn't stopping. "There's always ways to deal with anything. If you think I would walk away from you for that…then fuck you."

He stepped back and away from Seth, but Seth held him with hope in his eyes. "You think we could…somehow…?"

Casey didn't know what to say, his head was too full to process any of this. He shook his head then stared down at the table, gripping the sides in white-knuckled determination.

"Talk to me, C," Seth pleaded.

Abruptly, Casey knew what he wanted to say. "Do you

remember the day we first met? I was eight, you were just shy of your tenth birthday."

"You had that haircut with the wonky bangs."

"You could throw a football the whole length of the playground."

Seth snorted a laugh. "You said you liked girls."

"So, did you."

Seth smiled cautiously and Casey felt some of the ice in his heart melt.

"Then we were together," Seth said. "And I fell in love with you so hard, because you'd always been there for me, and you challenged me, and you were the other half of me."

Casey released the tight hold he had of the table and walked around it, watching as Seth moved on the stool and finally spread his legs a little so Casey could stand between them. The movement was instinctive and Casey was now only a few inches from the man he loved.

"Through everything," Casey said. "We always had each other."

Seth nodded and his eyes looked glassy as if he was trying not to cry.

Hell, maybe the idiot should cry, it would get rid of some of the poison inside him.

Casey cradled Seth's face. "Promise me we will work through this together."

"Why would you want to? After all of this?"

Casey held back his disappointment but he couldn't help the small amount that slipped into his voice as he spoke. He thought Seth had come to a point where he'd found his first step to healing. "If you have to ask why I want to, then maybe you aren't ready for me to be back in your life."

Seth stared right at him, his brown eyes wide. A million thought processes showed in his expression and he appeared to realize what Casey was asking.

"Hi," he finally said. "My name is Seth Wild. I'm struggling with pain, and depression, and I'm going to be seeing a therapist, because last year a building fell on me, which means my leg and lower back are full of metal, and I'm not going to be a firefighter anymore. And that is shit, because it's all I ever wanted. Although that's not entirely true…" He stopped, his breathing ragged. "Because all I ever really wanted was you." Casey pressed a kiss to Seth's forehead. "I need you to help me, C. Will you help me?"

Casey kissed each eyelid, each cheekbone, then slanted a touch to Seth's lips before sliding his hands down from cradling Seth's face to hugging him.

He had only one thing to say.

"Always."

They stood that way for the longest time, until both of them needed to sleep, and as soon as the meds Casey encouraged Seth to take kicked in they found their spot on the sofa with the ten kids sprawled all around them wrapped in blankets and fast asleep. Then, with Seth leaning on Casey and holding hands under their own nest of blankets, they slept.

"UNCLE SETH! UNCLE CASEY!"

Casey snapped out of a very nice dream involving whipped cream, with Jamie's voice in his ear.

"What's wrong?" he asked as Seth came around a little less quickly.

"We think we can hear the snow plow and some of the snow is moving at the front."

Casey extricated himself from the sleepy Seth and only relaxed when his husband joined him at the window. There was movement out there and the snow was being moved. Seth placed a hand flat on the cold glass.

"Time to go home," he said.

Yeah. Time to go home, and see if everything they'd managed to find here was real.

Epilogue

Seth found the weeks after the Snownado, as Casey had taken to calling it, were unbelievably slow.

Something had snapped in Seth when they'd been trapped at Shorefields.

He wasn't less of a man for having Casey help him, and being a firefighter didn't have to define him, although that was the hardest one of all. As of yesterday, he was officially no longer an active duty firefighter and he had the compensation check in his bank account waiting to clear. He was still at the station—a trainer, a marketing guy, an office support worker, a planner, he was everything and anything the fire service could give him without him actually going out on calls.

God, he missed the calls. The buzz, the life, the friends, but somehow in all of this, when he came home each day to Casey he could rationalize everything. He'd lost, then gained, at the same time, and the way it had happened was all due to Casey. Today he'd done something pretty fucking crazy. He'd been logging overtime on the PC, making sure each firefighter had the correct codes against their name, cross-checking to the budget and he'd snapped again.

He switched to Word and wrote the letter before he could even think rationally. Signing it and leaving it on the Chief's desk had been the exclamation mark on his statement.

He'd handed in his resignation. He was going to do something else. What? He didn't know. He stopped in at the gym on the way home and spoke to the manager there about ideas he'd had for a rehab program. He was met with doubt at first, and then a growing interest. This could work.

But what would Casey say?

Tonight, was an anniversary of sorts, a whole two months since the Snownado, since the whole East Coast of the US had disappeared under a blanket of white, a deadly covering that had taken lives and made heroes out of so many people, first responders and civilians alike. He let himself into their small house, shrugged off his jacket, and for the longest time he stared at the department-issued fleece hanging next to one of Casey's jackets.

Dinner was next on his list, nothing amazing, because he still wasn't the best cook, but maybe with more time on his hands he could do some of the things that interested him, like cooking, and gardening, and working at the gym maybe, and hell…maybe even going back to college and getting a degree.

"Hey, babe." Casey hugged him from behind and placed cold outdoors kisses on the back of his neck. Seth turned eagerly to face his husband and they kissed for the longest time.

Their sex life had been tentative, slow, and Casey had been impossibly patient about everything. How he did it when their sex lives had once been so intrinsic to them as a couple, Seth didn't know.

He'd refused the little blue pills; wanted everything back to normal.

And then it had happened, after a dinner, with soft lighting, and Casey kissing every part of his body, Seth had felt his cock plump up, and that was it. He wasn't losing the ability to do that again any time soon.

They'd actually exchanged hand jobs after that, for the first time since the accident, and the night after, and the next morning, and at lunchtime, and the day after. They couldn't get enough of reconnecting now they could, and a lot of that was down to the counseling.

Seth was blocked, his brain taking over when it was his instincts that needed to be at the fore, and they'd worked hard on reconnecting on an emotional level way before they reconnected physically.

It was working.

"I can see you thinking," Casey said.

"Dinner's okay to leave." Seth pointed at the food. "And I think we should celebrate."

"Celebrate what?"

Seth rested his hands on Casey's hip bones and rubbed patterns with his thumbs. "I want to show you the scars."

"I've seen them." Casey looked puzzled as well he should. Seth wasn't really making a lot of sense and he knew it.

Seth looped his fingers in Casey's belt and tugged him closer. "Up close."

"Okay."

Sliding to one side, Seth laced his fingers with Casey's and tugged him upstairs. Casey didn't ask what they were doing because it was obvious as soon as Seth stripped once they were inside the room.

"Counseling went well then?" Casey teased as he followed suit, pulling off all of his clothes and in an instant, moved into Seth's space.

"I need you to look," Seth insisted. He sat on the bed then scooted up so his head was on a pillow and he lay flat.

Casey chuckled and climbed on the bed after Seth. "Believe me, I'm looking."

"*Really* look."

Casey frowned momentarily and stopped his predatory prowl up the bed. "What's wrong?"

"Just tell me what you see."

Seth pointed at his groin and he felt a tug of something when Casey looked at his erection then grinned at him. "I see you're very pleased to see me." He leaned over and kissed the tip of Seth's cock as he said this and managed a cheeky taste before pulling back and sitting on his heels between Seth's spread legs.

"How awful are they?" Seth asked. "I mean, I see them in the mirror but…"

"Your scars?" That frown was back on Casey's face. "This is about your scars?" Casey peered closer. "They're not as red as they used to be. The one across your thigh is looking good, pale."

"Jagged."

"Yes, jagged. Guess that's what comes of having an entire building fall on you. And the other scars and burns?" Casey traced the one that ran upward to Seth's groin, following the path of his finger with his lips. By the time he reached the crease between groin and leg Seth wished he hadn't started this. But, he had to know, so he didn't disappoint Casey. Then he would tell his husband what he'd done today, after he knew whether Casey was happy to be near him. Call him a coward, but he had to know.

"And?"

Casey chuckled and nudged Seth's cock with his nose. Seth moved a little in the hope that Casey would get the message that he needed Casey's mouth on him. Then he stopped himself. This was about honesty, not sex. Casey closed his lips around him and suddenly all thoughts of taking this slow flew out of the window.

Wait...

The words that Seth wanted to say were locked in his head but the way Casey was using his lips and his tongue and *ohmyfuckinggod* his fingers appeared to release them.

"Casey, please...guh... I handed in my notice..."

Casey released the sucking motion he had going with one final lick.

"Okay." He looked up at Seth through his eyelashes. He didn't seem worried; he seemed as if he was waiting for Seth to say more.

"And I don't have any fucking idea what I'm doing next."

Casey said nothing; he simply moved up a little then cradled Seth's face and kissed him. "That's okay, we'll work it out," he said. "You should talk to Billy at the gym about a rehab program."

"I did."

"And go back to college."

"I will."

Casey huffed a low laugh. "Looks like you have it all worked out. So now we can get back to sex?"

Seth pulled his husband close. "You don't mind?"

Casey stopped in his path of kisses when he reached a nipple, pausing for a moment to nip and suck there before lifting his head. "I want you to be happy."

"As simple as that?" Seth questioned.

Casey smiled up at him then squirmed down until his mouth was level with Seth's cock. "Most things are kinda simple," he said. Then he swallowed Seth down and it was game over for talking.

Seth lifted himself up on his elbows—there was nothing better than watching Casey doing that thing with his hands and mouth and…this was going too fast.

"I want to be in you," Seth said. "It's been so long."

Casey didn't pause but a nod had Seth reaching for lube. He slapped it down onto the bed then yanked at Casey enough that he stopped what he was doing.

Casey kissed another path, this time up from cock to throat by way of a nipple.

"Are you sure?" he asked finally.

Casey kissed him to silence the words, then pulled back a little. "Pass the damn lube."

That little exchange done, Seth did as he was told and between them, they stretched and eased the way for Casey before he lowered himself onto Seth and after some time, slow-careful-time, Casey was fully seated and Seth thought he had died and gone to heaven.

He watched the man above him as they made love, wondering how he could have ever given Casey a moment to doubt him. But then it was all too much to think and the rhythm they had, the push pull, the touches, and hell, it had been so long since they'd done this. With a shout, he was coming and Casey wasn't long after, falling boneless onto Seth with a contented smile.

Finally, they had to move and with some awkward maneuvering, laughter, a sudden cramp, and a whole lot of kissing, they separated.

Seth lay flat on his back shifting a little so that his hip was padded against a pillow then looked sideways at Casey.

"I love you," he said. And he meant it. He meant every single letter of it and would mean it until the day he died.

Casey laced their fingers and squeezed his hand. "I love you."

"Casey?"

"Hmmm?" Casey sounded tired and Seth wondered if they would get back downstairs for dinner.

"Will you stay married to me?"

Casey rolled onto his side and rested his chin on Seth's chest. "Yes," he said. No explanation. No declarations of why or how or when, or questions. Just a simple yes.

Seth placed a hand on Casey's back and held him tight.

How could he have lost his way so badly and been so stupid? This right here was perfect. He'd nearly lost his life but he'd also nearly lost Casey. And that was wrong.

Because Seth/Casey truly was forever.

THE END

All The Kings Men

Humpty Dumpty sat on a wall,
Humpty Dumpty had a great fall.
All the king's horses and all the king's men
Couldn't put Humpty together again!

Prologue

CALIFORNIA IS ONE OF AMERICA'S MOST EARTHQUAKE-prone states.

The boundary between the massive Pacific and North American tectonic plates, the notorious San Andreas Fault, runs roughly southeast to northwest through much of California. In addition, a jumble of lesser transverse faults clutters the map of the state.

Sides of the San Andreas Fault move in the opposite direction, but at different speeds, causing geologic tension to build. That tension is released in the form of an earthquake. The possibility is always present for associated earthquakes among the nearby transform faults.

The U.S. Geological Survey says the state faces a forty-six percent chance of being hit by a Richter Scale magnitude 7.5 or higher earthquake in the next thirty years.

Possibly even today.

Chapter One

THURSDAY 6:52 A.M.

I'M COMING TO YOU... Early morning flight to LAX... I don't want to play phone tag anymore... I just want to see you face to face and talk... I miss you, Nate... I'm sorry... I love you.

Nathan Richardson leaned against the park gates and pocketed his cell after listening to his lover's voicemail for what must be at least the twentieth time. The message was emotional and Ryan's voice was choked as he spoke. Still, in the few words Nathan heard he got the message. He and Ryan needed to do one hell of a lot of talking.

They'd been together two years, Ryan a photographer and Nathan his model. It was the worst cliché ever and surely destined to fail. But not them. They were in love and going strong. Nathan wanted forever, commitment, a place they owned together, hell, even a ring. Ryan, older than Nathan by five years, had too many breakups under his belt to think that a happy ever after was even possible.

When Nathan was offered a part in a small independent movie, it had been the beginning of the end. Nathan had used modeling to finance acting classes and he jumped at the chance to join the cast of an independent gay film with a contract for two months' work and an audition for a soap as a new love interest in some kind of triangle.

Nathan expected Ryan to protest—for his lover to tell Nathan he couldn't live without him and not to go. Instead Ryan grew quieter by the day and merely encouraged Nathan to take the role. Nathan could see what was happening—Ryan was subtly saying he didn't want a forever kind of thing anyway. Ryan was ending their love affair while he had the chance to be in control of how it ended. They didn't fight. They drifted apart and Nathan let it happen.

That had been two months ago.

Two days ago Ryan had texted him. *I miss you. So much.*

Nathan didn't know what to type in return. Ryan wasn't exactly offering endless love and a ring. But when Nathan read those few words he knew getting over Ryan was unachievable. He loved the man, and always would. His friend Jason wanted him to move on. He could no more move on from Ryan than he could turn straight.

Ryan was the other half of him.

I love you, Nathan sent in reply.

I want forever, Ryan texted back.

I can go for that, Nathan replied quickly.

I can get a flight. Unspoken was asking if Ryan could visit Nathan.

Please.

Despite staring at the screen for an hour, there were no more messages.

Then the voicemail came when Nathan was on his run. Heartfelt and perfect. The two of them could make this real. Not long and his lover would be here, then they could clear the air and maybe he and Ryan could find a way to move on.

Ryan Ortiz said he was ready for forever and Nathan wanted that so badly.

He had run here, the opposite side of the US, to give Ryan time to think about what he felt and what he wanted. It had killed him not to be calling Ryan every day, but Nathan knew Ryan and knew his best bet was to not pressure his lover. His gaze passed over where he now lived, a place so very different from his and Ryan's former home in the chaos and noise of New York.

A small complex of four apartments, quiet and remote, the peace and solitude suited his frame of mind perfectly. He lived in this two-bedroom apartment in the hills beyond LA, rented from an absentee landlord, and had made it his own with photos of family and even one of him and Ryan in happier times. As much as he wished he could, he hadn't been able to cut Ryan out of his thoughts, or his life.

He stood in the roughhewn park carved out across the road from his home and looked away from his sanctuary to the nature that surrounded him. The park itself was a jumble of trees and rocks, grass and pathways, some steeply climbing higher into the hills, some gently curving and ideal for his attempted runs. The nearest main road was a quarter-mile away, and most people drove past the entrance to the small complex without realizing the road led to people's homes.

Jason and his girlfriend had put an offer on one of the two empty apartments. Having his best friend in LA living next door was a good thing. He needed that connection if he couldn't have Ryan in his life on a permanent basis. Although…maybe…somehow he and Ryan could make it work?

Nathan smiled as a cloud of birds rose gracefully from the oak at the edge of the park, heading skyward at an incredible speed. He loved that he was so close to the peace of nature, and the sight of the birds was both eerie and fascinating. He couldn't stop looking at it, wishing he had his camera with him, cursing at another amazing photo opportunity lost.

Suddenly, he couldn't wait to share what he'd seen with Ryan.

THURSDAY 6:59 am

RYAN ORTIZ SAT FORWARD in the cab as they rounded a corner. He was desperate to get his Nathan into his arms where Ryan could hold him and tell him that he loved him. The cab was moving too slowly and all the driver wanted to do was talk to him.

"What brings you to LA?"

"My boyfriend lives here." *Nathan.*

"So you're not a resident?"

"No, I'm here from New York, just for a few days." *Hopefully longer if Nathan will take me back.*

The questions continued to come. What did he think of the spate of forest fires in the LA hills? Did he think that Lindsay Lohan was for real? Did he have pets? Was he married? Did he want to get married? Was he fighting for equal rights? For the most part, Ryan managed to keep up until he realized that the driver wasn't actually listening to his answers, and so he was able to subside to a new level of tired grunts in answer to each new question. Still dazed from his early morning flight from New York, his mind limped through thought and memory, attempting to make order out of chaos. The views from the taxi, the vista of the city laid out through the misty smog, were gorgeous, and he itched for his camera. It was a very strange feeling not to have it with him, but the rush to get here, to see Nathan, had precluded organizing his extensive camera equipment. It was the first time in his memory he'd gone anywhere without at least one camera.

He missed taking photos of Nate. His gorgeous lover had started as his model for *Style* and hell, Ryan loved every minute of seeing Nate through the viewfinder. They'd slipped into a relationship, a fiery, intense love affair. Then his beautiful lover had revealed he wanted to try acting and even had a role lined up. Although when that had happened Ryan didn't know, as Nathan hadn't told him a thing.

"It's such a cliché," Ryan told him. "Model turned actor."

He was only teasing but Nathan took him so seriously. "It's just a dream of mine, and I'm lucky they let me try for it."

"Why didn't you tell me you had done this?"

"I thought they'd laugh me out of the door, I never imagined they'd say yes."

Ryan had pulled Nathan into a hug. "I'm proud of you, babe," he said firmly. Of course, inside he'd faced the finality that he was losing Nathan. No point in a future when they were separated on opposite sides of the US, and he certainly wasn't going to hold Nathan back. It had been easier for Ryan to assume they were ending with Nathan's move to LA.

Ultimately Nathan left his position with *Style* and moved permanently to LA, embracing his burgeoning acting career. The arguments increased at the same rate as the distance between them. Ryan had always been the one who picked the fights. *Fucking idiot.* Ryan fought insecurity and jealousy and the only way he could do that was to pretend Nathan leaving for a new career meant nothing to him.

Nathan got the role in the TV series, up and away from his independent film part, starting with a six-month contract. His picture was emblazoned on page twenty-nine of a teen magazine that Ryan's assistant left on his desk. The photo was one of Ryan's, and it was one of his favorites. Nathan, beautiful, shirtless, his lean body stretched with catlike grace, leaning back on his elbows. His jeans were pushed down and his hipbones teased at what was hidden. He was pictured gazing away from the camera thoughtfully, his soft dark hair in disarray around his face. The lighting had been faultless, each coppery highlight in Nathan's hair picked out in detail. The photo was simply perfect.

They had gone home after that shoot and made love

and it was the moment Ryan knew he was head over heels for Nathan. They'd exchanged *I love you's* and Nathan began to make plans for a future together, a house outside the city maybe, adoption, hell, the whole family thing. Ryan wasn't sure he was capable of all that, but he'd nodded and listened. Then he saw the damn photo again and he knew at that moment he should never have let his fears stop him from believing in what they had.

Ryan didn't hesitate when he saw that photo. He loved Nathan and they had been apart too long. Sure there was a relationship to save, he texted Nathan and Nathan had answered. Ryan impulsively booked a flight immediately —the first flight he could get to LA. He called Nathan from the airport and left a voicemail when Nathan didn't answer. Now he sat in the taxi as the driver steered it up into the hills. He needed to push aside his insecurities, drop to his knees, and beg forgiveness of the one person who made him whole. He hoped he wasn't too late.

7:12 a.m.

AFTER HIS PATHETIC, half-hearted stumble-run, Nathan decided he needed to get indoors and get a shower. He wasn't sure what time Ryan would get here but Nathan wanted to be at least halfway decent when he did.

He couldn't help the excitement that flooded him. He really wanted to see if maybe his ex-lover would want to find some kind of resolution. Maybe they could agree to split their time between the two cities?

He was just inside the main door when the floor beneath his feet moved, subtly the first time, slowly, a groaning, a creaking, and a soft shaking. The ground shift left him holding the doorframe. It only lasted a few seconds and was over before he could force a thought about it through the rest of the clutter in his mind. The checklist in his head clicked in automatically before the shaking had stopped. He smiled briefly. That earth movement would be dominating the news today. Hey, maybe today was a good day for him to walk proudly out of the closet! Surely revealing his sexual preferences would never be more newsworthy than an earthquake in Tinseltown.

He thumbed to the number of his brother out of state and hit Send. The phone at the other end rang once, twice, a third time, and voicemail kicked in. He decided not to leave a message. No one really needed to know that a minor shock had hit his apartment in the hills above LA. The trembler hadn't been strong enough to be worthy of hitting the news anywhere outside of California. Nathan had just been trying to be a good citizen, letting a family member know like the government said he should. He made a mental note to charge the damn cell when he finished his shower.

Seconds later, just as Nathan pocketed his cell, the earth around him ripped apart with such savagery that it was impossible to stand upright. Nathan scrabbled to hold the side of the doorframe, trying to find his feet. His vision blurred as dust and concrete fell about his head, knocking him to the ground. Before the shaking stopped, before the ceiling joists cascaded down and trapped his legs, he slammed into unconsciousness.

Chapter Two

They were about ten minutes away from Nathan's apartment when the pre-shock hit. The driver cursed as the car skittered sideways, and Ryan grabbed on to the door and his belt in confusion.

"What the hell?"

"S'okay, just a small one. We get them all the time out here."

Ryan knew what he meant. Earthquake. He'd never really experienced an earthquake before and it had felt weird, like the whole of the earth beneath the car had slid sideways, stones and loose gravel from the hills above them dropping onto the car in a crashing, rattling rain.

Ryan peered out the window at the sweeping vista of LA sleeping below him, wondering how many people woke up to the sound that was like distant thunder and to the shaking of the earth. The car had skidded to the edge of the road, and he shot a quick glance down the slope, thanking God that it hadn't been a major quake. Smiling ruefully, he sat back in the seat as the driver pulled away and angled back onto his side of the road.

A breath-stealing jolt yanked him from his musings.

The car was moving; no, the hill was moving… shuddering and falling…pushing the hapless car ahead of it. The rocks, vegetation…the *sky* tumbled. The car neared the edge, the driver shouting hysterically as it tilted sideways, large chunks of hillside falling to dent the car, beat at the car, push the car to the edge, to the drop, to the shaking and dancing of the moving earth.

Ryan clung with both hands to the grab handle over the cab's door and jerked at every noise, every motion. This wasn't good, not good at all. He stared out, snatching a quick look down at LA, and what he saw was burned into his mind. Explosions. He thought he saw buildings shattering and imploding, but that had to be his imagination. *What the fuck is happening?*

The car ceased its crazy ride and, for one second, remained poised on the edge, overhanging the drop. Then a final shove of moving dirt sent it careening, tumbling down the rise.

The car lodged against a natural outcrop and came to a sudden and bone-crunching stop, the thunder and passion of the earthquake still warring around it, the hill subsiding, plummeting, and falling in a haphazard storm of rocks and debris. The seatbelt saved Ryan's life. It stopped him from being thrown from the car and crushed under it as it rolled and slid, but it also ultimately trapped him inside the vehicle as the chassis twisted and buckled against the onslaught of the hillside. All too soon the noises around him started to slow, and he was left in the dark surrounded by dust and earth, his eyes burning with fumes. He needed to get out of the taxi *now*.

With a powerful resolution born of a desire to live, he heaved himself out of the belt and pushed at the door with his booted feet, tumbling out as it burst open. He crab-walked away from the compacted car, his eyes taking in what was essentially half a car. The front had been flattened and the driver crushed.

He was trapped in a nightmare. The remains of the cab perched precariously on a bed of dirt and rocks of all sizes. Flames licked up leaking fuel, eating at the crushed metal. Ryan knew he could do nothing for the driver. He was gone…crushed…dead…*fuck*.

Stumbling to his feet, he clutched at his forehead, pulling his hand away and staring in a shocked stupor at the blood. A head injury. *Crap*.

The car groaned as the metal heated. Half out of his mind with horror and dread, believing the car would explode, he twisted and scrambled his way up over the remains of the road, feeling the heat on his back as the fire continued to eat away at the mutilated car. The cab wasn't the only car destroyed. One that had been ahead of them lay crushed so badly no one could have escaped. Another vehicle that they'd passed on the freeway had plowed into an embankment and burst into flames. All of the vehicles had been tossed around like toys in the hands of Nature.

Finally he crashed to his knees, his back to the view below. There was nothing he could do for anyone in any vehicle here, and his gaze focused on what was left of the road. Reluctantly, spurred by horrified fascination and the need to face what had happened, Ryan pushed himself to his feet and turned slowly. Shielding his eyes with his hand

and coughing, he faced the nightmare vista of LA laid out before him. Fire. He could see fire, drifts of dark gray smoke, and clouds of dust. Debris. The ground still stirred uneasily beneath his feet. This was a living disaster movie, surreal, unbelievable. LA was unrecognizable. Everything had gone eerily silent where he stood above the rage of the distant fires and destruction, the motion of the earth around him having finally faded.

The taxi burned brightly, and he shuddered at the thought of the dead driver. Ryan didn't want to think about a world where death could be a blessing. He could have been trapped in that car, trapped in the flames. Fire: his worst fear, his nightmare.

Living, breathing fire tracked steadily on its way up the hillside following a dirty trail of oil and fuel that speeded its path. He really needed to move and *now,* but for a second, he stopped, dazed, still watching LA shattered by the ground on which it had risen. *Jesus, this looks worse than the Northridge quake of '94.* He recalled a spread in *National Geographic* that said the quake had only lasted thirty seconds, but he remembered it killed about sixty people and injured several thousand. Images of collapsed freeways and fires flashed across his thoughts, quick jumbled images of death and destruction. This looked bad, and this wasn't just a small part of the city. The entire LA downtown looked to be destroyed.

Below him lay LA, and around him, but not too near, he heard sirens and smelled smoke. Nathan was somewhere above him, perhaps hit as hard as he'd been. Maybe he was trapped, possibly dead—Ryan froze and refused to think of the worst scenario any more.

Should he try to contact someone? Who? Emergency

services? If the situation hadn't been so horrendous, Ryan might have laughed at the stupidity of his thought. There was no one else that could be right here and now; Nathan had him and him alone to depend upon.

He checked his pocket. Fuck, his cell was in the car, along with a hastily packed flight bag.

Tensing his muscles one by one, he tested for injuries. Each limb seemed bruised but worked. He was relatively uninjured, and nothing appeared broken. His breathing had become easy and regular. He thanked the heavens for the fact that he went running every day and was fit. Picking his way carefully, he started up the hill. Climbing over piles of stone and tossed trees and foliage, he managed to trace parts of the broken road, breaking into a run when he could. He'd been running for ten minutes when he came to an abrupt stop.

"Holy shit."

Mother Nature had destroyed all that Ryan knew as right and normal. The road twisted in on itself, decimated and ripped apart. It was difficult to see where he needed to scramble but as long as he moved uphill, he was going in the right direction. He imagined he was just over two miles from Nathan's apartment, in normal circumstances about twenty minutes at a steady uphill run. Over the unsettled wasteland he traversed, he knew the trip would last much longer.

Nathan could be hurt up there. Over the next rise could be total devastation. Ryan quickened his jog, his heart pounding as he jumped and climbed the fallen hillside. He didn't pass any other cars that had signs of life in them, just burned, twisted wreckage and bodies he couldn't stand to look at.

As he topped the last hill, to the place where Nathan's complex had sat, he stopped, horrified. The last time he'd been here, when Nathan first came to LA, the whole area was beautiful—landscaped and artistic design nestled into the hills. But now...

He gaped at a scene that looked like something out of a war movie. Everything was flat. Half the mountain had crushed the private entrance. The gates and what had been the parking area were torn in two.

"Fuck."

Chapter Three

Coughing and moaning pushed Nathan to consciousness, and it took him a few desperate minutes to realize it was him making the noises.

Earthquake.

A bad one if the destruction around him was anything to go by. He couldn't see much farther than he could reach. The masonry dust drifted around him heavily, and the ground still shook beneath him, dislodging cement and bricks. He could see light above him, daylight where there should have been another apartment. *Shit, this must be bad, really bad.*

He knew the apartment was empty, had been empty since Christmas, but the sky... That didn't seem right. It wasn't right.

He reached out with one hand trying to gauge what he could feel, what he could understand of the debris around him, but his movement was limited and the ground was still moving. It was surreal, frightening, and he could feel the edges of panic start to cloud his thoughts as he tested his extremities and realized he couldn't move his legs. Heavy steel lay across his hip and down past his knees. Breathing slowly and deeply, he pushed at the steel, but he might as well have been pushing a solid wall for all it gave under his attempts. All it did was raise more choking dust.

He decided to lie still, very still, until the earth stopped moving and the dust settled, maybe wait for emergency services. They wouldn't be far. They wouldn't take long; they'd be here soon. Jason would let them know. His friend and fellow actor was in downtown LA, quite a few miles from here. But he would know that Nathan was up in the hills if he couldn't get hold of him.

So, *shit*, he needed to let his out-of-state contacts know what had happened so they would stop worrying.

His cell. If he could get to his cell in the left pocket of his sweats… He could maybe tell Jason where he was, that he needed help, talk to his brother as well. He pushed his hand down, feeling his way, not even sure how far his hand was from the pocket, just knowing with enough grim determination he would get to the cell.

He could feel the cell, feel it in his pocket, the outline of it, but *shit*. The material was bunched and he couldn't get it out. Frustration made him whimper. This was not good, and he started pulling at the seam, desperate to reach inside. Picking, pulling, trying to ease the material apart. The ground had stopped shaking, and a sudden peace surrounded him that was unnatural. He heard no noises at all, and he held in a breath in anticipation of any sound at all, not wanting to move and miss it, as if any movement could be the death of him.

Nathan had managed to pick his way through to the inner lining of the pocket, cursing Nike for their fucking stitching. The pain in his legs was numbing, and he knew that was a bad sign. He had realized straight away that he couldn't sit up, and a combination of twisted steel and masonry made the space he was lying in impossibly small. He could still see the daylight, the early morning light spilling in to cast eerie shadows over his limited space. Taking stock of the situation, he knew two things for certain: he wasn't going anywhere under his own steam and aftershocks were inevitable.

There was very little between his fragile human body and the remains of his apartment torn apart by the forces of Nature. He hoped to hell that the shifting earth echoes didn't dislodge the steel that was holding together his cocoon of safety.

He heard his cell ring, the unique ring he had for his brother, Adam. He wanted to shout, "I'm here, I'm okay, someone help me." He just needed to get to the phone. Ease the threads apart…pull…pull…ease them apart, visualize the seam. His hand slowly made its way in, and he moaned in relief as his cramped fingers closed around his cell. He couldn't move his arm enough to see the phone, but he keyed speed dial from memory and hit speakerphone. His brother's voice was instant and threaded with fear.

"Nathan, what the fuck, the news… Are you okay?"

"Adam." Nathan knew his voice sounded small. It echoed in the silence around him. He needed to push his voice, use what he knew from acting and project his desperation and need for help.

"Nathan, for fuck's sake—"

"Adam, I need help…trapped, man."

"Shit. Fuck. In the apartment?"

"Yeah."

"I'm on it, Nathan. Hold on." He heard Adam talking to his wife.

"Nathan, Mary is calling this in. Hang tight, little brother. They've added your name and location."

"My cell." Nathan whimpered softly, hoping no one heard his fear. "I can't stay—s'battery…"

"Nathan, can you tell me what you see, what you know?"

"Light, I can see…light…trapped…steel and concrete…I think the rest is gone, Adam. I can see light."

"Okay, man, save the cell, help is on the way."

Soon please, Adam, soon.

FEAR THICK IN HIS THROAT, Ryan clambered down broken floors and through smashed glass, his bare skin tearing on exposed masonry and steel. Only a small part of the apartment complex had survived. The top floor had sheared off and lay in pieces. He had already found one body—a young woman, a brunette. She'd looked to simply be sleeping, but clearly she was gone from this world, because he felt for a pulse and found nothing. She was surrounded by photos and linens—life—but there was nothing he could do for her. She was way past any kind of help he could provide.

He tried to visualize where Nathan's apartment had been on the lower south corner facing the garden, but the whole site had slid, crumbling and snapping and tearing as it was swallowed by the hungry earth. There was only a small part of the structure left, buried in mud and debris, and Ryan was hoping for one thing—to find his ex-lover alive and unharmed.

He slid the last few meters to a pile of stones and wood—a fireplace. Electric cables twisted and popped as they snaked and touched each other, and carefully he picked his way to the final structure standing. He recognized nothing, no photos, no decoration, nothing that marked this as Nathan's in any way, but he knew somehow that this was Nathan's apartment. Knew? More like hoped—prayed.

Glass from a smashed window sliced into his hand, and he yelped as it dug and twisted into him. He stopped, pulling the glass out carefully, blood oozing to the surface. Distracted, he wiped it on his jeans, and judging where he stood, he carefully made his way into the sculpture of steel.

"Nathan...Nathan." *Come on, man, please be here somewhere. Please still be alive.* "Nathan, Nathan, Nathan," he repeated over and over, pausing in between to hear an answer. He picked his way past doorframes and kitchen cupboards forced open under pressure, spilling cans and crockery onto the floor. It was strangely intimate seeing the contents thrown and smashed around him, imagining them lined up carefully in the cupboard, Nathan putting them away, his gentle touches, his pride in his possessions, all destroyed in seconds. Ryan moved slowly over the broken cupboards, calling Nathan's name, stumbling, trying not to knock anything that might cause a mini landslide.

He stopped, realizing he was making so much noise that he wouldn't hear if Nathan was there trapped under the rubble. He had to stop panicking. He had to go against his instinct to scream and shout and just stand still.

"Nathan? Nathan?"

NATHAN GRIPPED the cell like a lifeline. Adam knew he was trapped; Adam would try and get help for him. He just needed to wait. He coughed; he tried not to, but his throat was lined with dust, and it was getting damned difficult to breathe.

"Nathan, Nathan."

Jeez, now he was hallucinating. Ryan's voice. He wouldn't be here at this moment. He'd still be on his way from the airport. God, he hoped Ryan was okay. It was stupid that he even began to worry about Ryan over and above all the other things he should be focusing on. Like survival. Like getting out of here to go and find Ryan. He really expected to die here. It was a remote location, time wasn't on his side, and he had no feeling in his legs. What did it say that this close to death all he could imagine was the panicked voice of his lover? He was seriously losing it big time.

He heard the voice again. "Nathan, Nathan."

"Stop it, leave me alone," Nathan said softly to himself. If he was going to die, it wasn't going to be with Ryan's panicked voice and regrets that they had been apart for the last two months. He wanted to focus on their friendship, on the love he had for Ryan, not on the time he had been lonely. He wanted to think about his family.

Chapter Four

RYAN HEARD SOMETHING—WORDS. *STOP IT. ALONE.*

Nathan.

Desperately, he scrabbled under bent beams, dodging dislodged brick and stone. It was hard to make sense of what he was seeing, everything upside-down, walls collapsed, ceiling and floor mixed in rubble and dust. There was no visible sign of Nathan, and he had almost lost all hope, standing in silence, trying to hear something —anything. There was a sound, a movement, and finally he could track it to a large steel beam that pinned Nathan down to the hard floor.

"Oh God, oh God, no," he stammered, falling to his knees next to the mess of twisted metal.

It was difficult to make out Nathan's features with his eyes closed and covered in gray dust. Ryan stared, shocked, for a few moments, then reality kicked back in, and shaking, he reached for Nathan's neck, locating a fluttering pulse. Still alive. He let out the breath that he didn't even realize he'd been holding—a sigh of relief. He dropped his head nearer to Nathan's face, feeling his breath and touching a shaking hand to his forehead. He was unconscious but alive. As Ryan considered what to do, where to start, Nathan's eyes opened suddenly, an intense green against his gray, dusty face. Ryan rocked back on his heels in sudden surprise.

"Nathan, oh my God, what hurts? Where are you hurt?"

Nathan didn't say anything in return. His unfocused eyes looked directly at Ryan, then blinked. He frowned, then it seemed to make sense, and his eyes widened as he coughed, starting to bring his head up to Ryan.

"Adam," he rasped, lifting his hand as much as he could. Ryan saw the imprint of the cellphone keys in his flesh. His voice was so quiet, but Ryan understood what he meant—tell his family that he was with Nathan, that Nathan wasn't alone.

There was a signal but the battery was low, and he tried not to focus on the fact that probably hundreds, even thousands, of people were trying to get through to loved ones and the network would be overloaded. He thumbed through the contacts, located Adam, and keyed the name, holding it to his ear, his palm resting flat on Nathan's head as he lowered it back to the cold stone floor. He was examining the area around the trapped man while the cell tried to connect. It took five tries, and Ryan sent his thanks skyward when it finally did. He knew what he needed to ask. He needed to know what the situation was with emergency services, what was happening in LA.

"Nathan?"

"No. It's Ryan, I'm here with Nathan. Battery's low."

"What are you—"

"I was outside when it hit. Tell me what's going on, Adam."

"Fire in the hills, spreading towards LA. You need to get away from the apartment, Ryan. I'm serious."

"What about emergency services?"

"Running evac. CNN is showing massive damage downtown. They're worried about aftershocks, but the fire in the hills, Ryan, the fire is the worst. It's spreading downwind to LA, right where you are."

"We're going now, trust me." Then, saying no more, he closed the cell, not wanting to waste the battery. What was the point in explaining in detail that it seemed that Nathan was trapped for the duration? No point at all.

He pocketed the cell, then started to feel around Nathan's trapped limbs. One beam had landed and pinned him from right thigh to his left ankle with no room to move. The beam was twisted and buried deep in a mountain of rubble and debris, and for the life of him, Ryan couldn't see how he was going to move the damn thing. He tried putting two hundred twenty pounds of gym-honed muscle into pushing it off, but that only elicited a groaning from the structure and a frightened demand to stop from Nathan, who was clearly in pain.

"Nathan, tell me where it hurts," Ryan said softly, kneeling at Nathan's side, cradling a hand into his dark hair.

"Pushing on…chest, ribs, now…it hurt my legs…but no more… I can't feel my legs." Nathan's barely there voice rose on a panicked note, and Ryan had to think on his feet.

"They're just numb, Nathan. The beam is resting on you; it's just cutting off the circulation."

"Swear to me, Ry."

"I swear." Ryan hoped he came across as firm and convincing. He didn't know for one minute why Nathan couldn't feel his legs, but he hoped to God he was right and that it was just pressure on them. "We need to get this off you. I need to make a…" He couldn't think of the word —something to pivot, to push off the steel. He realized Nathan had said nothing else, and that the man's eyes had closed again. Damn it, he needed to stay conscious. "Nathan, talk to me. Nathan, I love you. Don't start checking out on me."

"'M really tired." Nathan's voice was slurring, a combination of exhaustion and shock, and his limbs and torso were trembling visibly.

"Stay with me, Nathan. When I get this off you need to slide out. You need to brace yourself. Can you do that? Nathan… Nathan?" He watched as Nathan pushed with his hands, but it was no use whatsoever. He didn't have the upper body strength to push himself out, not with possibly cracked ribs and all sorts of other hidden injuries. Ryan certainly wasn't going to dissuade the positive attempt though. "That's good, Nathan, just stay still for me. We'll get you out."

Again Ryan pushed, but nothing was happening. He forced his entire strength against the steel, hoping for a break, hoping the thing would move enough to drag Nathan free. Almost sobbing with the exertion and frustration of it not moving and completely defeated, he slumped down, touching Nathan's forehead, listening as Nathan mumbled something incoherent. He lowered his ear to Nathan's mouth. His eyes caught the water bottle that he imagined Nathan had been holding. Somehow it was still intact and a quarter full, and he dribbled some water into Nathan's mouth. Water was good. He'd read that somewhere; water is always good.

Nathan coughed then spoke, forcing out words, staccato and urgent.

"Ground…not right…can feel…" The ground?

Ryan understood even as the ground started to move again, subtly rolling under them. It was another shake, and Ryan immediately thought of aftershocks as the entire apartment structure shifted again. Still it was enough to crack supports, and part of the ceiling started to fall. Ryan didn't think. He threw himself on top of Nathan, protecting his head and praying this wasn't the end. The ground shifting grew in intensity, shaking loose any item that had gotten wedged in the main quake, and dropping it onto the two men.

"Don't," Nathan tried to say over the noise of the falling debris. "You gotta leave, Ry, this is stupid. One of us…"

Ryan tensed as rocks and pieces of rubble crashed down on them, onto his back. He didn't hear Nathan cry out at all, and Ryan waited until blessed peace came at last following a few groans in the structure and settling debris. Ryan lifted his head, not even thinking of the injuries that had just cut into him, more focused on how the new tremor may have affected Nathan's position.

"Nathan, I think I can… I can see space here."

Space where there was none before. There was a clear gap now between the steel and Nathan's legs. He crouched low and tensed his leg muscles to give him solid purchase, and immediately tried to pull Nathan, but nothing happened.

"Nathan, I need you to help me. Can you help me? Relax, let me pull you out." He got a good grip under Nathan's arms, his own hands wet with blood, and pulled, heaving, digging his heels in, and finally, slowly, Nathan moved from under the twisted steel. There was no time for self-congratulation, no time to stop and rest. They needed to get out of here before the next aftershock. The structure about them was precarious at best, hanging on by a few beams and little else.

With the impetus of fear and the adrenaline of action, Ryan lifted Nathan as best he could. Ryan might be built and he might work out every day, but shit, Nathan was no lightweight. A lifeless man in shock was not an easy burden to carry.

"Help me, Nathan, help me—come on—we need to get out of here—daylight—we need some air—come on." Each word was punctuated with another step towards the hill outside what was left of the apartment complex. Exhausted and drained, Ryan finally slumped to the brown summer grass, sliding Nathan gently to the ground.

"Nathan." Ryan leaned over him, anxiously poking at his leg and seeing it twitch. He had never felt so relieved. They were outside, they were both alive, and everything was okay. The pain in his back was now a dull ache, but he needed to see what was there, needed Nathan's help to see if anything was open and needed attention. Thing was, Nathan was lying on the ground, gasping for air, moving his legs, reaching down to touch his chest.

"Ribs?" Ryan asked gently. Nathan opened his eyes and nodded, his eyes glazed and his face creased in a frown.

"Yeah, can't breathe so well," he said simply, "but that

is nothing compared to the whole leg…shit, my wrist, I…" He subsided into silence.

"Can you stand, Nathan? We need to move."

"I need some time, just need to catch a fucking breath."

"We can't stay."

"I can't go anywhere. Shit, Ry, we need to stay and wait for help."

"Adam said there are fires up on the ridge behind us, so we need to move. Move down, 'cause they're coming this way." Ryan swore as Nathan visibly paled, fully aware of what he had just revealed, that Nathan had been trapped in the path of a forest fire above LA.

"Fuck." Nathan struggled to stand, his legs not really letting him stand on his own. Ryan was up in an instant, helping him, linking his hands around Nathan's back, Nathan swayed for a moment, his hands coming to rest on Ryan's lower back, slipping and sliding against wet material. He finally grabbed a handful of material that gave him purchase with his good hand. His other refused to obey what he wanted it to do. Ryan tried not to grimace, urging Nathan to lean against the twisted gate to the park area.

"Turn the fuck round," Nathan bit out. He held out his hand in front of him and it was coated with fresh blood.

Ryan winced at the harshness in Nathan's words but turned nonetheless. "Ryan, fuck—your back is shredded."

"Is it bad?"

"Aren't you in pain?"

"Just tell me, Nathan, is it bad, bleeding badly?"

"More of an ooze than a gush," Nathan finally said.

Ryan sighed in relief. "Then it'll be fine. We will be fine."

"Shit, Ryan, it's… You need to get to a—"

"Nathan, shut the fuck up. If it's not bleeding badly then we don't have to do anything with it. We walk."

Walk? Easy for him to say, but Nathan did try, the numbness and aches in his legs causing him to limp badly. He had to stop frequently and retch into the grass.

Ryan stopped each time to help Nathan, but the need to move allowed no patience for Nathan being sick. He resorted to taking Nathan's weight against him and slowly they made their way farther from the complex. Nathan suddenly stopped, turning back to look at the devastation.

"Angie… She was…we need to find her…this morning, she waved at me."

"Young girl, brunette?" Ryan swallowed as he realized he had already found the girl.

"Yeah, pretty, actress."

"Sorry, man, she's gone." There was no other way to say it.

"Gone."

"Yeah. Is there anyone else here?" Ryan asked. But inside he knew they had to go, and if it came to a choice of rescuing others or getting Nathan down off of this damn mountain of destruction, then there really was no question as to what he would do.

"We should go and…" Nathan was rambling, pain bracketing his mouth as he attempted to turn back to look at the crushed apartment block. "We should get Angie to… her body…just away from the fire."

"She's gone, man. I checked her myself. There is nothing else we can do. Was there anyone else there?"

Nathan shook his head as if he could clear his head of

the horror. "No, just the two apartments out of the four, just me and Angie and Oscar."

"Oscar?" Shit. There was someone else? Ryan glanced at the destruction that had once been a beautifully styled complex. Surely no one else could have survived that.

"Dog, stray, kinda hangs out round the area."

Ryan breathed a sigh of relief. "He'll have been long gone, man. Dogs sense these things."

"Yeah...the birds." Nathan looked a bit spaced out, and Ryan snapped his fingers in front of Nathan's face, trying to bring him back to the present. "We need to leave Angie? Are you sure?" Nathan finally stuttered.

"I'm sorry, but please, we need to get away from here and down the side. We need to get to safety." He didn't realize just how much he was begging for them to just get a move on.

Nathan didn't say anything else, just leaned into Ryan's supporting hold and together they started to move downhill.

There was a steady noise in the distance coming closer, a *thwump thwump,* and four black-as-night helicopters flew overhead, down the hill towards downtown LA. Neither man said a word, and neither acknowledged that the Army was now clearly involved in whatever had happened below.

"I think I saw LA," Ryan finally murmured, more to hear noise than to actually speak. "I saw it when I got here. It was burning, there were...fires...and clouds of dust, debris—buildings at crazy angles."

"Jason is down there. He was on his way to Starbucks, I'd only just gotten off the phone talking to him," Nathan said softly. "That was why your phone call went to voicemail…"

"Your friend from the show?" Ryan asked without his customary jealousy at any other man in Nathan's life. He needed to get his head around not doing that. "I'm sure he'll be okay. I mean the whole thing happened really early. He'll have been in the open; he'll be fine."

Ryan wasn't convinced about what he was saying. After all, he'd seen the proud skyline broken and drunken in destruction. He didn't vocalize his fears and doubts—it was hard enough to walk, let alone worry about a situation in the city below that was way beyond his help.

Chapter Five

THEY STUMBLED SOME DISTANCE BEFORE THEY SMELLED the smoke. Nathan didn't want to turn round to see what he feared was behind them.

"We gotta step this up," Ryan urged. "Can you walk faster?"

Nathan swallowed; he was already pushing it to walk at this pace. Every movement was agony in his thighs where the beam had laid, and his breathing was labored. He knew *he* couldn't go any faster, but Ryan could. Ryan could run ahead, get out of the way of the fire, get help, maybe he could get back here in time?

"Ryan, I can't. I really am trying, but you need to go ahead and get help."

"You need me to help you walk. I'm not going ahead."

"You could get help."

"I'd never get back up in time, and they're dealing with a city in flames. They won't be focusing on the hills."

Nathan was tired and in pain. Why couldn't Ryan see

this and just leave him to sit on the side of what was left of the road. "Ryan, just go, I'll—"

Ryan spun so fast Nathan almost lost his footing, and he was suddenly hauled up against a desperate-eyed Ryan, his face inches away.

"Fuck you, Nathan. I didn't leave you to burn in your apartment. Do you think I'm gonna leave you to burn now?"

They stared at each other, Nathan's breath hitching, the pain in his chest flaring. Whatever Ryan's faults, he wouldn't leave anyone to burn alive. He would save whoever needed to be saved, not just Nathan.

"I just don't want to hold you up," Nathan said, wheezing.

Ryan relaxed, the fight leaving him as quickly as it arrived. "I love you and I'm not leaving you," he finished simply, and with this declaration from Ryan, they resumed their slow journey downhill, Nathan still itching to make Ryan go ahead, not wanting to hold him back. That was the second time he'd heard the words from Ryan and he needed to make sure, if they didn't make it out, that Ryan knew how he felt.

"I love you too, you know," he said. Ryan glanced at him with a smile. "I never stopped." They didn't talk anymore but at least they both knew how each other really felt underneath the insecurities.

Nathan really was trying so hard to walk faster, but the pain in his legs—the grating, sharp insistent ache as he walked added to the whole not being able to breathe thing—was making it impossible to push any more. Ryan was supporting as much weight as he could, but fuck, he wasn't Superman, and frustration that he wouldn't leave him and go ahead was bubbling insistently below the surface. Where only moments before he'd been speaking words of love, that warm feeling had subsided.

This was typical. Damn stubborn, irritating, controlling, insufferable Ryan. Always in control, always organizing, always so anal about detail. Nathan swore Ryan had OCD when it came to stubbornness and control.

Well, Nathan wasn't ready for that. Nathan was his own man, and he could organize his own life, thank you very much. He didn't need the Ortiz rules to live by. He didn't need jealousy, and he didn't need to be told what to do. Ryan should just leave him. Go. He didn't want Ryan anyway.

Fuck, he really loved the big idiot. Why was his head so screwed and why was he considering this when he should be focusing on getting down to civilization—or what was left of it in LA.

THE SMOKE WAS VISIBLE NOW. Wisps floated around them, a breeze following them down the hills, bringing with it a forewarning of the destruction that would follow. Each time a disaster happened—the fires, earthquakes, hurricanes—it felt remote and removed on the news, not like this, not personal and vindictive. He wished he was watching this on TV and wasn't right smack in the middle of it.

They had been stumbling downhill for at least half an hour when Nathan heard the barking long before he actually saw the scruffy mutt.

"Oscar," he breathed softly. The dog that hung around

the apartment building looking for scraps stood on an outcrop of broken and torn road, barking insistently.

"That's Oscar?" Ryan said. They stopped. Ryan tried to call him over, but the dog stubbornly stood where he was, his ears pricked, and his tail high. "Is he normally this active?" He winced as he turned to face Oscar and Nathan immediately worried Ryan was hurt worse than he wanted to admit.

"Nah, he's usually kinda quiet," Nathan confirmed. "Can you grab him, Ry?"

"We have to move, he'll find his way down on his own," Ryan said immediately.

"Please?" Nathan pleaded. Oscar had accompanied him on many a morning jog around the park and somehow, in the middle of all this, he wanted to cling onto normality.

Ryan cursed, then left Nathan propped against a fallen tree and crossed to the dog, who danced backwards and down the side of the twisted road.

Chapter Six

RYAN MADE HIMSELF LOOK AS SMALL AS HE COULD, stooping low to approach the dog as it moved backward, woofing softly and whining again.

"Wassup, boy, are we heading for a new aftershock, huh? Is that what you're tryin' to tell us?" Ryan couldn't believe he was talking to a dog. Oscar whined and turned, jumping off the outcrop and disappearing.

Ryan almost ignored him and crossed back to Nathan. He liked dogs as much as the next man, but if Oscar was warning of an aftershock then Nathan would need help just to stand, let alone to handle the earth moving.

Oscar appeared again at the top and barked twice. Something, some instinct to trust this barking dog, made Ryan turn back and scramble up the six-foot ribbon of twisted road, looking down at where Oscar now disappeared and to a scene of carnage he was sure he would remember until the day he died.

Five cars thrown from the road. Two were burned out with shadows of people inside. Two other cars had been crushed by road and rubble, and one car, like his taxi, had been half cut and pressed to nothing with huge rocks and chunks of road leaning precariously over it. Was anyone alive? Why was Oscar leading him down there? He wasn't sure he could handle this.

"Daddy, doggy," a small voice said. The sound was so small Ryan almost missed it. It came from the car cut in half. Calling back to Nathan that he would be back in a minute, he clambered down the other side of the newly exposed earth and climbed over God knows what to get to the car at the front.

"Hello?" he said. He couldn't see through the spider web of broken glass

"Daddy?"

Shit, a child was in there. He tried to move around to see in, finally finding a small part of the car that offered a glance inside. A little girl sat in a car seat, untouched, but with the belts twisted and stuck. The only way to get her out was to remove the broken glass. He didn't think about the fact that they should be moving, he needed to get her out.

"Hey, darlin', I'm Ryan. I'm here to help. Can you cover your eyes, sweetie? I need to break the glass." As soon as she moved her hands, he pushed the glass in, trying to ignore her shrieks of fear. Reaching in, he pulled at the belt, untwisting it and grabbing at the girl, pulling her out in one move. She was so tiny, no older than his three-year-old niece.

He heard Oscar whining, his gut instinct telling him that the dog wanted him to move. He was convinced that another aftershock was building under his feet, and desperately he moved away from the cars, the little girl sobbing into his neck, hanging on for dear life. He made it to the top of the rubble pile, sliding and slipping towards Nathan as another aftershock pulled at the earth, the hill that was left collapsing and crushing the girl's car. He felt sick. He hadn't been able to tell if her parents had been in the car, although he knew whoever had been in the front of the car was dead. There'd been nothing left of the front half of the car when he got there, and there was certainly nothing of it left at all now.

"Ryan, Jesus" was all Nathan could say. "What the—"

Ryan just shook his head. *Don't ask questions, just leave it.* "We need to keep walking." He switched the little girl to his left side and winced as her small hands twisted into the back of his torn shirt, pulling at open wounds. He gritted his teeth, then wrapped his right hand around Nathan. "Let's walk."

The smell of fire was overwhelming here, but Ryan couldn't tell if that was because of the burning cars or if it was the specter of death sweeping down the hill as they descended, trying to grab at the few survivors on the side of this mountain. He tried to quicken the pace. He couldn't even ask the little girl her name, because it made it too personal. What if he had a name to put to his failure to keep them alive? He couldn't handle that. What if he failed?

Chapter Seven

ADAM OPENED THE DOOR TO HIS PARENTS AND AFTER hugging them, led them into the front room where Mary nursed the baby and stared in horror at the screen.

CNN ran the same reel over and over, the devastation in LA, the iconic buildings and landmarks, some ripped in half, fire destroying the rest, estimates of thousands dead. The President issued a federal disaster declaration, the Army was in control, and a swarm of helicopters ferried people and medical help to and from the epicenter. It hadn't been more than ninety minutes and none of it seemed real.

There were stories being flashed on the screen. Stories of survival, miraculous escapes from destroyed buildings, even as an aftershock sent emergency services workers to their deaths as they struggled to help.

Adam didn't know what to say as they watched. They could do nothing. They had told the Ortizes that their son had contacted them. Ryan's family had thought he was safe in New York. Telling them otherwise was the hardest call that Adam had ever made.

The fires in the hills had merged into one huge forest fire, and emergency services from twelve different states had volunteered, joining the search and rescue crews, fighting fires, and helping with looting control.

"How long would it take them to get down?" his mom asked quietly. She was red eyed from crying and clutched his dad's arm with an iron grip. His dad was deathly pale.

"I don't know, Mom," Adam answered quickly. He didn't know anything except that his little brother was somewhere out there needing help. And that Adam living in Virginia put him too far away to help. "An hour? We don't know what it's like."

His mom sat carefully on the seat next to Mary. She stroked Emily's fuzz of soft blonde hair and bit back tears.

"He's never even met you, little one," she said.

"He'll make it out, Mom," Adam insisted.

His mom nodded. "He will. I am sure of it."

CNN changed the story with graphic scenes captured by low-flying helicopters. The core of it focused on the destruction in LA, but there were sensationalist reports of mortality statistics, eyewitness accounts, and information releases from the president and the governor. New, though, was the closure of two freeways north of Los Angeles and the manner in which the fires were being dealt with. Authorities had dispatched water-dropping helicopters, and there were more than two hundred fire engines as the blaze started to push towards the city.

The camera focused on an Officer Barlow of the LA County Fire Department as he made an announcement to cameras in in clipped, clear tones.

"About three hundred and fifty police officers are on the scene, patrolling evacuated neighborhoods and warning residents ahead of the flames."

"Nathan isn't dead," Adam said, his arms crossed, his voice calm. "I know he isn't; I would feel if he was." He said this for his momma as she sat, still as stone, transfixed by the disaster unfolding before her eyes.

Really, all he could feel was dread. And knowing Nathan was alive? He wished he could feel as convinced as he tried to sound.

It was a vision of hell that had been foretold since the San Francisco quake of 1906, but one that people chose not to think about.

But it was real.

Chapter Eight

THE SMOKE WAS NO LONGER A SUGGESTION OR A MAYBE. IT was starting to get into the air they were breathing and in their noses, the scent of burning pine and acrid smoke. Ryan did his best to hide the little girl's face in his neck, urging her to breathe gently, and with his other arm, he attempted to support Nathan more, hearing the rasping in his lover's chest, knowing he must be in so much pain.

Every so often he looked back. The last time he could swear he saw the fire jumping from one tree to another at the top of the mountain, his imagination hearing the spits and the crackle and the roar of the fire eating away at everything in its path.

He knew it was a mile, maybe less, to the base of the hill and to the highway. Surely there would be something there, some kind of rescue for those people like them that had been trapped on the side of the hills. The highway must provide a natural break for the fire. If he could just get Nathan and the girl to the other side…

He saw more cars tossed like children's toys to the

side, mostly empty, some with people—bodies—with no life in their eyes. Ryan couldn't bear to look, wondering how these nightmare images would visit him when they were safe.

He heard a voice. "Help, help me."

No, I can't hear that, I can't, hold Nathan closer, hide the girl's face.

"Please, man, just pull me out, please."

Nathan stopped. Ryan couldn't bring himself to not look. He saw a man trapped in the car, his face covered in blood.

The man's face was twisted in agony. A woman lay dead in the seat beside him, and the specter of the fire behind them danced, sending pinpoints of light onto the black polished metal of the car. Weighing his options—keep moving or leave a man to die—Ryan didn't hesitate. He placed the child on the ground and encouraged her to hold Nathan's hand. He instinctively pulled on the door handle of the distorted car. It wouldn't move, but with no glass in the way, he leaned in over the body of the dead woman whose eyes were wide, frozen in horror. He could hear the man's voice, broken and scared.

Ryan leaned in closer, cataloguing the extent of the damage. The engine had been forced back into the car, leaving the passenger dead and the driver, the man, with his legs trapped and mangled. There was so much blood and the guy's expression was dazed.

He would have to pull the man free, but he could see there was no way. Even the fire department with the Jaws of Life would take longer than he had. Tears pushed at his eyes, angry, frustrated tears, and he pulled back abruptly to return to Nathan, starting to slide an arm under his friend to resume the walk.

"Wait, we need to—" Nathan coughed, and Ryan lifted his chin, looking deep into green eyes wide with fear.

"I can't help him; there's no time. I have to get you and the girl to safety," he said clearly, feeling his stomach churn and heave at the thought that he was condemning a man to die.

"Tell him we'll send help. Please…"

Ryan's heart twisted. He knew what he needed to do. He needed to be hard, focused, but Nathan stood with agony carved into his face.

"Okay, I'll tell him." He crossed over the twisted road, clambering to the car, trying to get his head round this, pulling on every skill of pretense he had.

The man gasped, "You gotta help me."

"I'm Ryan," he said softly. "I can't get you out, man. We're gonna send someone back for you, okay?" The man looked relieved. He coughed, blood flecks spewing around his mouth. He looked close to death. "You'll be okay, man, we'll get you help." He raised a hand, gripping Ryan's in a blood-covered hold.

"David—Jackson, thanks."

Ryan pulled his hand free, stumbling back towards Nathan in shock at what he'd just done. There would be no time for David Jackson; the fire would be here before they could get someone.

He couldn't think, couldn't even begin to process the horror of what he'd just had to do, of the decision he'd made. He lifted the little girl, who looked confused, hoping to God that she wouldn't remember any of this if she lived through the day, and he grasped Nathan securely, encouraging his exhausted lover to walk.

It was all Ryan could do to center on what was happening, but every thought had to be focused on getting off this damn mountain. He didn't stop to think; he couldn't. The smoke was thick in his lungs, his head fuzzy.

Nathan rasped, clinging tighter to Ryan's arm and squeezing as hard as he could. Ryan prayed it would be okay; they just needed to get down to the highway, to the bottom.

Winds could cause the fire conditions to change by the second, by the minute, and he knew they had very little time.

NATHAN HAD WATCHED as Ryan reassured the driver, cursing his choice of apartments. The building had been so remote, so far away, when he imagined a burning LA, he felt a stark relief that he did live outside the inner circle.

The pain eating away at Nathan's reserves was leaving him unable to coherently think about anything. It was step after step after painful step, and more and more, he was leaning into Ryan. He tried not to think about the man in the car, about the girl's parents, about the fire. He tried not to think about Jason or his other friends in LA, in the city… He had to believe everyone was alive and out of the city now.

Then he recalled Ryan had said he'd seen LA burning, twisted. Jason was somewhere out there, somewhere in that carnage, in the center of a possibly destroyed city, and he desperately wanted to go back to yesterday and tell him to run. Now he wanted Ryan to run, take the girl and run. Ryan said he wouldn't leave him, but the child... That changed things, didn't it? Now Ryan had someone else, a child to think about.

"What's her name?" Nathan wheezed suddenly as if it was vital to him to know the little girl. The need to run had stripped Nathan of the niceties. Something in him was making him want to know her name before the fire caught up with them and they died. Ryan asked her gently, and she murmured something in return.

"Laurie," Ryan repeated, and she nodded.

"How old are you, Laurie?"

She held up three fingers then hid in Ryan's neck again. Laurie. Three. Ryan had made the right decision to grab her from the car. They needed to get her off of this mountain.

Chapter Nine

THE FIRE WAS COMING ON FAST, AND ALREADY IT WAS beginning to throw shadows. The air around them had become hot and oppressive, and it seemed as if there was a reflection of fire that only Ryan could see. Smoke—sickly sour, redolent with the smell of creosote—hung around them, and danger was uncomfortably near.

Nathan stumbled with a barely hidden shout of pain, pulling Ryan down, and Ryan, twisting at the last moment so Laurie wasn't squashed, ended up facing back up the rise, fascinated for seconds by the impassable wall of fire that was eating its way down the hillside. There were two separate fires—dancing, plunging, and racing at each other —meeting with a roar that must have been heard miles away. The fire was so much taller than the tree line, coming on with a rush and a roar, crossing and twisting and leaping from tree to tree, each bursting into crimson towers of flame.

The eerie quiet of the last few hours had changed, and the sounds had become a living, horrible noise of hissing and roaring flames. The crashing and splitting apart of falling timber was deafening, terrifying. It held Ryan immobile even as Nathan pulled himself to his feet.

"Ryan," he shouted urgently, and Ryan stood, stumbling upright and coughing.

The quality of the light had changed. The smoke covered the light from the morning sun, and the clouds were tinged with a surreal scarlet hue. The sun had become red in the smoke-filled sky. Ryan swore he could feel the heat at the back of his neck. He found himself ducking when water-dropping helicopters swooped over their head towards the heart of the chasing fire. They wouldn't have been seen, because the black copters were moving too fast to spot two men in the smoke below them as they swept over.

They must be close to the road. They must be by now.

Nathan stumbled again, pulling on Ryan's back, causing him to grunt in pain, shifting his balance to take more weight. Nathan shook his head, *sorry*, and tried to right himself, straightening his back and groaning as his legs had weight put on them.

It was Ryan who saw them first, thin shadows in the smoke moving closer and closer. Police uniforms. Neon yellow jackets.

Help.

LAURIE WOULDN'T LET emergency services touch her. She clung to Ryan and whimpered. She would only talk to Ryan, and he wasn't ready to let her go. If he let go, she would be lost in the system, and he needed to find her family so he knew she was safe. He had already lost sight of Nathan.

Nathan had been helped off, lifted onto a makeshift stretcher, pain meds already pumping into him. Triage was checking him over.

"What do we do?" Ryan said to no one in particular, refusing to let someone look at his back. *We need to go. We can't stay here. Surely the fire is close?*

"We'll move you and the girl down to the blockade." The man directing the crowd was distracted and waving at another officer, who was writing on a board, touching his ear, listening to narrative.

"I'm not leaving without Nathan," Ryan insisted quickly.

"Your friend, yes, he's cleared to travel in the truck. Fuck. At the moment, if you're alive, you're okay to travel in the truck. You'll be assessed fully at the blockade."

"There's a car, in the hills, with a man trapped inside. David Jackson." Ryan turned to face the hill again. The flames looked like a wall advancing down the hill. He saw the evac teams pulling back, pulling away. He twisted round to the guy who had taken Ryan's name, but he had moved away. He was talking to a family, urging them to the evac vehicles. Ryan stopped talking, stopped explaining. David Jackson was gone, surely.

A sudden grief welled inside him, and he was only grounded as Laurie whimpered into his neck. He wasn't finished yet; he needed to get Nathan and Laurie down off of the mountain. That was what was important. He needed to close himself down and focus.

They were herded to a 4x4 with other refugees from the fire. Ryan pushed his way into the front seat with

Laurie still hiding against his neck. They sat in silence. The only sound in the cabin was the disjointed noise of the radio. The ride was bumpy and precarious at times on the fractured road, the fire of a city on one side, the red in the hills on the other.

No one had anything to say. They sat in numb shock, in relief, in fear.

Chapter Ten

Jason had been one of the lucky ones. He'd been on an early morning coffee run and not in his building when the quake hit. The building that was no longer there. Everything he owned was in his apartment. Every memory he'd built was destroyed, but when he thought of his neighbors, none of whom could have made it out alive, material possessions meant nothing. He had followed the general evacuation, moving north, trying his family's and Nathan's cells repeatedly, but having no luck getting through. People scrambled around him, all trying numbers on cell phones, cursing at the lack of signal. Most were shocked and panicked, some just standing in the street, blind in the dust that choked lungs.

He knew he had to get away from the center of the city, out to the suburbs. To Nathan. He should try and get to Nathan, up in the hills, north of the city. It had to be safer there.

The crowd stopped at a designated evac point, as far away from the tallest skyscrapers as they could. An hour of half running, half stumbling brought them away from the worst of the fires; they were the lucky ones. An officer with a bullhorn called for calm. Army-uniformed men with masks mingled in amongst dazed civilians.

Jason tried to listen, moving to the edge of the crowd, but still he couldn't hear enough to have any idea of what was going on. He caught a few words over the whimpering and crying and stunned disbelief that hung in the air around him.

"Fires."

Jason heard the tail end of a man speaking behind him. He turned and saw an Army uniform speaking into a radio, his face streaked with dust and cuts. "…need to get people south. We have forest fires on the hills to the north. We'd be sending people there to die—south."

Jason didn't wait to hear more. Nathan was in the hills. What if he was trapped, what if the fires were… Nah, south was no good. What the fuck? North was where it was at, and slipping easily past the crowd in all the confusion and noise and past the Army sentries herding people south of the city, he started his way north and to his best friend.

He was about a mile from the base of the hill, just before the freeway, before he was stopped, caught, and herded away, all the time protesting that his friend was in the hills.

Frustrated, he stood at the barrier set by the fire department and the police, refusing to move, determined to at least stand as close as he could to his friend until he was found, or until all hope was lost.

Jason watched every arrival at the blockade, watched as each person was dealt with efficiently and passed on to separate teams who he assumed treated the varying degrees of injury or suffering.

He had counted one hundred twenty-seven so far—children, parents, whole families, individuals, some crying, some stoic, some still, some in flustered panic—but no Nathan.

He had listened. He wasn't stupid, and he knew the fire was past the valley edge where Nathan had his apartment in the secluded complex with the park area and the beautiful views.

It was all gone.

The next 4x4 arrived. It was Ryan he saw first, stumbling from inside the car with something in his arms. Ryan— *What the fuck is Ryan doing here?*

Jason ducked under the cordon, ignoring the shouts of the officers in charge, and dove towards the new arrivals, calling Ryan's name, watching as the tall man's head lifted and his eyes searched for the source of his name. His gaze finally came to rest on Jason, his shoulders straightening. Jason reached his side, pulling him into a one-armed hug, removing his arm as he encountered wet cloth and realized it was blood soaked.

"Ryan?" He searched Ryan's eyes, asking for a reason for the blood.

"Nathan—in the back," he said gruffly, his voice raspy and smoke damaged. Jason moved to the back door, opening it and looking in at his friend, pale, bruised, covered in blood, unconscious, as still as death.

"Jesus…fuck." He looked back at Ryan. "He's not…"

"No, we…" Ryan couldn't get the words out, and he pried away Laurie's hands, passing her protesting body to Jason, who took her without a moment's thought.

"Keep her," he whispered. "Don't let…process her… my back." Jason could see Ryan was losing it. He had felt Ryan's blood on his own hands, scarlet and fresh.

"I'll look after her." Ryan slipped to the ground against the car door.

People—doctors, officers, nurses—buzzed around them, pulling Ryan and Nathan this way and that, turning Ryan over, meaning that Jason could see his back. It was a mass of bruises and deep cuts oozing fresh blood, the material of his shirt stuck into the wounds. He had never seen anything like it and watched in sickened amazement as the paramedics attempted to peel back the material of the shirt to irrigate the wounds. At this point, it seemed Ryan had lost consciousness. Shit, Jason was surprised he'd even made it this far.

He hovered like a mother with her baby birds, feeling Laurie relax into him inch by slow inch. The fact that Ryan had handed her to him seemed to make him someone she could trust. They tried to take her away from him, but he refused. Laurie Allen, aged three, with a Christmas birthday, was staying with her new uncle Jason, and that was that. He answered the questions that he could. He knew almost everything about Nathan, and equally hardly anything at all about Ryan.

Next of kin for Ryan? I don't know, Nathan's family may know. Can you get to them through Nathan's family? Allergies? Nathan, no, Ryan, I don't know. It was a blur. *Where are you taking them now? The hospitals in LA. Is it safe? I'm going with them, Laurie too. I'm not arguing with you, I'm going.*

The earth chose that moment to shake, a mild aftershock, sending a ripple of fear through the civilians and causing frantic movement for the rescuers. Jason was waved through without comment, climbing into the same evacuation vehicle as both Ryan and Nathan. He tried his cell phone, and on what must have been his twentieth attempt, he actually connected.

"Jason?"

"Adam, shit, I'm with Nathan. He's fine, he's—we're in evac. They say some broken ribs. We're moving out; I don't know where they're taking us."

"Thank God."

"Can you pass on that Ryan is with us? He's cut up quite bad, but he's here, so tell his parents and text me their contact details."

"Will it get through?"

"Fuck knows. I'm not having a—"

Then static.

THEY ARRIVED at the next evacuation area to organized chaos. Jason was torn between following Ryan or Nathan, deciding instead to hover with the coordinator, Laurie still in his arms. The coordinator looked at him disapprovingly, but he stared her down. He wasn't moving. From where he stood, he could see CNN on a laptop showing the fires downtown and the evacuation, and it chilled him to the bone. It was as if he was watching a disaster movie—none of it was real.

The wind had changed, chasing the fire away from the highways, leaving devastation in its wake. Most of the downtown fires had been contained, but some were still burning. Reports of estimated death tolls were climbing every minute, five thousand, ten thousand, seventeen thousand, more. He didn't know what to focus on first. He leaned against the wall, Laurie asleep against his shoulder, even in the confusion and noise of intake.

He watched people enter Nathan's cubicle, then saw them leave half an hour later, heads together. He waited as they discussed something, then slipped inside. Nathan lay still and unmoving, his face deathly pale. At least his breathing was steady. Jason stood for a short while until the curtain moved, and the coordinator appeared, looking directly at him. He readied himself for a battle, but she looked exhausted.

"We are setting up for emergency blood donations. Can you donate, sir?"

"I can donate. I've been checked, so I can do that."

Chapter Eleven

RYAN CAME BACK TO CONSCIOUSNESS FAR TOO QUICKLY AS they were still stitching the cuts and slices in his back. He cried out in pain, and apparently gave the attending doctor the fright of his life as the doc jumped back with his own cry.

"Sorry, sorry, we're short on— Jeez, fuck, just sorry."
Where's Nathan? Laurie?

"I'm done." the doctor muttered, his words slurred and edgy. Ryan pushed himself up to sit, his back literally on fire with pain. "You need to sit for at least half an hour to let the meds kick in." He handed Ryan a fresh shirt, the top half of a pair of scrubs. Ryan looked at him, his head heavy, his throat raw, and his voice fading.

"Okay." *No way, just go, will you, so I can find them?*

"I'll check back on you," the young doctor said, dropping notes onto Ryan's gurney, sighing deeply, and pushing his way out of the tent.

Ryan counted to twenty and stood, shaky but determined to find Nathan and Laurie, and within minutes, he'd checked most cubicles, finding Nathan in the second from last.

Nate looked peaceful. They'd attached a drip into his arm—feeding God-knows-what into him, pain relief, glucose—and Ryan almost sagged in relief. Jason wasn't here and neither was Laurie, but all of a sudden, he just wanted to sit with Nathan, touch Nathan, ground himself in the here and now. The gurney was low to the ground, and it was enough to drop to his knees next to it, dipping his forehead to the cover, and sending a quick prayer heavenwards that they made it here.

"I gave blood," a quiet voice said behind him. He turned painfully to face the owner of the voice. Jason. *Where's Laurie?* He wanted to say it, but he couldn't, his throat was so tight and his head pounded with the pain.

"Laurie's with the staff, the other kids. I booked her in using my name." Ryan nodded, swallowing, wanting to push out words. "Who is she, Ryan?"

"I don't know," he rasped. It was important to get this information to Jason. "Found her—in a car, what was left of her car. Her family…" He couldn't say any more. None of it seemed real. Jason didn't push.

"They think Nathan's cracked a couple of ribs, but he needs X-rays, and they don't have it here. He also has a possible splintered hip bone, soft tissue damage from the hip to the knee, and a broken arm."

Ryan looked stricken. "I made him walk," he pushed out, his throat tight and his stomach turning in self-disgust.

"I don't wanna hear that, Ryan. You saved him, him and Laurie." Ryan dismissed the comment with a grimace of pain, fighting exhaustion and fear. Why wasn't Nathan awake?

He must have said it out loud because Jason answered.

"They dosed him up to relax his breathing. He'll be coming to soon. They said he would; they promised me." Jason's voice was rough.

Ryan reached past his own pain, smiling as best he could at Nathan's best friend. It wasn't fair to hoard the worry for himself. He could see Jason was wrung out. Jason looked back at him steadily, clearly seeing what Ryan was trying to do.

"I know we're in the middle of a freaking disaster but word to the wise," Jason started. "You need to be here when he wakes up, and for the record, Ryan, you need to fucking talk to him, sort this out. 'Cause you nearly killed him with the arguments you two had as effectively as this fucking earthquake. You're an idiot not to see what you have in Nathan and he was an idiot to walk away from you." Ryan tried to reply, but stopped and nodded instead. "I'm gonna go find Laurie."

Ryan rested his head back down, aware his knees were starting to stiffen, but the ache was nowhere near as bad as the pain in his back.

As the noise of the chaos around him started to fade, he slipped into an exhausted unconsciousness, the top half of his body lying across Nathan's bed, finally able to give in, just for a few minutes.

Chapter Twelve

"Ry?" Nathan's voice was so low, so quiet, hoarse and harsh. "Wha?"

Nathan coughed with a groan and a grimace of pain as his chest was on fire. "Your arm's broken," Ryan rasped as he jerked awake, his voice still croaky from the fire. "Ribs...your hip."

"Shit." *Is there anything that's okay?*

Nathan gripped hard on Ryan's hand. He wanted to say so much, wanted to thank him, to ask about Laurie, but all that came out was coughing.

"Nathan?" The voice came from behind Ryan, and he felt Ryan move to one side. *Jason? Jason is here, what the—*

Nathan couldn't speak, he tried, but Jason stopped him. "Hey, dude, I was kinda worried." He smiled crookedly, then crossed to the bed, grasping Nathan's hand and squeezing reassuringly.

"I'm going to find Laurie," Ryan said quietly. "I'll be back in a few minutes."

"'kay," Nathan managed to force out. He watched Ryan leave and caught sight of his back, fresh blood spotting the scrub top.

Jason was talking and he focused on what his friend was saying. "Gotta get you outta here and on to a hospital, but I tell ya, it's chaos out there, Christ knows when it'll happen. They've pushed us as far back as they can, but we are getting too close to downtown LA evac, so they're clearing a new break line."

Nathan nodded, the information a whirl of words that he didn't really hear.

RYAN HAD PASSED through two makeshift tents, his eyes down, avoiding anyone's questions with a blank look and a shrug, until at last he came to area that he supposed could be designated as the children's area. He circled until his searching gaze met Laurie's. Her eyes wide and frightened, she launched herself at him.

He scooped her up, and she resumed her position tucked into his neck. It felt good and safe. He turned to the harassed woman with the list as she looked at it, then looked at him, clearly out of her depth. Still she stood in the doorway, determined to release the little girl to only someone on her list.

"Your name please."

"Ortiz, Ryan," he said, his voice burnt and husky.

"Do you have some ID, some…" Her voice trailed off as Ryan just stood in front of her, in nothing but jeans, a scrub top, and bandages, holding out his hands to indicate he had nothing. "I'm sorry, I just…"

"—back to the main area, my—friend is there." Ryan was struggling to get the words out.

She looked at him, stricken. Ryan knew what she must be thinking. She looked over at the twenty or so children who sat around on the makeshift beds, every one of them alone, with no one. At least this little girl had someone, this Ryan.

"I need to check. I can't just let people—non-family—take the children." She watched as Ryan leaned back on the side of a bed, his posture clearly patient. He was willing to wait. "My team leader, he'll be back in a minute, needs to look at this."

"S'okay," Ryan said softly, his back tightening, the pain indescribable, and he tried to relax each muscle.

When the shouting started, Ryan simply held Laurie tight.

"Out, out, out, everyone, we need to get out… We need to get out. All those walking out…the fire…"

They held Ryan back, and they held the children back as they stood, screaming at the noise. Chaos erupted. He was pushed back, pushed away, over the ripped tarmac, pushed behind the new break line, the Army swarming as they had to deal with people screaming for loved ones, staring in horror as the fire was darting and jumping down the hillside to the makeshift evac area. Ryan was desperately straining to get through, back to Nathan, to Jason, to warn them, his back pushed and jostled, but it was no use. The panic was as good as a brick wall, impossible to force himself through.

He'd known that this was only a temporary evac area, an emergency, a stopgap, but surely they wouldn't have collected so many refugees in one area, medically attended so many injured people just for the fire to turn and burn them all to the ground.

He heard prayers shouted and screamed to the heavens, saw people still walking, running, crawling from the area in danger to the front of the break line.

"Move back. Everyone move the fuck back. Let people through."

Nathan, Nathan…

"Will it jump? Oh my God, will the fire jump here?"

"Pray to God it doesn't."

Screams filled the air as the fire cracked like lightning and moved into the area, and in seconds, the inferno twisted and circled, wrapping the tents in flame, and each one fell, destroyed in seconds.

Ryan could feel the heat on his face as he fell to his knees, a silent scream locked in his mouth.

Nathan.

Chapter Thirteen

Jason all but carried his friend out of the tent, never more grateful than he was right now for the extra height he had on Nathan. They were guided, herded, pushed out of the tent and down towards the new line break. Hundreds of people surrounded them, rushing and running to escape the approaching flames.

"I can't see him, J."

"He'll be with Laurie and the kids. Come on, man…" Jason looked at their path carefully, watching for the fire, as he tried to pull his friend to safety at the same time he worried about Ryan and the little girl.

People were shouting, screaming, begging for help around him, help to find loved ones, separated when they were processed for medical attention. Jason couldn't listen, couldn't hear. He concentrated one hundred percent of his effort in getting Nathan down past the new break the Army had made.

Two hundred yards… They were moving so painfully slow. Why was no one running?

One hundred and fifty yards… The fire cracked and spit behind them.

One hundred yards. "Let them through, everyone just move back."

Fifty yards away, a man in uniform took Nathan's other arm, and between them, they dragged him past the uninjured.

Twenty yards… An eerie quiet settled as the flames swallowed the evac area,

Ten…

Five…

Jason slumped to the ground, Nathan half falling on him, breathlessly thanking the uniformed man who had risked his life to help people over the line. The fireman gave them a small smile then he plunged back into the smoke and flames to help more people. Jason memorized his face, the name on his uniform. *Kowolsky*. He would find him. After all this was finished, he would find him and thank him.

Medics scampered over fallen bodies, some lost to the trampling crowd, some just not fit to be moved. They shouted urgent instructions, and they quickly scanned Nathan, assessed his injuries non-life-threatening, ordering that he move on.

"The fire is being held back. Get a fucking move on and move down as far as you can."

To the chaos that was the epicenter. They had no choice.

Jason helped Nathan to stand and began to slowly move down the hill, his eyes tracking the push of humanity, watching people reunite, watching people crying for others. He saw the children before he saw Ryan, a small group, sitting in a huddle with everyone walking around them.

"Ryan," Jason breathed softly, looking at the man who sat, huddled, his knees drawn up, Laurie clinging to his legs, his face a mask of grief. "Ryan!"

Ryan lifted his head, blinking, recognizing his name, but so lost in his grief, obviously not certain he was hearing right. He stumbled towards them over split ground, Laurie still clinging to him.

"Nathan." Ryan forced the words out and fell to his knees as gracefully as he could, and Jason helped Nathan put his head in Ryan's lap.

Nathan turned his face into Ryan's body, grunting with the exertion of movement, and Ryan carded a hand through his short hair.

As they sat huddled close, Jason didn't say anything that flickered through his mind. Nothing was as big as what they were facing. No petty paths in life, no worries, were as important as the struggle for life that was being won and lost around them.

"I'm gonna find out what's going on," Jason started, stopping only when Ryan grabbed at his hand.

"Thank you," Ryan forced out, coughing.

Jason just shook his head imperceptibly. Nathan was his friend. He didn't even stop to think of leaving the fire without him.

"I wanna know what happens next," he said simply.

Smoke and shadows swallowed him as he strode with purpose back up the hill to Army Control. He hovered behind the small group of Army personnel and firefighters who were discussing what was happening.

"We can move the walking wounded down to level two and join them to the evacuation," a fireman said.

"I can spare maybe two men to work through that."

"Jeez. The level three movement is up from the City. We're just moving them from one danger—"

"I don't need commentary on the obvious; I need solutions."

"Level three? Jesus, what about aftershocks? What is the intel on—"

"We don't know; we have nothing."

"Start moving as many as we can down to level three."

"Sir."

Jeez, we are fucked.

He listened as best he could before forcing his way back through the milling crowd back to Nathan and Ryan. This level three didn't sound too good, but shit, anything was better than sitting here with the fire frustrated and furious, hovering and spitting over the other side of the break, waiting for the right moment to cross, threatening and evil.

Chapter Fourteen

Jason stopped, resting a hand on Ryan's arm. "We need to get up. They're moving us to a new evac area."

Ryan looked down at the barely conscious man in his lap, glancing at his hands twisted in Nathan's hair. "Meds?" he said softly.

"Yeah, they kind of knocked him out. His hip is clumsily strapped, but we need to get him to a hospital or some sort of facility where they can X-ray and get him some real help. I'll get Laurie, and we can move him down."

Jason stood, obviously scanning for Laurie. She sat not far away with a group of other children, all unnaturally quiet. He crossed to scoop her up, and Ryan watched him stop as other children stood to follow him. Ryan heard him trying to explain.

"I'm not...you can't...I can't..." But in the end he shrugged, and the group followed behind him back towards Ryan and Nathan.

Ryan shook Nathan. His green eyes were revealed

slowly, blurred, and for a moment, it was almost as if he didn't recall what had happened. Then, just as suddenly, he seemed to remember, started to struggle upright. Ryan helped him as best he could, trying not to wince as the newly reopened wounds on his back stretched and pulled. Jason stood in front of them, Laurie in his arms, helping Ryan to stand, supporting him as he swayed, obviously seeing the fresh blood on bandages, but not saying a word as Ryan stared at him, entreaty in his eyes.

Between them, Nathan stood, wavering on painful injuries, waiting as Ryan threaded an arm under his. No one said anything. No words were needed, not even when the eight children started to follow Jason. Ryan just looked over at him, and Jason just shrugged again.

They stumbled and followed and made their way down, people urging them on, guiding them to the next evac area. Even with fractures, Nathan was still considered walking wounded, but Ryan guessed he wouldn't want anyone's assistance anyway and vowed to help him keep going. There were people hurt far worse than them, with burns and lots of other injuries.

They had almost made it to the new area when another milder aftershock hit, nothing major, nothing that made anyone stop walking. Numb to the disaster around them, it distracted Ryan enough to not watch where his feet were going, and he stumbled on loose bricks, righting himself quickly, and seeing other bricks laying around him. In the spectral smoke, images started to form—a building, windows, more buildings, walls, shattered, heaved, and thrown like a giant's playthings around the weary refugees.

Half of a sign lay on the ground—*spital*—and gave them enough to know where they were. Ryan was overcome with a strange kind of anger, a grief. What was the point? How were they going to receive medical attention in a hospital that was clearly destroyed? How was this place safer than the last? They might be away from the fire, but they had moved straight into earthquake central.

Three hundred people, four hundred, maybe even five, moved in a column onwards past the main hospital to a building hardly touched by the destruction around it. It was covered in the grays and browns of moving earth but seemed intact, safe, standing. He recalled that in '94 after the Northridge earthquake, many hospitals were destroyed or rendered unusable. There was chaos in transferring patients, and he had watched a TV show focusing on it only a few weeks back. Something about the state legislature passing a law about California hospitals, making them ensure that their acute care units and emergency rooms were housed in earthquake-proof structures. Thank fuck for the law.

As they watched, a large Army transport helicopter landed a distance away from them, and a group of people in scrubs started to move stretchers from the intact area to the waiting arms of Army medical personnel. This was the evacuation point for the terminally injured or those who needed special attention, and none of the newly arrived refugees walked to it or watched it or even seemed to have any desperate hope to be on the waiting craft.

It seemed as if, as one, they knew that to be leaving on this flight, this particular evacuation flight, would mean they were close to death, and no one was ready enough to accept that fate. They huddled in small protective groups as Army personnel started to move in amongst them, singling out the sick and the injured for medical attention.

It was an hour, maybe more, before it was Nathan's turn to be checked in the emergency area. He clutched at Ryan, insisting he was seen too, forcing his friend to turn round and expose the horror that was his shredded back. They were assigned a group and a doctor who was organized, quiet, and somber. Jason waited with Laurie and the children while Ryan and Nathan were hurried in through to the emergency department where doctors, surgeons, nurses, and volunteers waited. They were the witnesses to untold horror. The light had dimmed in their eyes, and their faces showed their exhaustion from their continual work.

When would this day ever end?

Ryan lay on his front, numb, quiet, knowing Nathan was in the next cubicle. He had heard what the doctor told Nathan. His X-rays showed a fracture in his arm, three broken ribs, some extensive soft tissue damage around a fracture in his hip, through his leg, and down to his knee.

The doctors hadn't been as forthcoming with him. X-rays weren't needed to reveal what his problem was. Where the concrete and glass had fallen on him, there were deep cuts, in three places to muscle, which explained the intense spasms of pain he was having. He had internal bruising and some damage that they were concerned would slow down the range of motion in his neck.

Where he'd tried to protect his head, his hands were now swollen and bruised beyond recognition. There were no suspected fractures, but a particularly bad cut appeared to have sliced into a tendon. He needed stitches and a multitude of tests for reaction time when the doctor expressed concerned about unusual swelling at the top of his spine where he'd received the worst hits.

The doctor said he was lucky the concrete hadn't been an inch or two lower as it may have damaged his spinal cord irreversibly. Ryan didn't say a thing, not even realizing that Nathan could hear as clear as day what the doctor said just as Ryan had heard Nathan's prognosis.

It wasn't until the doctor left, the nurse running to find more bandages and thread, that Nathan stood next to him, a crutch under his arm, his chest bare, his arm in plaster. Ryan couldn't turn over.

"Ryan." Nathan was whispering, unable to talk any louder, his throat still raw.

"Hey," Ryan said in an equally small voice.

"I heard what they said, Ryan. You wouldn't even have been injured if you... You shouldn't have put yourself in harm's way like that."

"Why?"

"You're hurt. Your spine... What if you'd received permanent damage?"

Ryan twisted his face to turn away from Nathan so he couldn't see his tears. "I'd do anything for you," he mumbled.

NATHAN COULDN'T HEAR, so he could either hobble round the other side of the bed, or actually get Ryan to look back at him.

"Please look at me, Ryan."

It took a few seconds, but he did at least turn. Nathan

touched the tears on Ryan's face. "Are you in pain?" he asked softly.

Ryan shut his eyes. "No, yes… No, that isn't why."

"Can you tell me?"

"Have we…destroyed it all?"

"You mean us?" Nathan sighed, moving his thumb to trace Ryan's lip and down to his bruised and swollen neck, a touch so gentle, even though Nathan knew they must have numbed Ryan's back. "No, Ryan. We need to talk, but when we need to talk… Jesus, it seems so small and pathetic compared to all of this."

Nathan bent down, wincing at the sharp, insistent pain in his chest, his lips inches from Ryan's, a single tear tracking a path to the corner of his mouth. "I love you, Ryan. Doesn't matter what happens. I will always love you. I can't begin to understand what changed us, but I know we'll realize one day. Maybe we were scared, I don't know, but it will be fine when we talk. I promise I won't fly off in a huff, and you won't need to come into an earthquake zone looking for me."

He smiled slightly at the irony in his words, his own eyes wet, then he dropped the smallest of kisses to the corner of Ryan's mouth, tasting the saltiness of his tears. Ryan tried to lift his head to chase the kiss, but his face reflected the magnitude of his pain. Nathan, however, sensing the need in Ryan, ran a collection of butterfly kisses over marked skin, feeling the muscle beneath, relearning the taste.

"I'm sorry," Ryan tried to say, his voice so small.

"Ryan, don't."

"No, let me…let…fl…" Ryan slurred the words.

"Ryan? Are you okay?

"I shine…fees shi…she fine." Ryan buried his face in his hands, groaning. He mumbled something that Nathan couldn't hear.

"Seriously, Ryan, it doesn't matter. Whatever you need to say, and the things I need to say…Ryan? Ryan?" Nathan suddenly felt fear clutch at him, Ryan was so still, so quiet. Had he just fallen asleep or was he unconscious? It didn't look like he was moving at all. He had slurred his words. Was he even breathing?

"Can I get some help in here please?" Nathan hobbled to the curtain, "Help, my friend, Ryan, I don't think he's breathing. Can someone help him?"

What happened next became a part of the nightmare landscape as Nathan watched helplessly.

"His airway's closed. Does he have any allergies?"

"I don't think so…I don't know…"

"Stand back, get out of the way. Shit, he's coding…the neck, too much swelling. Who assessed this man? Next evac chopper is here. He's not gonna make it out if we don't… Scalpel… For God's sake, twenty milligrams…"

Jason, what's happening? Where are you? I need you… Is Ryan dying?

Chapter Fifteen

It took two hours. They used paddles, shot electricity through his heart, cut into his throat, opened an airway... Pressure had built up at the base of his neck, edema, restricting air, starving him. It took two hours, then he was evacuated, unconscious but alive, in the main evac helicopter that hovered ominously in the smoke-blackened sky for one precious second before wheeling away from them.

Jason was scared. Nathan had stopped talking, stopped asking questions, seemingly stopped breathing. He was so still.

"Nathan," he said softly, pulling the younger man back into the emergency area, not knowing what to say. He had Laurie wrapped in his arms as well, tears rolling down her face as they took Ryan away. Jason wanted to cry too.

They wouldn't let Nathan go with them, saying there was room for emergency evac patients only. It was at that point that Nathan went quiet. Ryan was being taken to a better-equipped emergency unit, another rung up the damn injury chain. It was five miles farther away, across the tip of the worst destruction. Fires were still burning, eating into the hills, and other fires were around that would probably burn for days in the destruction of LA.

"I'm getting to that hospital," Nathan said, his first words for what must have been close to an hour.

"Nathan."

"I've decided. I want to be doing something positive, and that sure doesn't include me sitting around here with my thumb up my ass. The whole travel area is empty. It's just buildings, and I'm going—"

"No more running," Jason said. "We stay until there are empty spaces on the next evac out of here. I'm not arguing, damn it."

Nathan went to move, but Jason gripped him tight. He was an uninjured man, taller and heavier than the injured Nathan, and Nathan lost his fight. Grumbling and grimacing in pain, Nathan stopped moving, allowing his weight to shift, leaning against Jason.

Jason continued, trying to be as persuasive as possible. "We can help here, man. Wait until there is space on the next evac helicopter. Are you with me here?" Nathan stared at Jason, then back at the nine children sitting, looking at him expectantly. "Nathan?"

"The kids," Nathan said suddenly. "We can process the kids, get some details, maybe look into reuniting them." He sounded a little unsure about whether that was a good plan or not. "I need to be doing something positive." Jason smiled, seeing light in Nathan's eyes.

"Yeah, that is a good idea, dude, a good idea."

RACHEL WAS SEVEN, from LA she thought. Her mom was at the last evac area, injured. When they ran, she didn't know where her mom had been. She was very scared.

Alex, five, and his big brother Jack, eight, were separated in the rush from crashed cars. Their mom was at home in the suburbs. Their dad had been driving, and he'd passed them over to a rescuer just as an aftershock had thrown the ground around. Jack was convinced his dad was fine, and that any minute now he would arrive to take him and Alex away. Well, that was what he was saying in front of a clearly worried Alex.

Cory and Peter, both nine, were neighbors, evacuees running together as their parents battled to save their houses. The last words from their parents had been, "Stay together, stay together…"

Patsy, nine, she was staying with an aunt in the same area as Cory and Peter. She'd been on a sleepover, painting nails and doing hair, and her aunt had gone back for the dog. She didn't know what had happened to her aunt, but her family was in Arizona.

The last three were all under five, so it was difficult to get details. Apart from names—Susie, Lisa, and another Jack—Nathan had nothing.

Then of course there was Laurie, three, a Christmas baby whose only concern was where Ryan was.

Nathan started with Rachel. If her mom had been at the last evac, injured, then maybe she had been pulled down here. Maybe it could be a happy ending.

After a half an hour of searching and following the medical trail, he found her.

Still and cold in the makeshift morgue.

It was then, as he stood in the cold, silent room, surrounded by white-shrouded bodies, that it hit him just how real this was.

JASON CAME BACK from his travels around the hospital to report his latest findings, Rachel, Cory, and Peter trailing him, to find Nathan sitting, his back against the wall, his legs in front of him, asleep. Laurie curled on his left side, and Susie and Lisa were on the other side, sharing his lap. The other kids were huddled in a heap of coats and blankets, all asleep like a pile of puppies. Nathan's breathing, even in sleep, was labored, and Jason winced—his friend's ribs must hurt like a bitch.

He didn't know what Nathan had found out about Rachel's mom. But when Nathan had come back as white as a sheet and just slumped down the wall, drawing up his knees and wrapping his arms around them, Jason assumed it wasn't good news. He had painkillers in his hand, knew it was time for Nathan to take them, and trying not to disturb the children, he shook his friend's shoulder gently. His green eyes opened slowly, then he slightly startled even as Jason indicated *shhhh*. He handed him the tablets then the water, and once he'd seen Nathan swallow them, he backed off, allowing his friend to relax into sleep again.

Laurie turned into Nathan's side, mumbling something in her sleep and twisting her hands into Nathan's shirt. She obviously felt safe. Jason looked around him at the children sleeping, knowing in his head that it must have been nearly twenty-four hours since the first earth tremor, but understanding in his heart, for Los Angeles, a lifetime had passed.

Chapter Sixteen

Jason watched as Nathan opened his eyes and smiled down at the lap full of small children, all asleep and probably as warm as hot water bottles. Jason sat against the opposite wall, an answering small smile on his face. Nathan yawned and blinked.

"S'ten," Jason offered softly, knowing Nathan would ask. Twenty-seven hours since the quake.

"Sleep at all, dude?" Nathan asked, and Jason nodded. No sense in letting Nathan see he had hardly slept at all.

"Some. Was helping around a bit and some of the kids were kinda restless."

"You should have woken me, Jase, I coulda maybe helped."

"Nah, I handled it. Anyway, we are so outta here in two. Some new med staff came in, volunteers, and all the wounded have been triaged and moved. We're kinda some of the last left at this station."

"Where they moving us to?"

"They have a center, a children's center, they want us

there. Well, they want the children there, and I'm staying with them." Jason didn't ask if Nathan was staying as well. He could see the conflict in his friend's eyes, the desperation to see Ryan, to make sure he was all right, warring against the need for the kids to maybe be reunited with their families. Finally, he saw a decision in the calm set of his friend's face.

"I'll come with you and get the kids to the center, but then I'm going to find Ryan," Nathan finally offered, closing his eyes briefly, a frown on his face. Jason sighed inwardly. It hurt him to see his friend like this, hurt him to see Nathan so desperate to make sure Ryan was mending but being unable to reach him, the two sites having no direct communication. Batteries had long since died in cells, reception was sporadic, and the only communication they did have, via the Army, was restricted for emergencies only.

Jason had known Nathan for so long. They had met in acting school and just fell into friendship as easy as breathing. To his mind, he'd never seen Nathan so conflicted. It had always seemed to Jason that Nathan saw events in black and white. He was so strong in his beliefs and his opinions—always so quiet unless he had something he needed to say, kinda shy, and desperate to keep to himself. Jason often pointed out that the Virginian farm boy had sure chosen the wrong career if he wanted anonymity. Nathan had argued back that it wasn't anonymity he craved, just a small amount of personal space.

And now, looking over as Nathan began to wake up the children one by one with quiet words and hugs, words of reassurance slipping from his tongue, Jason had his first real look at the desperation in his friend's face whenever Ryan's name was spoken. Every child asked where Ryan was. Jason sighed and made to stand, helping to peel off each sleepy child, finally helping a sleep-stiffened Nathan, his leg straight in front of him to protect his hip, to his feet.

"Think I may need some more," Nathan wheezed, his free hand moving to his chest, "pain killers." He was breathing steadily, but his face was pale, and a sheen of sweat glistened on his skin.

"I'll grab some. Can you stand okay?"

"Standing…not a problem…breathing more so." Then Nathan smiled, a wry smile, a sarcastic Nathan-smile, and it made Jason feel less deathly worried and more just normally worried.

"Come on, man, let's go get these kids back where they belong and go find Ryan, yeah?"

"Yeah."

They all clambered aboard the next transport through the smoke hanging in the air and the dust clogging their mouths and noses. Each child was passed up carefully from Jason to Nathan and, assisted by crew, strapped into place. Jason jumped up and sat next to Laurie, holding her hand and whispering something to her as the rotors started and they waited for the speed to pick up.

The sudden stomach-falling feeling of lifting from the ground made Jason's head spin, and he felt several sets of small hands clutch at his Army-issue jacket. Sooner than he wanted, they were airborne. The men had been warned they would be taken above the low-level smoke, that they would cross the top edge of LA, and that they would see things that maybe the kids should be kept from seeing. They tried.

The climb through the spinning, wheeling smoke was disorienting and brutal. It sent shivers down Jason's spine, like the climb to the top of a roller coaster before the fall. He didn't want to see LA destroyed. Not his city. He needed to see, but he didn't want to.

At first it was difficult to make out. The ground below was hidden by the low-hanging pall of smoke and a large debris field, but LA was tall. LA had buildings that kissed the sky in their grace and beauty—or it once had. Now they had mostly vanished. Some remained, the glass gone, tilted, slanted, their backs broken, as if a small breath would topple them to the hidden floor below. Blinds hung out of eyeless frames, and desks, chairs, and jumbled furniture were only briefly seen as the chopper climbed higher, escaping the height of the tallest remaining buildings.

An insistent glow of orange travelled the tallest skyscrapers, fires burning unceasingly inside, fuelled by the normal parts of office life. Surely these buildings would have been virtually empty so early in the morning. Surely hardly anyone had died. The people who commuted would have still been at home, and they wouldn't have been at desks, trapped... Would they?

Jason realized he couldn't identify much of what was left, couldn't make out the skyline from the ruins below, and part of him wished he had a camera to capture the stark destruction, to understand where the LA he knew had gone. He looked over at Nathan, seeing tears in his friend's eyes, wishing he could cry himself, wishing he had something in him that would snap and let out the emotion that was eating away inside of him.

He couldn't indulge in his own fears and sorrow, not in

front of the kids. He recognized Nathan's protective way of dealing with things had taken over, shutting him down, and his usual safety valve to release the tension—Ryan—was nowhere near him. Nathan had said in their alcohol-fueled talk a few days before the quake that he could always rely on Ryan to talk him out of his isolationist coping mechanism, prank him out of it, joke with him, make him laugh, kiss him… Jason wanted to help in the same way, but it was impossible.

Nathan was clearly desperate for information on Ryan, frantic to see him. Jason hoped they would find Ryan whole and awake, not the still, white-bandaged body they'd flown away the night before.

Jason turned away from Nathan, because he couldn't bear to see the tears on his friend's face. Instead he looked over the vista that was a burning, destroyed LA. He felt empty.

WHEN THEY ARRIVED at the new area, Nathan sat down tiredly. Jason took care of booking the children into the children's center, but Nathan kept Laurie on his lap. She was the very last to be processed. Nathan didn't want to let her go, and Ryan wouldn't want him to.

"Sir, Mr. Richardson, we just need to process this little one now."

"I know…" He paused. "Her name is Laurie, Laurie Allen, and she's three. We found her up by Dryden, in the hills, in a car."

"Can you describe the car, sir? Or any other details?"

"I didn't see, I'm sorry but my partner did. Ryan, Ryan Ortiz…"

"Can you spell that for me, sir?"

Jason took over, spelling and giving as many of Ryan's details as he could. Nathan took advantage of the time, pulling Laurie in for one last hug before standing and passing her over to the kindly woman taking the details.

"We can check back." Nathan knew he wanted to see if Laurie was happy, if she had been reunited with someone…anyone.

"You can, sir, you can."

Nathan and Jason watched as the last of their babies were taken through the security doors. They had seen inside, knew it was a better environment than following around two tired men, but still, to see Laurie waving over the woman's shoulder was not good, not good at all.

"Nathan, let's go find Ryan."

Chapter Seventeen

THE HOUSE PHONE RANG. THERE WAS NO REPLY, BUT THE message was simple: If this is Ryan, or someone with news about Ryan, please contact Kathy, then there was a number, her cell.

Ryan didn't leave a message, just rang his sister's cell, his fingers clumsy on the small buttons. He was suddenly overcome with emotion as she answered, breathless and quick.

"Ryan?"

"Kathy." His voice was so raw, and his throat, where they had cut, so raspy, he could hardly make sound.

"Ohmygodohmygod Ryan, Ryan."

"Kathy…" Ryan didn't know what to say, and his voice filled with tears.

"Ryan, are you okay, where are you?"

"Hospital…throat." From his position lying on the hospital bed, he awkwardly handed the phone to the aide who stood next to him. She briefly explained the problem without making it sound dramatic, nodded, exchanged looks with Ryan, then as suddenly passed back the phone, a stricken look on her face. Ryan put it to his ear.

"…with you? Ryan, Ryan, man, is Nathan with you?" It was Adam; they were obviously playing pass the parcel with the phone and clearly Nathan's family and his had somehow met and stayed together through this. It made sense he supposed; only one state line and some eighty miles separated both families, and they had evidently pulled together in the face of the two men being lost to the fires.

"S'okay." Ryan lied. He didn't know if evac was being organized, but he prayed it was, and that Nathan would be here soon. He looked at the aide, who breathed deeply and took the phone back, explaining that, no, Nathan wasn't at this facility, and yes, he was fine, and yes, he was being brought here soon. She handed the phone back.

"Adam," he rasped painfully.

"Your mom," Adam said softly, then the noise of the phone being passed.

"Ryan, I know you can't talk, Ryan—oh my God, baby."

DOCTORS AND NURSES fussed around him. "Ryan Ortiz, presented with blah blah blah…"

Ryan sighed inwardly. All he really heard when they were discussing him were long words that meant, bottom line, they'd had to cut his throat. That translated in his head to blah blah blah. *Lovely.*

They asked him to roll on his front again. Deft fingers lifted his bandage and checked his back. The pain shooting into his shoulder made him wince. The owner of the hands apologized, and he tried to shake his head, he really did, but jeez, the top of his spine was on the really bad side of painful.

They left him alone after injecting something into his drip, probably some kind of sedative as he hadn't really slept properly. They didn't seem to think unconsciousness counted. He felt as if he was drifting, but he was able to focus on the fact that Nathan wasn't here with him and that Jason and Laurie were still somewhere out there. God knows when he'd be able to find anything out about his friends apart from the fact they were safe at another hospital.

He tried really hard not to focus on Nathan, tried not to worry, but it was so damn difficult. However hard he tried, his last thoughts, as always, were of Nathan. Wondering where he was, if he was okay, if he was wondering the same thing about Ryan or whether he might be feeling he'd had a lucky escape.

I love you, Ryan whispered in his head and let the stealthy warmth pull him into sleep.

NATHAN WATCHED Ryan fall into sleep from the side of the curtain. He'd been warned by the nurse not to interrupt, as according to her the patient hadn't slept since he was brought in. He wanted to talk, to make Ryan see he was here, but instead he waited until the mask of deep sleep fell over Ryan's face then he moved in, carrying a chair and slumping into it next to the bed.

His eyes traced the injuries on Ryan's back. The nurse explained some of them had been left uncovered as opposed to bandaged as they watched hourly for infection. Antibiotics were being pumped into him. They were concerned about the neck injury, because the edema had been a shock, the swelling that closed his throat sudden and frightening to Ryan. Nathan couldn't even begin to contemplate the fear.

Suddenly uncomfortable in his own skin, he stood, shaking, desperate for touch, desperate to give comfort. Leaning over Ryan, his lips inches away from Ryan's face that was turned to one side, so perfect and still in sleep, he lowered his lips, touching a kiss to cool, clean skin, his lips touching chin and cheek then into the tangle of hair laying across his forehead. He relearned the muscles in Ryan's strong shoulders, every muscle that wasn't bandaged, and every delicate bone that moved under the skin.

His fingers trailed after his kisses, tears falling unbidden from his eyes. The kisses he pressed to Ryan's skin were promises, pleas, prayers, and they patterned to his long, smooth neck, the bandages from the emergency surgery, the swelling, the faint veins, the pulse fluttering in a rhythm that Nathan could taste against his tongue.

He pulled back slightly, the tears pushed from a grief so deep as gently he traced each defined muscle and injury on Ryan's strong back. That he had come for him, put himself in harm's way, didn't leave him, and had almost died to help him proved something. He knew Ryan loved him. How could he not love him back? Or ever doubted?

He trailed his fingers from the base of Ryan's spine, kissing and cataloguing each injury, the cuts crisscrossing his smooth skin, the field stitches stark and pulling pale torn skin together in a parody of art. Tears still fell silently, and Nathan absently brushed them into Ryan's skin, just learning and touching, happy and content to follow each mark and remember the act that put them there.

It was after a few minutes that Nathan sensed Ryan was waking. He felt faint tremors, a tightening of skin, a subtle movement of muscles, then Ryan raised his head, looking directly into Nathan's eyes staring back at him, his pupils wide. Nathan placed a finger carefully in front of Ryan's dry lips. "Shhhhh."

Nathan wanted to say so much, wanted to shout at Ryan for throwing himself in harm's way, wanted to hug him until he couldn't breathe, wanted to taste him, love him... He didn't know where to start. How could he say all this, do all this?

Gently, Nathan moved back, face to face with Ryan, kissing him gently, once, twice, soft, simple promises, before moving back to sit in the seat, a hand still touching Ryan's arm.

"Go back to sleep. I'll be here when you wake up."

FLICK.

"...three days since what has been described as the worst natural disaster ever to hit the mainland United States—"

Flick.

"Now standing at just over six thousand dead, with what is thought to be in the region of one hundred times that homeless, and now we cross to Graham at—"

Flick.

"...heartbreaking thing is the children. Thousands of

children have been split from parents in the frantic rush to escape from the—"

Click.

Nathan threw the control down on Ryan's bed in disgust, the sleeping man not even moving at the sudden movement on his covers. The news coverage didn't change. It hadn't changed in the last hour, and it probably wouldn't change in the next week. People would be eating and breathing the disaster in LA for quite a while; they had no choice.

When Nathan had spoken to Adam and to the Ortiz family, they had said CNN kept them in touch with what was happening, how rescue was being coordinated, seeing survivor stories. But all Nathan could see was the chaos around him, people still being airlifted in, pulled from the rubble, knowing they would perhaps be some of the last people to be pulled out alive.

CNN put the dead at six thousand, but the quake had hit the Latino areas heavily, and no one really had a handle on population there. The news seemed to focus on the fact that so many lived because the quake happened before the morning rush to work, giving hope where Nathan failed to see much now. Too many body bags, too much death, too many lost children.

Nathan didn't say a word of this out loud though. He didn't tell Ryan; he just spoke to the doctor who pushed up discharge as much as he could, primed Nathan with meds, and wished them Godspeed. This time tomorrow they would be on their way out of LA, although how, they didn't know.

"I'm gonna go see Laurie," Nathan announced to his unconscious friend, snagging his jacket and leaving the room. He left the same message with the harried nurse holding a clipboard and she made a note on the paper. He was still wearing his emergency scrubs, his jeans cut off when the blood and the gashes and the broken ankle had demanded it. So many people wandered around the same, in mismatched, ill-fitting clothes. Nathan wondered where they would find clothes to fit six-four Ryan when he was booked out tomorrow. Not even the scrubs fit him very well.

Ryan still couldn't talk properly. They had exchanged very few words when he was conscious. It was mostly just Ryan listening to the bits and pieces of news that Nathan managed to pick up on his travels in and around the hospital.

Nathan was more worried about Ryan than he allowed himself to show. His back was still so torn up, and some of the marks were so deep and red, and he seemed low, not just in pain, but low like the spark had been snuffed out of his expressive brown eyes. They hadn't talked yet, but Nathan had been there for him, telling him he loved him, kissing him gently to sleep.

He just knew Ryan's memories wouldn't be that he had saved Nathan, saved Laurie… It was the ones he couldn't save. In particular the man he had to leave in the car—David Jackson—would haunt him, dragging him down, and Nathan didn't know what to say. Nathan was the one that had made Ryan go back, look into that man's eyes and tell him they were sending help, even as the fire crept towards him. It was Nathan that had made Ryan do that, and the guilt building inside him was like an acid.

He'd spoken to Ryan's family on his behalf, stuff Ryan tried to get him to say, making the rest of it up and saying what he thought they would want to hear. His own family had been easier. He'd just told them he was good. He didn't whitewash the whole trapped-under-a-beam business, but he did at least give it the Hollywood ending, something that was in short supply around here at the moment.

Stepping out into the California sun, he was surprised to see the heavy smoke had started to dissipate this morning. The fires in the hills had been brought under control, and a lot of unreachable fires in LA were starting to burn themselves out behind fire lines. Some were so deep in rubble they couldn't be reached. He stopped briefly at the outside wall where a collection of missing person photos was starting to build. He had started to count the hours he was here by the size of the groupings, reading some of the details, wondering if any of these people would be found. Unconsciously he found himself looking for the name David Jackson, but it never appeared.

It was only a short walk to the children's center, short enough to make it easy on his ankle, long enough to actually get some air, smoke filled or not. They knew him at the front desk. He signed in. He knew where he was going, and before he knew it, he was at the dorm that held, at last count in this long, thin room alone, twenty-two children under the age of four. The guard who sat and watched and the group of nurses who huddled around various groups kept on doing what they were doing. No one stopped Nathan, and he spotted Laurie way before she spotted him. A woman was cuddling her, her back to him, hunched protectively around Laurie.

"Nathan," Laurie said happily, and in a flurry of

movement, the woman stood, sweeping Laurie on to her hips and looking startled.

"Hey, Laurie Lee—" Nathan smiled. "—you okay, sweetie?" Laurie just grinned back, but she didn't hold her arms out for her usual hug, instead gripping tight to the lady.

"Mr. Richardson?" The woman held out her hand.

Nathan shook it even as he acknowledged the name with the usual, "Nathan." He was still bemused, but assumed she was some sort of volunteer. She just stared at him, her eyes red, from smoke or crying he couldn't tell.

"I only just made it up here. I've been trying to find… I don't know what to say to you…your friend. They told me…" She stopped, her eyes filling with tears. "I'm Laurie's mom. Laurie was visiting her dad and his wife… I want to thank you; I want to thank you for my daughter… And I don't know how." She burst into tears, and Laurie snuggled in as her mom pulled her tight.

That was wonderful. It was what he and Ryan wanted, for Laurie to have family, for her not be on her own, but he didn't know what to say, how to vocalize just how happy he was. "You don't need to thank us," he said softly, because really she didn't, because when it came down to it, it was Laurie that had kept both him and Ryan going.

"I do… What you did, you and your friend, Ryan… Laurie told me, they told me here, that your friend pulled her from the car, that you carried her down… I don't know how I can ever repay you."

"You don't ever need to, but there is… Can you just do one thing for me? Can you come and see Ryan?"

Chapter Eighteen

RYAN WAS PISSY AND TIRED. NATHAN HAD PULLED HIM OUT of sleep and was helping him to sit up, and he hurt, damn it. He hurt from the base of his spine to the tip of his head, and why? 'Cause someone wanted to meet them, probably some doctor who wanted to poke and prod at him. Well, it wasn't as if he was in top form. All he wanted to do was—

"Ryan!" Laurie's voice.

Ryan's heart lifted, and he held out his hands as the three-year-old scrambled up on his bed and threw little arms around his neck.

"Laurie, babe, you okay, sweetie?"

"S'momma," she mumbled into his neck as Ryan lifted his eyes and met dark brown eyes so similar to Laurie's that he knew in a heartbeat who the woman was.

"Your momma, darlin'?" he said softly, trying not to wince as she pulled on the back of his neck tightly.

"Uh huh."

He pulled her in for a hug, kind of knowing inside this might be the last time he got to do that. He owed this small child so much. She and Nathan were the light in the dark, the ones that kept him going when he could have stopped, and all those other clichés that were clutching at his heart right about now. The tears started way down inside, twisting his stomach. A skipped heartbeat and the agony of failure and seeing the enormous vista of destruction about them flared deep inside. He couldn't let the tears out. He had to be happy; he *was* happy, happy to hand Laurie back with a squeeze and a kiss to her mom. Her mom, who was saying something, words that refused to filter through the noise buzzing in his head. *Thank you… Sorry… Forget.*

He saw Nathan write something down and smiled somehow. He heard Nathan making medical excuses for him and heard him make promises before helping Laurie and her mom out of the room. He was only gone a while, but Ryan stayed sitting up. He needed to say something to Nathan when he came back. He wasn't sure what, but something to somehow explain the situation and what was in his head, starting with apologies and reasons.

Nathan came back into the room, crossing immediately to Ryan, and sitting down to face him, drawing one leg up and leaning in worriedly.

"You okay, Ryan?"

"I…yeah…I'm cool," he whispered, saving his voice.

"I was blown away when her mom said who she was and—"

"Sorry, Nathan, sorry," Ryan interrupted, swallowing then grimacing in pain. "I got scared. I couldn't have faced it if you moved away and then found someone else."

"Ryan—"

"I treated you like shit, didn't let you in. It was easier to push you away. That isn't me…it's not me. I trusted you, but I let my own insecurities stop me from telling you."

"Ryan, I know, but I saw it too late. I was scared as well. It was easier to get the parts and move on without having to be honest. You pushed me away and I thought you hated me." He paused, watching as the light in Ryan's expressive brown eyes dimmed. He shook his head. "I know you didn't, even when we argued, it wasn't the real Ryan who said he didn't love me."

"I do love you."

"You were jealous, yeah, but nervous, anxious, and sad as well. I know that. I just wanted my Ryan back, the Ryan that made me feel, the Ryan I fell in love with, and I didn't know how to find the real you. Then there's me. Why would you waste time waiting around for me? You had your own life. I never expected you to still want me. And that's the killer: I talked myself out of you still loving me."

They fell silent, Ryan breathing heavily, Nathan resting his forehead on Ryan's, breathing in synch, waiting.

"Want us to go home," Ryan whispered.

"HI GUYS," Jason said from the door. "I hear they're getting you two out today." He smiled.

"They're going to try," Nathan said. "And you."

"I'm staying," Jason said. "I'm uninjured, and I can help."

"You do realize you only played a doctor on TV and that you aren't actually a doctor, right?" Nathan deadpanned.

"Ha ha," Jason said with a grin. He crossed to Ryan

and held out his hand. "Look after him," he said. His voice held warning.

Ryan barely nodded. "I will," he said.

Jason hugged Nathan, then with a final wave, was gone.

"Where are they taking us?" Ryan asked.

Nathan shrugged. "Your guess is as good as mine. All I know is the area is twenty miles outside of the city and there are hotels that are taking in refugees. We can stay there until we can get a flight to your place. Meet up with the family."

"You want to go back to mine?" Ryan said wonderingly. He looked like he didn't believe a word Nathan was saying.

"Well, I always thought of it as ours," Nathan offered. Then he smirked. "Anyway, my place isn't really something we can live in," he added.

Ryan closed his eyes and made a sound of distress that had Nathan next to him in an instant.

"Don't say that," Ryan said. "I could have lost you."

Nathan regretted what he had said in jest and held Ryan's bandaged hand gently.

"But you didn't, you saved me. You need to focus on that." He leaned forward and kissed Ryan gently. He only hoped he could take his own advice.

THE DOCTORS DOSED Ryan up with painkillers, and Nathan took some that he had pocketed earlier himself. When they managed to get to the city limits, it was already early evening, and the regime of painkillers was due again. Ryan looked really ill, and Nathan doubted he looked much better. They had passed through checks and roadblocks, following the small trickle of people in vehicles heading out of the city. They were part of a convoy sat in the back of an Army transport, and Nathan had shamelessly begged to use the comms system and had managed to get in touch with Adam. He was relieved that he had managed to pass on messages to both families. It was another tick in the plus column, and Nathan could see Ryan unwind inch by inch as they moved across the county and to wherever people like them were being taken. Out here everything was so normal. No death or destruction and no smoke.

When they arrived it was dark and the Hilton sign was a welcome sight. Their room was on the first floor and the staff couldn't have been more helpful.

When the door shut behind them and it was just the two of them finally, Nathan relaxed and exhaustion stole over him.

Chapter Nineteen

RYAN REFUSED THE PAIN MEDS THAT NATHAN HELD OUT—they made him sleepy, and he didn't want sleepy and disoriented. He wanted real. He wanted to try and kiss Nathan, hug Nathan, sleep next to Nathan, and he needed to feel tonight, really feel.

Somehow Nathan had managed to help him shower, covering his neck, washing his hair. He'd left Ryan sitting on the edge of the bed wrapped in a towel, promising he would be back soon.

When he returned, he was laden down with spicy smelling hot pizza and Walmart bags that revealed new jeans, clean T-shirts, sweatshirts, and heavens, new boxers. It was like Christmas. Nathan grabbed the quickest shower in history, foregoing a shave, then they both dressed in the new Ts and boxers. Ryan felt almost human and they sat cross-legged opposite each other on the bed, eating pizza, Ryan struggling a bit but managing to eat some of it nonetheless.

When he finished, Nathan placed the box on the floor

next to the bed and returned to what appeared to now be his favorite pastime, staring at Ryan. Ryan, for his part, decided he needed to touch, needed to feel, and he ran hands over broad shoulders and against hot skin, relearning Nathan's body, cupping his face and leaning in to touch lips. They couldn't do much more. Nathan still struggled to breathe with his broken ribs, but Ryan was content to touch, to be touched. Soft breaths were exchanged with eyes closed and fingers seeking anchors in soft T-shirt material.

"Love you," Ryan whispered against Nathan's lips. Nathan caught the words close to him, savored the feel of them, and craved their warmth.

"I love you too."

Ryan traced Nathan's lips with the tip of his tongue, darting in for a quick taste before retreating to lie back on the bed on his front, encouraging Nathan to lie as close as was comfortable. Nathan switched off the light and pulled the covers over them. Sleep claimed them both before they even had time for conscious thought.

RYAN WOKE IN THE NIGHT, unable to move from the pain, and must have made a noise because Nathan was instantly awake and right there with water and medicine. He helped Ryan to lie on his stomach, when before he had been lying on his side, and Ryan sighed in thanks. Some of the tension knotting in him started to dissipate. He turned his head to face Nathan, knowing this was a conversation he needed to have, but Nathan beating him to it.

"Some of these marks on your back may scar," Nathan started softly. "I am so sorry."

"No…'pology," Ryan muttered.

"I should never have run. If I'd stayed in New York then none of this would have happened," Nathan pointed out, sorrow filling his voice, his hands twisted in his short hair, a kind of raw despair on his face. Ryan pushed through the pain, lifting a hand to capture one of Nathan's, easing it down to hold it as tight as he could.

"Made…you…run." He pushed the words out, pronouncing each as clearly as he could. Tears formed in his eyes from a combination of pain and distress at what he was saying; Nathan could have died on that mountain, the same way that David Jackson had, trapped in the burning and twisted metal. It didn't bear thinking about. The thought of losing Nathan, of losing him to the fire, his body… It was too much to even think about, let alone articulate.

"Ryan, you need to sleep. Shut your eyes."

Ryan closed his eyes, his hand still loose in Nathan's, and he let Nathan's voice wash over him as the painkillers started their work on his tortured muscles and stretched tight, hot skin.

NATHAN CARRIED ON A ONE-SIDED CONVERSATION, willing Ryan to relax and let sleep take him to a place where he could begin to heal. "Do you remember when we first met, when I had that first callback, and it was just us, you and your camera and I was alternating between being pissed I had lost the last job and overwhelmed that I had gotten to work with you?"

He waited for Ryan to nod, a sleepy smile loosening his tight, pain-thinned lips, before continuing.

"You walked in; I had Googled you, checked out your portfolio, and you were nothing like what I was expecting. I mean, the gossip columns said you were tall, but when I stood up and you were still like towering over me, I felt so small. Then to add insult to injury, your hands, dude, so big and warm. When we shook hands, you won't believe what went through my head. Do you know there and then I knew I was screwed, I mean, I had to do the whole model thing, and I was crushing so hard on you. So yeah, screwed."

Nathan looked down at Ryan's face, his features relaxed in sleep, his breathing even and shallow. "Worst of all though, Ryan, it wasn't lust. It wasn't really crushing. It was like I knew you were the other half of me, and I just had to wait for you to see that I was the other half of you."

He shifted and winced in pain. His damn hip was giving him grief and he hoped to hell he'd get full movement back in it soon. His chest hurt, every part of him seemed bruised, but contented, he lay down as close to Ryan as he could get and let sleep take him as quickly as he could.

IN THE MORNING Nathan had to help Ryan dress entirely as Ryan's muscles kept spasming, and pain was etched on his face. Nathan handed him water and meds, which Ryan downed immediately with a grateful smile.

They had decided they were going back to New York and had arranged for both sets of parents to meet them there with the extended families. He was desperate to meet his new niece, and so thankful he was alive to do so. Nathan was utterly convinced with quiet certainty that for the foreseeable future, where Ryan was, Nathan would be. No, not even just for the near future, but on a much more permanent basis. Splitting their time between New York and wherever Nathan ended up with his acting was something that they agreed on.

Finally they could get the happy-ever-after they had nearly thrown away.

DAY twelve after the earthquake was a milestone. They were still in the hotel but the heavy bandages and stitches that had been applied to Ryan's back in the field needed removing, and Nathan knew Ryan was apprehensive. In fact, on the way to the closest hospital he admitted he scared to death wondering what the doctor would find on his back. He hadn't let anyone touch his back or his throat, and Nathan was struggling to understand why.

"Because you might hate it," Ryan blurted out suddenly, his throat infinitely better. At least he was talking, not quite at full Ryan level, but slowly getting there. This odd response was a result of Nathan's insistence on wanting to be in the room when they assessed the injuries. It wasn't the first time Nathan had pushed, and if he didn't get his way, it wouldn't be the last, but those words were so at odds with what he thought Ryan might say it stunned Nathan into premature silence.

"Okay, I'm shallow," Ryan continued. "I know it's stupid, but people say I have a nice back, soft, smooth, strong, and I was kinda proud of it." His breathing hitched, and Nathan knew the signs of an oncoming Ortiz breakdown.

"Proud of your back?" Nathan tried not to sound incredulous, but he must have sounded just that way because the response he got from Ryan was instant and messy. Ryan slumped down onto the bed.

"I don't really mean that; I don't know what I mean. I just don't know."

Nathan fell to his knees in front of Ryan, peering up at his him through his hair. "It's not shallow to worry about what you look like, Ryan. Jeez, my whole career kinda depends on it at the moment."

"I'm not—" Ryan swallowed, his eyes still leaking, his hands twisted in the covers on either side of him. "Jesus, fuck, Nathan, I don't give a shit about…what I look like… I don't know what I mean."

"Ryan, you're not making any sense."

"Like I don't know that. This is all screwed to hell. Ignore me, I'm just…will you stay with me?" Ryan stared straight into Nathan's eyes, his brown eyes sparkling with unshed tears.

"Of course I will, Ryan, you know I'll go in with you, hold your hand," Nathan reassured gently.

"I-I didn't mean that, not really, I meant, even if I am scarred and shit, will you stay with me?"

Nathan sat back on his heels, feeling as if a huge weight had just knocked him sideways. This was what was upsetting Ryan? The thought that Nathan couldn't love a less than physically perfect body? Nathan's first reaction was anger. Did Ryan really think he was that shallow? His next reaction was that Ryan's head wasn't right. They had literally been to hell and back. No wonder he was screwed up.

Then it kind of hit him all at once. Ryan had hinted several times that Nathan didn't have to stay with him, that it was okay if was too badly hurt and scarred and Nathan felt it was all too much. This latest outburst was just another way of giving Nathan an out, and it was the last time that this was being brought up if Nathan had anything to do with it.

"When you found me in the apartment, Ryan, when I was pinned down by my legs under that steel, what if I'd been paralyzed when you pulled me out?"

"Fuck, Nathan."

"Seriously. Imagine there was no fire and someone came to help and I got out, but what if I could never walk again? What would you do?"

"Do?"

"Would you leave me?"

"No!"

"And what if I'd had some kind of scarring from the fire? On my face? I wouldn't have a career as an actor anymore. Would you try and understand why it all happened or would you have run screaming for the hills?"

Ryan looked shocked. "Shit, I wouldn't do that, you know I wouldn't," he said. Clearly realization hit him as to what Nathan was saying. He looked down at his lap.

"So, time to get you to the hospital and get you sorted, pretty boy, yeah?"

THE DOCTOR TOOK SOME DETAILS, simple stuff,

nothing too heavy. Questions that even Nathan could answer. He strayed into some heavier questions, made some brief suggestions about therapy, both physical and psychological, and Nathan sensed Ryan tensing next to him. He filed the reaction away for further thought.

Then it was time. Time for the doctor to start peeling away the dressings. He called in a nurse, donned gloves, pulled a tray closer and gently reassured Ryan. Nathan pulled a chair over to sit next to Ryan's head, and the doctor began, keeping up a running dialogue of what he was doing. "…difficult to see through some of the swelling… If we cut this away… Can I have some local here? Looking good… What we have here are some very healthy-looking wounds, Mr Ortiz. …did a good job. You may have a scar there, nothing plastic surgery won't fix…"

"I won't be doing that. If it scars, it scars," Ryan said, wincing at the pain and smiling at the same time.

"What about your pretty back?" Nathan smirked, reaching over and touching Ryan's hand softly.

"Are you ever gonna forget I said that?"

"Never."

"Bastard."

"Yep, but you know you love me."

"Yeah, I do."

Epilogue

THE FLIGHT HAD ONLY BEEN THREE HOURS but it was enough for Nathan's hip to get all achy and make him miserable. He missed Ryan and three weeks was too much time apart. Since the earthquake they hadn't been apart a single night but a clash of filming for him against an assignment in South America for Ryan meant twenty-one nights alone.

As soon as the plane stopped taxiing, he was up and out of his seat, wincing at the pain in his legs. He had one suitcase and he knew Ryan would be waiting. The luggage for his flight was taking ages to come around. His cell vibrated and he smiled when he saw Jason's name.

"Hey," he said as he tried to peer over the heads of the other passengers waiting for bags. He wished he had Ryan's height sometimes.

"Hey, you left your sunglasses next to the bed," Jason said in summary. Nathan had stayed in Jason's spare room in his new Portland apartment. He just knew he'd forget something.

"Don't worry, it's not like I'll be needing then in the Big Apple, it's rainy and cold as hell. Did you hear back from the center yet?"

"Not yet."

The center was Jason's idea. A central hub for kids affected by the quake. It had been nearly a year since that awful day and there was more than one child alone because of it. Nathan and Ryan helped fund it and final planning permission was due today or tomorrow.

"Call me as soon as you know everything's gone through okay."

"Even if I interrupt you and Ryan and the homecoming? It's been twenty-one days, you know." Jason was teasing but Nathan felt his cheeks heat. He missed Ryan like he would miss breathing. "I'm joking. Say hi to Ryan for me."

Nathan hurried as fast as his bum leg would let him and was out in the arrivals area and searching for Ryan as soon as he could.

"Nathan!" Ryan called.

They met in the middle and Nathan dropped his bag and let go of his case as Ryan swung him up and around then kissed him solidly in the middle of JFK arrivals. There were some comments, a few wolf whistles, but they were only two of hundreds of reuniting couples.

Chatting about everything they'd missed eased them into the here and now and they collected Ryan's car and spent at least ten minutes just sitting in the car kissing. All Nathan could think was that he was glad the SUV had tinted windows and that the parking level was dark.

The journey home was delayed by traffic but Nathan

relaxed back in the leather seats and simply enjoyed being with Ryan.

"I've missed you so much," he said as they neared the place they called home. The two-bedroom apartment was small but perfect for the two of them. Nathan couldn't wait to take a shower and show Ryan how much he had missed him.

"I missed you too," Ryan said distractedly. Nathan frowned at the tone. Ryan sounded like he didn't mean it, and he had this serious expression on his face. What was wrong? They certainly greeted each other like nothing had changed. But it *had* been twenty-one days, that was nearly a month.

"Are you okay, Ry?" he asked softly. Ryan glanced at him then smiled.

"Sorry, I was miles away, I'm fine, just have things I need to sort in my head."

"Thinky Ryan-type things," Nathan teased. They both had moments since the quake where they were sometimes best left alone. All the therapy in the world wasn't going to scrub their brains of some of what they had seen.

"I heard from Laurie," Ryan said. "Or her mom, anyway. She sent us a painting for the fridge." He indicated left as he spoke, then took the turn and they were so close to home that Nathan could feel the tension of the flight leaving him in a rush.

Ryan took the case and Nathan the bag, and finally they were inside with the door shut to the world. Nathan immediately began to kiss Ryan, twenty-one days was too long to go without kissing. When Ryan gently pushed him back, Nathan knew he was pouting. He laughed.

"We need to talk first."

"About what?" Nathan said immediately. He hated that his first instinct was to assume it was something bad. You'd think that after all this time of talking and healing together that he could feel absolutely sure Ryan was happy.

"Come sit down." Ryan guided him gently to the sofa and Nathan sat down as asked. "I've been thinking," he began. "I love you so much, and the last three weeks just made me feel like my life was unraveling again."

"I know," Nathan said in a small voice.

"I don't know if I will ever stop thinking about what happened, or why I wasn't right by your side when it did happen. One day we'll be able to rationalize it all, but for the time being I want us to focus on the good."

"Okay," Nathan said to fill the pause. He wasn't sure where this was going. Yes they were closer now than they had ever been—tragedy had pulled them back together where they belonged.

Ryan sank to his knees on the floor in front of Nathan and pulled something from his pocket. A small box. He held it out on his palm.

"I've been waiting for the right moment. I waited for Valentine's, for your birthday, for mine, then I realized the day isn't important. Because every day with you is important. Nathan Richardson, will you marry me?"

Nathan blinked and realized his mouth was hanging open. They'd talked about forever, but this really was *forever*.

"Yes," he said quickly. "Yes, I'll marry you." He leaned forward and opened the box. Inside sat two matching platinum rings and when he tilted it he saw they were engraved inside with the simple words *through fire*. Perfect.

They kissed then Ryan stood and pulled Nathan with him. Together they walked to the bedroom and Nathan tugged his T-shirt over his head at the same time Ryan did. They laughed and in the laughter, they kissed then fell back on the bed. The kisses grew heated and finally they were naked and pressed close together.

Making love was familiar and secure and everything Nathan wanted. With smiles and the press of lips and hands they explored each other like it was the very first time.

"I love you," Ryan whispered against Nathan's throat. Nathan moaned low as Ryan prepared him and touched a path of kisses from his throat to his belly then took him deep into his mouth. Nathan nearly lost it there and then and he pushed at Ryan's head. Ryan's lips curved into a smile as he climbed back up to carry on the exploration of Nathan's mouth. In a smooth move he was pushing inside Nathan, and there was no pain, only the burn that Nathan craved. Ryan kissed and made love to him and all Nathan could do was go along with the ride.

"I love you, I love you," Nathan whispered as orgasm climbed inside him. His hands tracked the scars on Ryan's back, each one of them a badge of courage. When he reached the peak, he gripped tightly and shouted Ryan's name with Ryan coming close after.

They cleaned up and cuddled close and Nathan closed his eyes.

"Do you think Jason could be joint best man, and that Laurie would be a flower girl for us?" Ryan said thoughtfully.

Nathan smiled and inhaled the scent of his lover. Everything about Ryan made Nathan smile and want more of him.

"We'll ask them tomorrow," Nathan murmured. "We're busy today."

Ryan stole another kiss then pulled back. "Very busy."

THE END

Alpha, Delta

Chapter One

"This is the second fucking time we've had to do this, and I'm telling you now, I'm not staying for the whole thing."

Finn Hallan glanced over at his teammate and wondered if he should check him for any visible weapons. Erik was one of those guys who was never happy about sitting still, let alone in a seminar dealing with health and safety.

"Cap's not going to like you backing out of this," Finn warned. He was just as restless, more familiar with action and getting on with things than sitting in a briefing room listening to changes in policy. Thing is, this shit was statutory, and Cap had made Finn and Erik attend, in case there was anything important about oil platform safety. Finn was certainly not going up against Cap, and he knew Erik needed to keep his ass in the chair if he wanted to stay on the team.

Delta was a highly sought after group of people to join

and if you made it, you didn't refuse to sit in meetings that you'd been ordered into.

"We need a serious emergency," Erik groused. "A hostage negotiation or at the very least a terrorist threat."

The woman in front of him turned and frowned at the words, but she took one look at both Erik and Finn and turned back to face the front. Finn knew they looked out of place. Both in the dark dress colors of the Delta uniform, not long off duty, they probably gave the impression of some kind of hardass security detail. Certainly, not the kind of guys you told to shut up. She would know who they were, members of the ERU, code-named Delta, and the ones who policed for terrorist activities in Norway and out into the Norwegian Sea. Which, incidentally, was where most of these NorsDev employees in the briefing worked.

Erik grinned and raised his eyebrows suggestively before cupping his groin and looking pointedly at the back of the blonde's head. Finn shook his head. She was a NorsDev exec, and everyone knew the high-ups at the energy company had nothing to say to the ranks. If only she knew how much Finn and Erik could do for her if she were in trouble. If only she was aware of the kind of men they really were—ones who never sat still—then maybe she'd be a little more understanding of the boredom factor.

The presentation on the large screen at the front of the room switched to a new slide with a name in block capitals. Niall Faulkner. Not a name that Finn recognized and he couldn't help the groan when he saw the line under the name. *Platform Decommissioning Engineer.*

"Oh Jesus fuck. Save me from nerds with clipboards

and PowerPoints. I think my last brain cell up and died," Erik muttered.

The speaker indicated the slide, "And now I'd like to hand it over to Niall Faulkner. Some of you will recall Niall was responsible for the X220 additions." A ripple of murmurs around the room indicated that at least some knew what the hell that meant. Evidently, this Faulkner guy was someone with a name at NorsDev. A man stood in the front row of the lecture theatre and made his way up the four steps to the stage, tripping on the last step and grabbing at the retreating previous speaker as he left. Luckily the new guy, Niall, Finn assumed, didn't fall flat on his face, but he couldn't help the smile on his face. It was funny shit seeing someone fall over.

Niall made his way to the lectern, looking down at his notes and shuffling them into some kind of order. The main spotlight flickered then focused directly on him, and Finn had an instant gut reaction to the man on the stage.

Short and slim, with dark hair and glasses, he was the hottest safety officer Finn had ever seen.

"Woo boy," Erik said under his breath. "You thinking he's way to pretty to not be utterly and entire gay?"

Finn didn't dignify the comment with a response. Erik was the only member of the Delta team who knew Finn himself was gay and that comment was directly aimed at Finn and the fact Erik kept trying to get Finn hooked up with someone. *Anyone*. Last week it had been this short guy with glasses who worked in legal A month ago, it was a random stranger who fixed Eric's car. The guy didn't stop.

"Even if he is, he's not my type," Finn lied very quietly. Actually, this Niall guy was pretty much the epitome of Finn's type. Preppy with a side order of nerdy was just exactly what Finn liked under him, or over him, or hell, anyway which around him. And the glasses? Hell, glasses got him every time.

"I totally think he's batting for your team," Erik said, obviously waiting for Finn to shout him down. Instead, Finn went the opposite way just to fuck with Erik.

"Absolutely," Finn deadpanned.

Erik's eyes widened, and then he frowned and peered to the small stage below. "Seriously? You can tell from here?"

Finn punched Erik in the leg, "No, fucker. I can't."

Erik huffed and pulled out his cell phone, putting it in his lap and shielding the glow with his hands.

"This is all bullshit anyway," he announced. "I'm out of here," Erik was clearly booking out of this presentation. On the other hand, Finn found himself absolutely fixated. He wasn't entirely sure what Niall was saying because he wasn't listening to the words, but Finn could listen to Niall's soft Scottish accent all day. Kind of a cross between Ewan McGregor and Sean Connery.

All too soon this Niall guy, who apparently could remove oil platforms in a responsible and environmentally sound way, had finished the presentation. There was a polite ripple of applause before he threw the meeting open for questions.

Finn had a lot of questions, only none of them were to do with...he peered at the last slide...ethical decommissioning.

Erik leaned over, "Bathroom," he said. "Or maybe I'll just fuck off and find a bar."

Finn gripped his friend's jacket. "Cap will kill you for flunking again."

Erik shrugged free. "Cover for me," he hissed, then left out the side door. *Fucker*. The woman in front turned to face him, but this time she didn't turn away. In fact, she was looking at him expectantly, as was the whole row. He scanned them, wondering exactly what to say.

"Sir? Did you have a question?" The soft sexy burr of the Scottish voice asked over the microphone.

Shit. Evidently, Erik's leaving had caught Niall's attention, and he thought the kerfuffle was a freaking question. The woman in front smirked at him, then raked him with her eyes with a large dose of disdain. She was daring him to say he'd been fucking around with Erik and hadn't listened to a word the presenter said.

"Yes," Finn said smoothly. The woman looked surprised, but she didn't turn in her chair. "Is decommissioning of oil platforms what you always wanted to do?"

And no, he had no idea where that came from, but it seemed like a reasonable question. People asked that kind of thing? Right?

Niall stared out at him with a look of consternation. Finn waited for that moment when Niall said that in all of his *however many years* he had never had such a strange question. Then Niall's expression cracked and he shook his head ruefully.

"I wanted to be an astronaut," he admitted. "But mild vertigo and a propensity for being sick whenever I flew meant that wasn't going to happen. Seemed to me the ocean and the unexplored depths was the next best thing."

As soon as he'd answered, another question came from

the front row, from the lick-asses who actually paid attention in these seminars. The pressure was off Finn. Damn woman was still looking at him, although the rest of the row had turned back to face front. Her expression had changed, and she was looking at him with a speculating gleam. He leaned forward toward her.

"Can I help you?" he half whispered.

She lowered her lashes at him. "I don't know. Can you?"

Finn leaned even closer. "Unless you have a cock under that pretty red dress, then I'm not sure I can."

Her eyes widened, and she turned her back to him with an audible huff. It was all Finn could do not to laugh out loud, even if he did feel a bit of a dick for saying that. But then, she had been the one staring.

The rest of the seminar passed in all it's boring glory, a combination of industry information, safety notes, and that speech from Niall-with-the-accent. When Finn turned on his cell phone, he saw he had three missed calls from Cap, and a picture message from Erik of a cup of coffee and a Danish. Just seeing the food made Finn's stomach grumble and knowing Erik was sat somewhere relaxing pissed him off no end.

He listened to Cap's messages. If the matter had been urgent, then he'd have been pulled from the seminar, but these messages were more on the line of is-Erik-there and I-just-saw-Erik-with-coffee.

Like I have any control over Erik.

He sent off a quick text to Cap, assuring him that Erik must have been on a break, then another to Erik saying he'd been spotted. Let Erik and Cap fight that one out. As for Finn, he'd earned points today by staying through the whole thing, and he'd seen the edible morsel that was Scottish-Niall, so it was a win/win for him.

In the breakout area with coffee and snacks, Niall was holding court. A gaggle of women surrounded him, all talking, and Niall looked like he was doing okay. Laughing and smiling and talking, and Finn wanted some of that. Using his best seek-and-destroy tactics, he made his way around the edge of the room until he was behind Niall and a single step forward had him up close and personal with the man. He realized a few things in quick succession: Niall smelled of a fresh aftershave, he was a good six inches shorter than Finn, and his voice was even sexier close up.

Please if there is a god, let Niall Faulkner be gay, or at the very least bi or curious.

"So astronaut, then," Finn inserted in a lull in the conversation. Niall looked at Finn sharply, then, obviously realizing he was looking right at Finn's chest because of their height difference, his gaze travelled upward, then down to groin level, then back to Niall's face. Quickly, but with enough focus to have Finn thinking that Niall was checking him out.

Oh yes, he certainly checked me out.

"Until I was eight at least," Niall said with a small smile.

Finn wasn't letting this drop. He wanted to tease Niall, and he sure as well didn't want Niall turning back to the NorsDev women who surrounded him. "I wanted to be a cowboy like Clint Eastwood."

"But you ended up a cop," Niall pointed out with a nod to the uniform that Finn was wearing. "ERU? That's the special team out of Oslo, right?"

"Yeah, and same thing," Finn said. "Fighting the bad guys."

"Except you don't have a horse."

"I had to leave the horse outside. He never pays attention in seminars." Finn held out a hand. "Finn Hallan," he introduced himself. "On loan to the Norwegian Emergency Response Unit."

"On loan from where?"

"Metropolitan, London."

"A Londoner working for the Norwegians. I didn't know the *Beredskapstroppen* opened to non-Norwegians."

"My father is Norwegian. And you're Niall Faulkner, the decommissioning expert from Scotland, if I hear right? And you work for NorsDev." There, that turned the whole conversation about what Finn could or couldn't do on its head. He'd much rather hear what Niall had to say about himself. And the interesting twist of a Scot using Norwegian words was just the sexiest thing ever. The women around him, all four of them, melted away and just about on time Finn was in a one-on-one situation with the sexy engineering guy.

"Were you actually listening to what I was saying today?" Niall asked with a tilt of his head to punctuate the question. He had the most intriguing eyes but the light there was too bright to properly make out the color. How did Finn explain he was looking at Niall and listening to the tone of his voice rather than taking in the content of what Niall was saying?

"Of course," Finn lied. "You're an expert in the field of decommissioning."

Niall raised an eyebrow, silently mocking Finn.

"And you're ethical as well," Finn added.

"I can summarize for you now," Niall said. He opened his mouth to begin, but a man stepped up next to Niall with a plate of snacks and coffee.

"Eat something," the new arrival insisted. He spared Finn a quick glance and a smile then focused back on Niall. "Seriously, if you don't eat you'll fade away to nothing." The new guy had a similar Scottish accent to Niall, but it wasn't enough to hold Finn's attention like Niall's. Finn didn't imagine the look of exasperation on Niall's face, nor did he think for one minute Niall would fade away. He may be a little on the small side, but then, most people were next to Finn with his six-four in height to be fair. But there was something solid about Niall, he was all lithe muscles and slim build…in fact, he was built for—

"Mr. Hallan, this is my brother Ewan," Niall said. "Ewan, meet Mr. Hallan—"

"Finn."

Niall ignored him and carried on with the introduction. "He's with the ERU."

Ewan whistled and looked impressed. "A real-life Delta in our midst. You here for your annual health and safety briefing?"

"Just picking up what we need to know."

"Might help if you listen to me then," Niall deadpanned. "I was examining the fact that when we're deconstructing the oil platforms that security is lower and there's a skeleton staff until handover and that this could well be a security risk."

Finn wasn't entirely sure what to say to that. His role in Delta was the backbone of the war against terrorists in Norway and the locale, which covered the oil rigs in the

Norwegian Sea. He should really have listened to Niall. So how did he apologize, then ask for a recap without looking like a complete dick?

"I heard all that," he lied.

"Yet you asked me about what I wanted to be when I grew up?" He stepped out of the light a little and Finn was blown away by Niall's eyes, a stunning mix of golds and browns. They were damn near twinkling with the teasing.

"I didn't exactly phrase it like that," Finn defended himself. Then he backed down. "Maybe I could get a private consultation," he said slyly. This was the perfect time to test the waters with the decommissioning engineer, or whatever he was called.

"Call your team, and I'll do a group talk before I leave on Friday," Niall offered. "It was good to meet you, Mr. Hallan."

"Finn," he repeated in the hope he would hear his name on Niall's lips in that soft bur.

They shook hands again, then Niall was lost to the crowd, his brother at his side guiding him around the different people. Finn resolved to look Niall Faulkner up when he got to a quiet space. There was something intriguing about the man with the hazel eyes and the soft steady voice. Oh and his pants, there was something about what was in his pants, and the way they hugged his groin tightly…and that ass…

Chapter Two

Niall allowed Ewan to guide him away and was thankful for the interruption. "Thank you," he said in a quiet voice.

"Was he making you nervous?" Ewan asked with a backward glance at the man they had left by the back window.

Niall considered the tall, broad, in-your-face, dark-haired, blue-eyed man. Nervous no, a little turned on, yes. That Delta ticked every single one of Niall's items on the checklist. Taller. Bigger. Stronger. Fuck, even his libido had his cock hardening in his pants and he couldn't do allow himself to get turned on like some horny teenager. Not here. In this place, he was a respected engineer with years of experience behind him and his opinion was requested. He held a high position leading a team of engineers at NorsDev, one of the biggest energy companies in the world, and he wasn't even thirty yet.

He did not have time to fuck that all up by mooning over Mr. Tall and Sexy in his uniform. And hell, that uniform. It stretched in all the right places, and add in the trim waist and flat stomach, and Niall was a goner. God knows what he would have done if he'd actually gotten a look at Finn's ass, but it had to be fine given the way his uniform pants clung to muscled thighs and—

"Earth to Niall," Ewan interrupted is thoughts. "You okay?"

"Yeah, I'm fine…and no, he didn't make me nervous. So, who's next on the agenda?"

"Adam's here from finance, something about budgets."

Oh. Hell. No. "You have to get me out of here," Niall said urgently. "That man will kill me with boredom."

Ewan turned to say something but it was too late, Adam was there, folders under his arm, and Niall abruptly saw an hour of his life disappear into a black hole. When he glanced back at where he'd left Finn, he saw the man was still there. He was leaning back against the window, arms crossed over his broad chest, and he was staring right at Niall.

Flustered, it was all Niall could do to concentrate on Adam and his wish to cut three million from the budgets for decommissioning the Forseti platform. When next he got a chance to check on Finn, the sex-on-legs guy had gone. Niall couldn't help the bite of disappointment. Yes, Finn Hallan made him feel all kinds of nervous, but it was a good nervous, and he already missed the sight of him.

And what did that say about the attraction between two people? Because Niall was ready to jump the man's bones and they'd barely shaken hands.

"I'm going up to get some work done." The time had long since passed eight p.m., and he was off the clock now. Someone else could be the expert, the one who answered questions, all Niall wanted was a tumbler of whiskey, his PJs and his laptop. And sleep.

Ewan passed him another plate of whatever leftovers there were on the main table. Niall took them because he knew it was a waste of time arguing with his little brother. After all, Ewan was just looking after him.

"I know you won't call room service," Ewan said with a sigh. He tucked a plastic bottle of Coke into Niall's laptop bag and handed him the whole thing. "Go. Before someone corners you again."

Niall did as he was told, edging his way out and making sure not to meet anyone's gaze. He only did these safety audit assessments once a year and it seemed like everyone in NorsDev wanted a piece of him. When he made it out to the main corridor juggling plate and laptop bag it was like the last day of the summer term, and he had the long stretch of weeks ahead of him. Okay so it was only one night but that was a long time in a really nice hotel with a shower built for two.

Unbidden, thoughts of Finn in the shower had him groaning at the rush of lust. Jesus, he was losing it big time today. He pressed the button for the elevator and stood back. He was on floor seventeen of the Radisson Blu with a wonderful view of Oslo, and he couldn't wait to see it all lit up in the dark again. The elevator was way up there at twenty-four, but he wasn't moving. He'd have a long wait, but climbing up seventeen flights of stairs would probably mean he'd be found near dead on floor thirteen. He chuckled at the thought but stiffened when a familiar voice spoke behind him.

"Niall," Finn said softly. "You going up?"

Niall turned very slowly to face the object of his

fascination and he swallowed. Finn had changed out of his uniform and into jeans that hugged his legs like a second skin, and a scarlet T-shirt that stuck very close to every single muscle. In uniform, he looked edible, but dressed like this with damp hair from the shower he looked like every gay man's wet dream. His eyes were so damn blue, his lashes long and dark. He may have showered but he hadn't shaved, and stubble darkened his jawline, which gave him an almost dangerous look. Niall needed to say something, Finn had asked him a question. Something about the elevator.

"Seventeen," he said.

Clearly, that was enough, Finn nodded. "Are you finished for the day now?"

Niall nodded and heard himself sigh. "All done for another year."

"Except for my one-on-one," Finn pointed out.

"I didn't say a one-on-one. I said I'd talk to your whole team."

The elevator arrived and they both got in. He pressed seventeen and stood back with the expectation that Finn would press for his own floor. When he didn't Niall assumed that they were on the same floor. That was until the doors shut and Finn stepped right up in his space.

"I wasn't talking about the security briefing," he said all sexy-growly. Niall moved back until his back hit the mirrored wall and Finn stepped forward.

Abruptly Niall was flustered and words failed him. "Wh-what were y-you referring to."

Carefully, *oh so gently*, Finn used a single finger to tilt Niall's chin up.

"Our one-on-one," he said.

"Ours…" *Oh God, oh fuck, I am going to break the zipper in these pants.*

"Unless I read this wrong and you don't want me to hold you down and suck your brains out through your cock."

Finn hadn't moved any closer. In fact, it appeared he was deliberately well out of Niall's space. This was the moment that Niall had to make a decision. He could brush this off, ignore the erection pressing painfully against his zipper, forget the fact that desire and lust fought for every inch of his body. *Hold me down. Fuck…* Or he could take everything those blue eyes promised and have one night of the kind of sex that he imagined he would have with Finn. He heard his brother's voice. *Go for it. No one is ever promised a tomorrow. What do you have to lose?*

Swallowing, Niall shifted the weight of his computer bag from his shoulder, distracted by the flash of numbers as the elevator passed twelve, thirteen…he had to make a decision.

"You didn't read it wrong," he said. His voice came out surprisingly normal despite the fact that his tongue felt too big for his mouth.

The elevator came to a smooth stop, and Finn moved his finger and stepped back.

"Is your room okay?" he asked softly.

Niall attempted to remember how he'd left his room. The maids would have been in to tidy, but Niall wasn't the neatest. He'd been in the hotel three days and was still living out of his suitcase.

It seemed suddenly sensible to set guidelines. "Yes. Tonight, just tonight. Okay? And do you have…are you…"

The elevator doors made to close but Finn held out a hand and stopped them. "Condoms, lube. Check." He didn't address the whole one-night thing.

"This all seems a bit clinical," Niall said, simply for something to say.

In answer, Finn held out a hand and took the plate of food. He stepped out of the elevator and waited for Niall. When Niall let them into his room, he had to concentrate on getting the card in the slot and disengaging the lock. He considered the sad fact that he wasn't exactly coming off as the most competent engineer in the world.

When they were in, Niall placed his laptop bag on the floor under the desk and watched as Finn placed the food on the desk then shrugged off a small runner's backpack. That must be where the condoms were because there was absolutely no room in the pockets in Finn's jeans. Niall didn't know what to do next. He'd never really had a one-night stand. How did it happen? Did they just get on with it? The first times he'd had with all three of his boyfriends had been after dinner where wine had played a part. "You look really worried," Finn said. He was using a soft tone like you would with a child and that gave Niall a bit of confidence to prove he wasn't actually in need of the tone.

"I don't really do this." He waved between them.

"Have sex?"

"Have one-night stands."

Finn stepped in his space again, and this time, with the desk at his back, Niall had nowhere to move. Then Finn did something that had Niall near melting into a puddle. The damned cop cradled his face gently.

"I never actually agree to one night." He tilted Niall's face and leaned down at the same time. With his hands cradling Niall, he kissed him. The kiss was firm but not pushy. There was none of the shit that happened in clubs whenever Ewan managed to drag Niall to one. Seemed like all that happened there was tongues and teeth and a whole lot of demands. This was...

Different.

Finn touched his lips with tongue, pressing inside. With a whimper that Niall hoped to hell was just in his own head, he opened his mouth and tentatively matched the movements. He didn't know what to do with his hands. Should he leave them at his sides, or could he touch...? He rested them on Finn's biceps but couldn't stop with that touch. Instead, locking his hands at the base of Finn's spine and pulling him closer. They kissed that way for the longest time, and Niall was so hard it was painful.

Finn moved one of his hands from Niall's face and trailed his fingers down Niall's back, finally coming to rest on his ass, pressing and lifting so that Niall was near on tiptoe. If they didn't do something soon, release the pressure, if he couldn't undo his pants, then he might do serious damage to his cock. As if he'd somehow telegraphed the message, Finn's hand moved and this time it was to slip under the top button of Niall's pants. He lowered the zipper, finally pushing his fingers into Niall's jersey boxers and closing around Niall's hard cock. Niall pulled back sharply from the kiss and cursed loudly.

All Finn did was chuckle, *the bastard*, then guide Finn back for more kissing while twisting his fingers and tugging on Niall. Niall could stand like this until he came, held up just with the desk at his thighs and Finn holding him upright, but he wanted his hands on Finn, and he wanted it now. Copying Finn's movements, he loosened the tight buttons on Finn's jeans and finally managed to get his hands inside Finn's pants. Just the feel of his hands on Finn was enough to have him deepening the kiss, more frantic in his need to taste Finn. Then Finn released his hold of Niall's cock but before Niall could complain, Finn yanked at Niall's hand on him, releasing the hold, then lifted him, hands under his ass, and carried him the short distance to the bed.

They tumbled onto the wide mattress, bouncing and awkward and a mess of uncoordinated limbs. But all too soon they were stripping clothes until finally, they lay naked and hard against one another. There were questions in Finn's eyes and Niall instinctively wriggled and spread his legs, letting Finn settle between them. He wanted a lot, he wanted everything: Finn's mouth on his cock, Finn's fingers in his ass, more kissing, fucking. He wanted it now. Finn slid off and grabbed his bag, emptying the contents on the bed. Lube and condoms showered the quilt and in a quick movement he covered his erection and had his hands slick with lube.

Crouching over Niall, with his fingers pressing against Niall, he paused. "Are you sure?" he asked.

Niall didn't say a word. He simply grabbed a pillow and pushed it under his ass, lifting himself, then held onto to the metal framework at the top of the bed. He didn't want to turn over. If he was going to break all the rules and have some muscled cop fuck him into tomorrow, then he wanted the visuals to go with it. Finn groaned and kissed him, a single finger breaching Niall, the burn of it a discomfort that edged away. For the longest time, they played. Finn kissing a path from Niall's lips to his throat then from one nipple to another, all the time pressing his fingers inside and adding lube.

"Now," Niall said a little desperately. He didn't know what he was asking for. Finn's lips were so close to his cock, but the fingers in his ass were making him want to screw down on them, and he was torn.

"If I suck you, will you come?" Finn asked raggedly and breathing heavy.

Niall whimpered. "Yes, I don't want…need you inside…please…fuck me…"

There was time for blowjobs later. There *had* to be time for blowjobs later.

Finn sat back on his heels and used more lube on his sheathed cock. He shuffled forward, his muscled thighs lifting Niall that little bit higher and guiding himself to Niall's loosened hole. Then he pressed and slowly he moved inside. Niall inhaled sharply. He would never get over this first intrusion, the feeling that this wasn't going to work. Then abruptly that stopped, he relaxed, and he tilted his hips and inch-by-inch Finn was inside until finally he stopped and hunched over to steal a heated kiss.

They kissed until Niall couldn't breathe and he realized Finn was moving, slowly, powerfully, he was pushing Niall to feel. Finn gripped the headboard hard, the slide of pillows under his ass and head meaning he couldn't control his movement. No, the control was all Finn's. With every push, Finn talked. He praised Niall, thanked him, his voice increasingly ragged as he was getting closer.

"Touch yourself," Finn said. Niall didn't argue, circling his cock. He set a counter rhythm that made sense in his head, pushing down onto Finn then up into the circle of his hand. Above him Finn tensed, staring down at Niall, his lips parted. Then he was coming, great pushes into Niall's body and the sight of this big man tensed and hard, his face contorted in pleasure, was enough to have Niall coming hard over his belly. He closed his eyes at the last minute, savored every ripple of orgasm as it hit him.

Finn collapsed against him, taking care to rest just to one side. Then, as he softened, he eased himself out and dealt with the condom. Niall didn't want to move, but someone had to deal with the trail of wet on him. He grabbed the tissues by the bed and wiped himself down.

What happened next? Was Finn going to take his twenty or so remaining condoms, his lube and his tight body and go back to his own room? Or would they cuddle? Or maybe some more kissing?

What actually happened next was not on Niall's list of scenarios. Finn reached for the plate of food and set it on the bed before sitting cross-legged, unashamedly nude, his softened dick still an impressive size against the dark curls there.

"Want food?" he asked.

Finn scooted to sit in a similar position. Something about the decadence of this, of a one-night fuck, of sharing what they had just shared, had him not caring he was naked with a near stranger. Super-Confident Niall was running this show. Of course, it wouldn't be long before Introverted Niall took control, but he'd work with what he had now.

They picked at grapes and cheese and biscuits and shared the bottle of water. Neither spoke much until Finn opened his mouth and said something that was an unexpected to Niall as sitting naked was.

"We have to do this again."

Chapter Three

"You seeing Finn this weekend?" Ewan asked.

"Hmm?" Niall entered the last row of data and saved the spreadsheet. That was the last of the preliminary workups on the Forseti platform, and he had the buzz of achievement. Numbers were not his thing. Pipes and oil and steel and the mechanics of decommissioning, that is what he was good at.

"Tall, dark, cop, gruff English accent, all around bad guy, three months of monkey sex."

"He's a good guy, not a bad guy." Niall chose to comment on that one point on a yawn. He pushed himself back and away from the desk and stretched tall, his fingers just scraping the low ceiling. "And no, he's training this weekend up in Urskar."

"It's been a few months you've been seeing him now. You getting kinda serious?"

Niall huffed a laugh. Finn was the farthest from serious that a man could get. He was all fuck and leave. Yes, they talked, yes, they sometimes shared the same bed, but Finn wasn't all hearts and flowers. He was a Delta, and that meant he was on call in the hairiest of situations in Norway. Terrorist threats, hostage negotiation, riot. All the big bads that no one expected in a beautiful, peaceful country like Norway. But it was the oil at the end of the day, the platforms in the Norwegian Sea, the proximity to the UK, all of this created a volatile mix that Finn was in the middle of.

They'd only managed five hook-ups in three months. Niall knew this because he counted. Seven days was all they'd enjoyed, but hell, those seven days had been more than enough to keep Finn's orgasm tally at a healthy level. A combination of alpha male who loved to be in charge, with Niall's capacity for apparently being able to push all of Finn's buttons and made their sex explosive. Added to that they talked about a lot of things from engineering to being a cop in London. Niall had fallen in love, and he hated the feeling that he wasting his heart on someone who could never care.

"I'm out of here," Ewan said. He picked up his laptop bag and the files from his desk. What very few people knew was that Ewan held the same degrees as Niall, that he was just as much of an expert as Niall was. Ewan was just happy being the one in the background. Not that Niall particularly enjoyed all the talks he had to give or the conventions he needed to attend, but he was, after all, the big brother and he'd taken his responsibility well enough. "I'll pick up the bags and meet you at the helipad."

"Yeah, okay. But, Ewan is Mel okay with you coming to Forseti with me?"

"You already asked that twice today."

Niall shrugged. "I'm just making sure."

"She said, and I quote, 'It's a boy, and if he takes after his father he'll be late, and I'm having a baby, not dying', so I think we're okay."

Ewan left with a small wave and Niall closed everything down before turning off the lights and locking the door of their shared office. He had about an hour to collect his luggage from his apartment then it was his least favorite thing about working on the oil platforms. Getting to them.

The Super Puma was on the helipad, rotors unmoving, the pilot talking to his co-pilot with a clipboard in his hand. There were six passengers. Niall was there before Ewan, who arrived five minutes later, still talking to Mel on his cell phone and gesticulating wildly.

Niall crossed to his brother and caught him just outside the white ring of the landing area. "What's wrong?" He'd never seen his brother as upset as he looked at that moment.

"They've taken her in, I told her she looked all puffy, and she just cried, and I didn't mention it again, but her blood pressure is climbing, and they're saying it could be the start of pre-eclampsia."

Niall laid a hand on Ewan's shoulder. This was a three-week stay on an oil platform in the middle of the Norwegian Sea. This wasn't a quick five-minute drive from home to hospital. Quickly, he assumed big brother mode.

"You stay here with Mel. I can handle this one."

Ewan blinked, his mouth open. He was going to argue,

but Niall said nothing and waited. He could see all the decisions going on in Ewan's head. The work Niall and he were doing on Forseti and the scheduling for decommissioning was something that with two would take three weeks, but with one would take longer.

"I could come out when Mel's been seen," Ewan said finally.

"There is nothing more important than Niall Jr.," Niall said with a reassuring smile.

"We're not calling him Niall."

The brothers exchanged a hug and grins, and Ewan stood on the pad until the Puma wheeled up and away, and both his brother and the station were ever-decreasing dots in the blur of rain.

Sitting as comfortably as he could between the others on the copter, Niall took a moment to look around. The other four passengers were all in the standard black jackets of security and would be relieving the other team looking after the platform. Forseti itself had run dry two years before, and the decision to decommission instead of move led to all the oil workers, except for a skeleton crew of six, being moved off.

Now it was Niall's turn to go in and make decisions. And these would be the men he would be spending the new few weeks with. They were all big men, and he realized they all had the same look about them as Finn did. Determined, sure of themselves.

That just made him miss Finn. Which was stupid. They were fuck buddies, nothing more serious, and the fact Finn disappeared like a thief in the night after most of their hook-ups just underlined that.

He couldn't talk to his companions; the blades were thunderous in the spare metal interior. He was more interested in what was out the window anyway. Rain and more rain. The wind didn't appear to buffet the helicopter, but it was enough to cause great blasts of rain against one or other of the windows. He wriggled a little to get comfortable and pulled out his cell phone, selecting a playlist and hoping to hell it was loud enough to drown the noise.

They landed in wind and rain, a dramatic moment when the helicopter had to hover away from the platform for a few seconds, but not enough to worry Niall. He'd had worse crossings.

The leaving security team exchanged nods as they climbed into the Puma and suddenly it was just Niall, the new security team and a rather agitated man in a thick slicker waving them over to the sheltered area. The security operatives went their separate ways, and the guy in the slicker grabbed Niall by the hand and shook it hard.

"Welcome," he shouted over the noise of the driving rain on the steel. "Let's get inside."

Niall followed him in, never happier than to be inside from the cold and rain, slipping off his bulky coat and shaking the other man's hand.

"Jeff Fjelstad, Chief," he said. His words were heavily accented Norwegian, and Niall smiled at the tone of it. He'd worked for NorsDev for six years now and loved splitting his time between Edinburgh and Oslo. He spoke more than enough Norwegian to carry on a decent conversation at work if needed but the NorsDev way was English as a common denominator.

"Niall Faulkner."

"Welcome to Forseti, Mr. Faulkner."

"Niall. Call me Niall."

"I'll show you to your accommodation then we have the initial planning meeting set up in the media room. Is that okay with you?"

Niall and Jeff made small talk about the state of the oil industry, about NorsDev, about the Forseti platform itself, but nothing that took too much thought because Niall was already in engineering mode. Decommissioning a platform wasn't just a numbers exercise, and it wasn't about dismantling the steel structure. It started a long way before that and could take up to two years to complete. From dismantling staff accommodation to ecological impact on a wider scale, this is what Niall was here for as team leader. The platform would be his home on and off for the next six months at least. A week here, a week there, and how much time did that leave to meet up with Finn? Not much at all.

At least he got a private room. Well, two rooms actually, given Ewan was supposed to be there. The door between the two rooms opened up, and that was the first thing Niall did just to get more space. The office was another door off of his room, and he opened it to have a look inside. A large well-lit space with three flat screens, plenty of wall area, and storage. This would be one of the last places dismantled before the main structural work, and this was where he would be doing all his planning.

He slipped on his glasses and took a moment to stand at the window, the northern gales smashing into the rig, the rain so hard it sheeted down, and Niall couldn't make out individual raindrops. Because of that, he could see the structure ahead of him, part of the platform and views of the heaving sea beyond. Behind him, out of sight, were the machines and pipes, the steel and concrete, the electrics and the decisions he had to make, but outside of the window was the very thing his job sent him to protect. Mother Nature in all her finest anger.

He stopped in the small bathroom and washed his face; his cold skin was prickly with the heat of the water and he stared at his reflection for a moment. He often wondered what people thought of him. He wore glasses, was an engineer with all kinds of letters after his name, a nerd, but he was respected. Just, sometimes, being so small and skinny he was perhaps not seen as able to handle the sea or the oil or, hell, anything.

Except for Finn. Finn thought Niall could handle anything given to him. Just the thought made Niall smile. He removed his inner jacket and instead pulled on a thick cable knit sweater. Tomorrow was soon enough to go traipsing around the exterior; today was all about meeting the skeleton crew, talking to security, and learning who his team would be.

He sent off a quick email to Ewan asking after Mel, even though he couldn't tell when it would go. Communications would be secure and connected from the drilling deck or the media room when he finally got there. At least he'd made some effort at checking in and he'd send something else as soon as he set foot in the communications area, or as he knew it, comms.

With a last look around the two rooms, he made sure Ewan's door was locked, then his own before he stepped outside. Then, shoulders back, he made his way up in the direction where he recalled the media room was placed. He got lost a couple of times but finally made his way to the same deck as the media room at least.

A loud bang had him startled from his relaxed *I know my way* vibe. Then a rumble and a shake that could only have meant that lightning had hit Forseti. *Thank fuck we landed earlier.* Niall sent a quick wish that the helicopter had landed safely back in Grane and carried on. He rounded the last corner, and another explosion rocked the path he was taking. He stopped and steadied himself against the wall. That didn't sound like lightening?

Cautiously he stepped forward to the corner and came face to face with one of the security guards from the ride over. He didn't know who was more startled. The security guard was armed, pointing a gun upward, not at Niall. Then the guard reacted, pointed the gun at Niall, and his demeanor screamed to Niall that he should run.

In the split second it took for all that to happen another explosion rocked the walkway they were on, and both men knocked heavily into the wall. The guard flailed and fell back, a bullet embedding itself in the wall next to Niall's head. With years of experience on walkways that weren't stable, Niall regained his footing. Without hesitating, he turned and ran. Time didn't slow down; it was a frantic terrifying stumble to the next door in the corridor, and a desperate heave through the space, kicking the heavy metal door shut and turning the exterior lock. A bullet hit the door, and the guard, red-faced and determined, was at the handle trying the lock.

Niall stumbled backward, hitting the wall and sliding to the side, falling to his knees and facing the other corridor. Jeff was there. Sprawled on the cold floor, his sightless eyes wide open, a bullet hole in the center of his forehead, and blood pooling around his head.

Terror gripped Niall and shock drove him to stand and back away even more. What was happening? He could see the armed man through the tiny glass porthole in the door and for a split-second Niall froze, looking into the dark eyes of the man who had shot at him. Then he turned and ran again. Left, right, along, down—the schematics of the accommodation block changed from one platform to another, but once he was into the bowels of Forseti, he'd be able to stop and breathe.

His breathing was tight, but his thoughts were suddenly clear as he jumped the last flight of stairs into the drilling deck. He had to grab his glasses as he realized he was losing them and he removed them and shoved them under his sweater. He'd be blind without them.

This is a terrorist threat. This is a hostage situation. He stopped at the base of the stairs and forced himself to focus. Whatever the fuck was going on he had to follow protocol. Information and communication. He bent at the waist and supported his arms on his knees, his breathing easing. He was fit, but he wasn't a freaking marathon runner. His long hair flopped in his eyes and, irritated, he swept it back as he stood.

Communication meant one thing. The drilling deck, where the brains of Forseti was, or the media room, where the workers contacted families.

The media room is compromised, he told himself. *What would Finn do?*

Decision made, he jogged through the maze of the drilling deck and stopped only at the main door out into the open air. The rain hadn't let up; he wasn't going to make it to the other side of the deck without being soaked through. He could go down two levels and come back up in the comms room, but that would add time to this.

What if the comms room is compromised as well?

He stepped back away from the window and pulled out his cell phone. It was just a regular iPhone, and there was no way there would be anything in the way of a connection. If he couldn't get to the main deck to connect to NorsDev then he had to find a satellite phone and hope to hell the weather subsided enough for a message to get through.

What if all four security guys on the Puma were in on this? What if they were working with the crew here? What if they have guns trained on the top production deck? What do they want? Who wanted to take over an oil rig in the middle of the damn ocean that didn't even form part of the active pipeline for oil? It didn't make any sense.

Time outweighed the worries and Niall pushed open the door onto the deck, the rain finding and drenching him in seconds. He carefully shut the door behind him and edged his way around the large half-football-field sized area, crossing in and among steel and plastic, thanking God he hadn't switched out his boots for his work shoes, and wishing to hell he'd taken a coat to the briefing.

Why would you have even done that, idiot?

A sound over the noise of the rain had him stopping with fright clogging his throat, but it was just a loose plastic cover snapping under the weight of rain. If it was a working platform, it would be dealt with, but the deterioration of care was the first thing that happened on decommissioning. The sharp edges of it tugged at his sweater, and he yanked away before, in a motion of desperation, he yanked at the plastic itself and tore off a thick swathe of it. Stiff and uncompliant, it was the only weapon he could think to find. What he wouldn't give for a steel pipe, or hell, a gun.

He reached the comms area and crouched by the window. In there was a way to contact NorsDev, to contact Finn, anyone. He couldn't see movement, but that didn't mean a thing. Then, just as he made to move, he caught sight of a man pacing the comms room with a wicked looking automatic weapon in his hands. He'd been behind a pillar and out of view, but now he was plainly there to see. Niall ducked down. Great. There went comms, which only left the satellite phones. Where would they be? *In the comms room. Idiot.*

But wait. *IT maintenance…*

Working his way back around the main deck, he approached the comms room from another direction, straight to the maintenance room, and after a considered look in through a cracked window, he cautiously moved in. When he shut the door behind him, he stopped still, gauging if anything was there. No signs of movement, no sounds, just an empty room full of storage boxes and a couple smashed PC screens. He opened the nearest box, nothing but ID card holders. Another box held paper, yet another held energy bars wrappers, but no actual bars. His stomach rolled, reminding him he hadn't even got breakfast and it must be way past lunch by then.

Finally, maybe six boxes later he found what he was looking for and pulled out three satellite phones and a couple of chargers. Pushing them back in, he lifted the box and glanced at the piles of remaining boxes. There could be more but could he chance it?

In the end, the need to get out of the situation alive trumped everything, and he was out of the security room, and scrambling down open stairs. Icy rain stung his eyes and skin as he moved to the lower production deck and into one of the main storage rooms. There he finally stopped long enough to realize he was shaking with cold and he couldn't feel his fingers. When the door was closed against the elements, it didn't make him feel any better physically, but on a safety level, he felt like he could give himself a few minutes to breathe. He pulled off the sweater, which dripped with water. Then, ignoring his wet pants, laid everything inside the box on the table in the darkened corner. Using his cell flashlight, he lit the area, hoping no one was checking the random abandoned rooms on this deck. He'd deliberately chosen a room with three exits, and it was enough so he could focus if he knew he had at least two alternative ways out.

Two of the satellite phones were broken, the backs off and the electrics loose, and only one charger had a light glowing to say it worked when he plugged it in.

"Fuck."

He blew on his fingers, trying to get some warmth into them, but his whole body was so cold it was impossible. Wires slid through his hold, the delicate connections a mess that he couldn't at first make sense of.

Frustrated, he stopped. He needed to warm up before he could concentrate. Walking from side to side in the room, over and around crates, he finally felt like he was warming. All he could do was be thankful he didn't appear to be teetering on the edge of hypothermia.

The wiring was easy after that. The box contained satellite phones for maintenance, and he was able to cobble together enough to get one phone that might work. Finally, with the handset on charge, he hid everything under crates and crawled into a space he made, dragging his sweater with him and huddling against the interior wall, which was warmer to the touch than the cold floor.

All he could do now was wait.

Chapter Four

The call came in just past fourteen hundred hours, Erik beating him to ops by about two seconds, both men pulling on vests and arranging holsters.

Finn had been reading, spending the quiet down time before dinner trying to get his head around some of the shit that had gone down today. Time at the Urskar training facility was hard work but it wasn't hard physical work that was bugging Finn. He knew exactly what it was.

Niall.

They'd talked this morning; he was working on the Forseti platform in the Heidrun oil field for the next few weeks. They wouldn't see each other for a while, and that was fine. Finn was good with that. Of course, he didn't like the fact Finn was flying in this weather. The storm passing through near the Forseti platform was a big one. And yes, he had to admit to himself he'd checked. And that was the problem. He'd checked the storm, he'd worried about the flight, and he was already missing the feisty, nerdy, sexy engineer enough to have it consuming his thoughts. All the what-ifs and the whens, and mostly the whys. He didn't usually do serious, but Niall could make him change his mind. One guy with a soft voice and a wicked mouth comes along and suddenly Finn was losing control of his *touch but don't keep* policy.

Then, that morning he'd fucked up. Big time.

He hadn't been paying attention and he'd seriously blown things in training. He'd let his guard down and got a helmet full of pink dye with a spot-on head shot from a crowing Erik. It wasn't so much the kill shot, it was why Finn had been distracted. He'd been thinking about Niall, and not in the *I want to fuck that sideways* kind of way, but in an *I hope he's okay and I'll miss him* kind of way.

Then Erik had to go and manage to kill him. It was the first time Erik had ever gotten the drop on Finn in training. It had taken three hair washes and vigorous scrubbing to get the pink out of his hair and off his left temple.

Fucker.

When they reached the briefing room, Erik grinned at him, that shit-eating grin that told Finn he wouldn't be living it down that Erik's team had taken first blood in the mini war game they were taking part in. The grin didn't last long, subsiding as soon as Cap walked in. After all, it didn't matter what had happened that morning; instead, they were all about whatever had caused them to be alerted.

"About thirty minutes ago, four bodies were found at the Grane oil terminal, identified as security assigned to the NorsDev Forseti Platform."

Cap stared straight at Finn and for a brief moment Finn wasn't really understanding the words. Then one thing hit him square in the chest. Forseti. That was where Niall was.

Rising to his feet he didn't know what to say as fear gripped him. "Four?"

"We have reason to believe these four men were replaced so that a team of hijackers could get onto Forseti."

"That's being decom'd." Erik sounded puzzled. "What kind of collateral does an empty oil platform have?"

"Only four?" Finn interjected. "What about the engineers? Niall Faulkner and his brother Ewan?"

Erik looked up at him, and Finn could see the moment the information made sense in his head.

"Fuck. Niall is on Forseti?"

"Both of them…Niall and Ewan. Did they go? Does someone know if he…?" The rest of the team all stared at him, Cap included, and Finn realized he was coming off as a mad man. He subsided. No one could get information out if Finn was raving like a fucking lovesick moron.

"The pilots are back, they took one engineer and four security replacements. So, souls on the platform are one engineer, six skeleton crew, and the four security replacements. Eleven souls in all."

The bottom fell out of Finn and dread stole his breath. Was it Niall or Ewan on Forseti? With who? Terrorists?

"Intel is showing no communications or demands, but chatter has it that this is an isolated cell connected to the Hofstad Network out of Denmark." Cap slid his finger on the laptop, and the screen changed behind him to show four faces. Three fair-haired, one dark, all in fatigues with long addendums at the bottom of the photo. Ex-Marine, one former SAS. The names a blur. Except for one.

Svein Roberg.

"He's dead," Erik said in disbelief, echoing Finn's

thoughts exactly. Roberg had a long history of fighting the good fight for whichever side paid him most. Ex-Special Forces, he had finally been taken down by the ERU two years before, just after Finn joined the team. In fact, it had been Finn who faced him down after tracking him to a small holding in Alta. They'd chased him to the Alta Dam, where the murdering fucker had died.

The bastard had tried extortion in the name of environmental concern and had killed three oil workers in an explosion at one of the dry land containment depots. Finn would never forget Svein's face. He didn't even fight when Erik and Finn had him cornered, simply dropped his weapon and raised his hands.

In the best traditions of all grandstanding bad guys he laughed then said, "I live to fight another day," repeating this over and over as he fell to his knees. There had been madness in his words, and cunning in his silver eyes. Only when Finn had stepped forward did the madness manifest in a blur of motion, the two men grappling for the weapon and a bullet leaving Finn's gun and carving into Svein's neck—blood spurting. Time had slowed, and Finn had watched in horror and a curious fascination as the terrorist leaped in a grotesque twist of muscles over the dam wall and down into the churning water below.

"They never found his body," Finn said softly. But Finn hadn't cared then. The fucker had a bullet in his neck and had fallen over six hundred feet. He had to have been dead.

"Until four weeks ago, his file was silent, but chatter indicated there was movement and he was implicated right in the center of it all."

"And no one thought to brief us?" Finn demanded hotly. "Why the fuck not?"

Several others in the team, Erik included, added their alarm.

Cap held up a hand and quieted the room. "Wheels up in ten," he said.

And that was it. They knew nothing. They didn't know why Forseti was the platform involved or why Svein Roberg had shown up. But, whatever information they received, they would be ready for action when they knew what the hell to do.

Erik grabbed his arm as Finn made to leave. "Finn?" he asked. The question was loaded. It was, *are you sure you're okay*, *do you know the man you've been seeing is on Forseti*, and *can you handle this*, all in one word.

Finn nodded. Didn't matter how he felt or what he actually said to voice any of it, he was going with the team and he wasn't putting doubt in Erik's head.

"Let's get this done."

THE HELICOPTER TOOK them to Grane terminal from Urskar, and Finn stayed quiet the whole time. Intel was trickling in, definite that Svein had survived being shot and was on Forseti, with camera footage from Oslo and at a gas station near Urskar. It hadn't escaped Finn's attention that Svein made no effort to hide his face. He was buying at the counter in the convenience store and looking directly at the camera.

Was he sending a message to Delta? That yes, he was back, and that they should come find him?

Still, why Forseti? Eco-terrorists chose live targets, not

empty monoliths in the middle of the ocean. What kind of statement could Svein make with no pipeline to threaten? Maybe they wanted some kind of impact of the attack in the press. NorsDev had managed to avoid being caught up in any kind of hijacking so far, the bigger names were the victims, companies like Lundin Petroleum and BP. But, somehow Finn knew. People were the only collateral that Svein had on Forseti.

And people meant Niall or Ewan.

As soon as they landed the team jumped down and gathered around Cap, Finn caught sight of someone walking toward them in the gathering rain. For a moment, he thought it was Niall, then realized the person was taller. Ewan.

Ewan hurried straight to them. "My brother is on that platform," he said with panic in his voice. Then he saw Finn and stumbled. "Niall is on there with them."

Finn grabbed at Ewan and held him. The man looked white with fear and Finn had to be the responsible one who kept control of everything and didn't let what he was feeling inside be obvious on the outside.

"We'll get him back," he reassured Ewan.

"What do they want?" Ewan asked.

Cap made his way to Ewan and stood between him and Finn. "We don't know anything as of yet."

"But we know it's hijackers," Ewan snapped. "What are their demands?"

Cap raised a hand and Ewan fell silent. "We need to take this inside."

The men went inside, a situation board was already in place, and Ewan was there with a couple others who all looked as worried as Finn felt.

"This was just posted," a man to one side said then turned the screen so Delta could see as well as everyone else. He pressed Play and a familiar voice echoed through the tinny speakers.

Svein Roberg's face was impassive as he stared out from behind a steady camera. Finn swallowed his anger and frustration that the man was even still alive.

"I have taken the NorsDev Forseti platform. Listen carefully. At midday tomorrow, I will destroy the platform and take it to the bottom of the sea where it deserves to rot. Let the sea swallow it whole." He stopped and smiled. "Come stop me," he added. Then the video stopped.

The threat was there, implied. He hadn't mentioned hostages. Just that he was destroying the platform. There was no oil to leak, no fires to start, the only collateral were people.

"Why would someone be so hell bent on sending over sixty thousand tons of steel and concrete to the bottom of the sea, uncontrolled?" Ewan asked a little desperately. "And how the hell do we get my brother off of there."

"We need to get on the platform," Finn said immediately. The noise level rose as everyone put in their point of view, varying from "we're fucked" to "let's do this" depending which team was talking, be it the ground crew, or the Delta team.

Delta huddled around maps. Every single one of them knew Forseti; it had been another training post only last summer. One of the most isolated platforms, it was a relic to the 70s standing over a tapped well in the Heidrun oil field.

"He's daring us—"

"No point in going in by Puma—"

"Sea it is—"

"Boat—"

"Drop—"

Every member had something to say, every man on the Delta team was a specialist in their own right.

"Can we get in touch with the crew? Are there comms to anyone on the platform?" Ewan asked a little desperately, and loud enough to be heard over the noise of discussion. Finn bit his lower lip. Svein hadn't made a call for money or demanded news coverage. Finn didn't have to think too hard to know that Svein was only on there to destroy everything, to what end Finn didn't know. There was no mention of a hostage trade-off. Which meant every civilian could be dead on the platform already.

Including Niall.

Cap answered for everyone. "No comms as yet, from the crew or from the engineer. Apart from the video we've got nothing."

"He wants *us*," Finn said. He didn't have to say it out loud, but everyone in Delta knew it. This was wrong, this wasn't delicate negotiation nor did it have a strong hope of resolution. It had to be nothing more than a trap for Delta.

Svein's twisted revenge on a team that took him down.

"He never got over the fact we killed him," Erik deadpanned. Graveside humor, blacker than black, was how the team worked but something in the pit of Finn hated it.

Niall was on there.

My Niall.

"So, we're walking into a trap," Cap summarized. "We know that. He knows that. We may as well land a freaking Puma on the helipad and just walk out, weapons drawn."

"Which is what he is expecting because he'll know we know." Finn did his own summarizing, and it made sense in his head. "So we split, half in the Puma, half by sea." He pointed at the main boat deck where they could safely dock a boat. Then he traced the side around and up and under the lower production deck. "Here, we land it here. He'll be expecting it, but there's only one way on and off this platform by sea."

"We need a distraction."

Erik huffed. "Landing a Puma is a pretty big distraction."

Cap glanced at each one of his Delta team, his eyes narrowed, and Finn could see the decisions being made second by second. "Erik, Finn, you're by sea, keeping the team small," Cap announced. "The rest of us will do the frontal assault, land the Puma, draw their fire. We go in, we take Svein and whoever he has on assist out of the picture, try and get the crew out alive."

There was deadly calm in Cap's voice, and Finn nodded his agreement like everyone else did. There was one word Finn was refusing to accept. There was no *trying* to get the crew out, and by default Niall. He would rescue everyone or die trying.

That is what Delta did.

Chapter Five

THE BATTERY LIGHT FLICKERED RED, AND NIALL HAD never felt such a keen sense of relief in anything before. A red light wasn't enough to use it, but at least the phone was charging. He just had to hope that whoever had decided to attack Forseti hadn't somehow affected communications and he could get a clear line out.

What would Finn do, what would Finn do…

A sound had him shrinking back behind the crates, but it was nothing more than buffeting wind and rain smashing into the thick walls. Whoever was hijacking the platform would know he was still alive and that he'd gotten away. And was it just one man with a gun, or was this more than one. Niall had only seen a single man with a gun face to face, but there was another armed assailant in the drilling deck control room. So that was at least two.

If the bad guys were worried about finding him, if they thought he was of any use, or hell, if they just wanted him dead, then he wasn't safe wherever he was hiding.

Worst comes to worst I could jump into the sea.

And die in seconds, slammed against the superstructure, or pulled underneath the tumultuous waves, freezing in seconds.

No jumping into the sea unless I have to.

The red light flickered for a second from red to green but then settled back on red. What happened if he used the phone? Would the unknown attackers pick up the comms trace and find him? Niall was an engineer, give him sixty-three thousand tons of steel and concrete and he could imagine every inch of it and know it like it was his own, but electrics and telecoms were something he couldn't get his head round. Hell, he could twist a few wires together in a rough approximation of fixed, but the phone looked like it was going to last about three minutes.

Maybe I should try for the accommodation block. That was self-contained and could be shut off from the rest of the platform in case of fire. It would be safe in there.

Unless the hijackers were in there.

Frustrated at the turn of his thoughts he banged his head against the wall and winced when it fucking hurt. He pushed his glasses back up his nose and huddled into an even smaller ball, shivering with cold, and waited.

He imagined Finn next to him, holding his hand, telling him everything was going to be okay. Keeping Finn in his thoughts was a good move; the strength he admired in his lover was enough to keep him calm. At least until the light flickered to green and stayed that way.

Niall immediately picked it up, not knowing who the hell to call. This wasn't a two-way radio, this was a phone and the only number he remembered off the top of his head was Ewan's, and Ewan was in hospital.

Fumbling in his tight pocket, he pulled out his cell and

peered at the screen. It was soaked through, water behind the screen, but when he pressed the power, it worked enough for Niall to get a number for Grane Terminal. He might have one chance to get a message through and everything counted on this one moment.

Shakily he pressed the digits for Grane but there was silence, before a crackle, then the sound of a connection being made. The call was answered and before they said a thing Niall launched into what he wanted to say.

"Niall Faulkner, Senior Engineer aboard NorsDev Forseti platform in the Heidrun oil field. Unknown armed assailants, two by my count. One crew dead. I'm cut off from everyone else." He waited for a response but could hear nothing. "Over?" he added cautiously. The phone crackled in his hand, and he wondered if there was even any point to this. Was it going through to anyone who could help? "Hello, this is Niall Faulkner, Senior Engineer aboard NorsDev Forseti platform in the Heidrun oil field. Can anyone hear me? One of the crew is dead." Nothing. "Please. Is someone there? One crew is dead. Two unknown armed hijackers."

He repeated the message over and over, forgetting the ice of cold, or the wet, or the fact he could be found. If someone was out there listening, if this was actually a connection, then he was damned if he was stopping.

"Niall Faulkner, Senior Engineer aboard NorsDev Forseti platform—"

"Niall!"

Ewan's voice? Was Niall going mad? That sounded like his brother's voice.

"Ewan."

"Thank God, hang on—"

Another voice came on the line. "This is Emmet Adams at Grane Terminal. Is This Niall Faulkner?"

"I'm on Forseti," Niall managed. "Send help."

"Can you talk?"

"I'm safe," Niall said. He didn't feel very safe, but no one had found him yet. And he'd managed to connect to the outside world, that had to count for something, meant that the comms weren't totally down.

"I'm patching you in with the ERU," Emmet said.

Niall waited. The ERU meant Finn, but it wasn't Finn's voice, another man spoke crisply and calmly.

"Talk to me," was all he said.

Niall imagined talking to Finn, what he could say that might make Finn's job easier. "Two armed men that I know of, one with intent to kill." That much was true, the guard he'd met wasn't exactly asking him to put his hands up, he'd gone straight to point and fire. "Guard one outside media room, guard two armed in drilling observation, I didn't see the crew."

"Assume all four from flight this morning are part of hijack cell," the voice warned.

Niall had already come to that conclusion on his own. He didn't need a random ERU member telling him that. His instincts told him he'd be lucky to make it out alive and that no friendly visitors would point a gun at him.

"What do I do?"

"Stay low. We're on our way."

More crackling then a different voice was there. "This is a big ask, but could you give us a distraction?"

"A what?" Niall startled as another bang on the wall outside had his heart racing.

"We have Delta two at your position in thirty minutes,

can you make some kind of distraction to pull assailants to the boat deck for sixteen twenty without putting yourself in harm's way?"

"I can…can do that."

Could he? He could think of a million ways to cause a distraction, from steel to fire, but could he actually move from here?

"Stay safe. If you can't manage this, then get yourself somewhere isolated and stay put. Agreed?"

"Agreed."

The phone went dead and at first, he thought it was just the end of the call, then he saw the red light and the sparks from the wires. The whole thing was fucked, and there wasn't anything else in the box that was halfway salvageable.

Sixteen twenty. Niall checked his phone, wondering if that was even keeping time with the wetness. The screen showed just before sixteen hundred and he just had to trust he was going to be doing the right thing. Fear curled in his belly as he carefully pushed all signs he had been there, boxes and wires, into the very farthest-most point in the dark corner. He wasn't the hero hanging from a rope setting explosions as a distraction, hell he doubted there was anything to cause an explosion. All the power around there was in water.

And why the boat deck? Wouldn't the ERU use the boat deck? What about a helicopter? What if they couldn't get there at all?

Closing his eyes, he focused on what he could do. Then it hit him. Water. He could use the valve for the…

Decision made, he still couldn't bring himself to leave his dark space. He was scared. The memory of Jeff dead on the floor with a bullet between his eyes was enough to have him not moving.

"What would Finn do?" he asked himself out loud.

Sucking up every ounce of courage he possessed, he threw his sweater back on and crawled out from the space. He cautiously made his way to the main door from the production deck outside. His hiding place was damn near all the way over on the other side of the vast platform, and the rain hadn't let up. Carefully, he removed his glasses, blinking as everything blurred a little. He thought about what he needed to do. Section seventy-nine was his first stop, if he could make it there then he could loosen the valve, move around the edge, under the walkway, and to the main boat deck. Follow the pipes to section forty-seven, locate the outlet, loosen it, wait for the pressure to build between the two.

He could do this.

He straightened and pushed back his shoulders, then opened the main door. He had to keep close to the sides as much out of the rain as he could for fear of being blown off the platform. Cautiously, he made his way to the edge of the connections for the main rig right to the steel jacket that kept Forseti secure in three hundred and fifty-meter depths. The going was treacherous, the howling wind making him wish for the safety rope he may well have thought to use in this situation. He wasn't the kind to take chances like this. He was the solid, safe one—the one who looked out for everyone else. Rain sliced into his face, blurring his vision even more and he stumbled to a stop.

He guessed the only good thing about this was that the bad guys had as limited visibility as he did. And he had one thing they didn't—he knew his way around these rigs with his eyes closed.

He didn't stop to check the time, couldn't stop, couldn't even take his hands off of every handhold he could find. He felt like he was walking against a brick wall one minute, then sagging to the ground in the next when the wind shifted, pressing him down to the metal floor. He just hoped to hell that he was close enough to the first valve now to at least make it to the second. He'd need leverage to turn the valve, and he doubted there was anything official to hand like a wrench. Inspired, he grabbed at one of the small water outlet draining pipes and levered the item until it came apart. Armed with a foot of hard metal he continued onward.

Feeling his way along the pipes, picturing the layout in his mind, he couldn't help but think of Finn. Was Finn landing by boat? Was he even part of the ERU Delta team? Did he know it was Niall on the platform?

Last week they'd spent a whole night together, Finn on his way north for training, and Niall in seclusion working on project deadlines. They'd eaten out, made a whole date of it, hell, most of it even seemed normal. Finn was stealing a small piece of Niall's heart every time they were together, and Niall bet Finn didn't even realize what he was doing.

And the sex? Niall slumped to the nearest pipe and gripped hard, knowing he was only maybe six feet from the first valve. He could think about the sex, about the way Finn made him feel, about the way Finn could hold him and make everything outside what they were doing seem unreal. Then he could focus on what he felt like when he stared into Finn's beautiful green eyes, or when he dug his fingers into Finn's dark hair like he never wanted to let go.

The valve was easy to grab, and Niall leaned into it. All he needed to do was turn it enough so the seal was broken. With the lack of oil running through the platform, the pipes instead were holding back water pressure. *This would work.* He was sure of it. The valve moved a little, or was that just Niall's wishful thinking? Then, using the metal bar as a pivot, he leaned with his bodyweight, abruptly wishing he were a lot bigger than he actually was, and it finally gave way.

That was the first part done, and he gave up trying to walk to the boat deck. Instead, he was near crawling on his hands and his knees, the metal pipe, twisted and buckled, pushed under one arm. He'd gone beyond just shivering, he was growing colder by the moment, his fingers numbing, and his head fuzzy.

I'm going to tell Finn I love him. Over and over he thought the same thing, focused on surviving, getting off the platform and telling the stubborn cop exactly what he thought of him.

"I can't love someone," Finn had stated when they woke up in each other's arms last week. "It wouldn't be fair."

"Fair on who?" Niall asked. "You? Me? Who the fuck would even know?" He was furious, and he couldn't help asking. He loved the man, and all he wanted was a commitment to go alongside the sex. Not forever, but an acknowledgment that Niall meant something to Finn other than just being there for only sex.

The rain eased as Niall rounded the last wall before the boat deck and he lay on his stomach in the wet until he could see through the spray to what was below. There was no sign of Delta, no sign of Finn, and there was no one with a gun. He belly-slid forward until he could see over the edge of that part of the platform and despair hit him. There was a hijacker there, still in a guard's uniform, just inside the door to the boat deck, staring out at the water with a rifle in his hand. He was sideways to Niall, but that didn't make it any easier. The valve was between Niall and the hijacker and Niall needed to get closer.

Part of him wanted to check his phone, but hell if it would even be working if he did. Would any of this be any easier if he knew he had five minutes or ten? He crawled a little further to the right, the valve in his sight and the rain sheeting at full force as he moved out of the shelter of the overhanging deck. He reached it and hoped to hell no one was above him waiting to shoot him in the back of the head.

What would Finn do?

Utilizing the bar, he used his full body strength to attempt to move the second valve. As soon as it was open enough, he needed to back the fuck off. The buildup of pressure would angle down into the boat deck, and the force of it would be enough to grab the hijacker and physically throw him to the ground. Or at least, that was what was in Niall's head.

The rain eased a little causing an eerie silence that made Niall's chest tighten. He would be seen. All the hijacker had to do was look up and to the right and that would be it, Niall would be dead, and he would never have gotten the chance to say anything to Finn.

I love you, I love you, he murmured to himself as he moved as slowly as he could to get his body weight behind this valve as well. Movement out of the corner of his eye and he swore he could see a boat in the stormy sea. The hijacker stirred. Had he seen the same thing?

Temper made Niall strong. He wasn't going to let the Delta team down. He was getting them on the platform, and he was fucking well going to make it home so he could pin Finn to the bed and force his lover to say how he felt.

I love you, I love you…

The valve creaked and groaned as Niall pushed but it was moving, and he saw the rifle point up at him at the very same moment the valve gave way. The force of its movement pulled him to one side, and the pain as he slammed to the floor was enough to steal his breath. A spark, a sound, and he was being shot at, the bullet missing him by inches. He couldn't move, the metal he'd used in the valve had pinned his sweater, curled into the thick mess of wool, and as much as he yanked he couldn't get free. He was like one of those butterflies in a display case. Any second now he was dead.

I love you.

The pressure built underneath him; he could almost imagine the water pressing and forcing, gathering enormous strength until it blew. He struggled to get free, the sweater pulling, tearing, and he knew he had to get away as soon as he could. An explosion of air and water rocked the small part of the platform he was pinned to, metal wrenching under the force of it. Niall could hear screaming and knew it was himself.

I love you.

Chapter Six

FINN ADJUSTED HIS HEADSET UNTIL HE COULD GET A CLEAR reading on what the hell was going on. Cap laid it down, Niall was alive and he'd somehow managed to get communication out of Forseti. The storm snagged and threw the small boat, and he gripped hard as a sickening lurch had him cursing.

"Fucking bitch," Erik cursed from the front. He was cursing Mother Nature and her ability to literally pick the boat up and slam it down into the sea like it was nothing. Finn didn't want to hear Erik's cursing; he wanted intel. About assailants, firepower, hostages, but most of all he needed to know about Niall.

Pride flooded him at the thought Niall had somehow eluded the hijackers and had contacted the station. He'd shown clear thinking in what must be a terrifying situation. Especially for an engineer more used to the fear of a failing superstructure than facing the end of a loaded weapon. Then that same fear insinuated itself inside Finn's calm acceptance of the situation. This was nothing new.

They were trained for this. They could get on the platform, become a formidable team against God knows who. But that was when they knew the parameters. This wasn't the same.

Svein wanted Delta with all the hate-filled focus of a thwarted bully, and he was using innocents to line up Delta in his sights.

The boat surged upward on a swell and Erik guided it through as best he could. They were only a short distance from Forseti, but the vast oil platform was barely visible in the churning storm that was trying to kill them. To get on the platform would take no small amount of skill and Finn had to just sit there and accept that Erik knew his job.

"Asked the engineer to create a diversion to drive the hijackers to boat deck," Cap confirmed.

Finn's chest tightened. Erik glanced sideways at him; he'd heard the same message. A diversion to the boat dock meant his half of the Delta team had to come around the back, no soft landing. Not that they expected it. They were clearly moving to plan B.

But what scared Finn the most was the casual way Cap had said the engineer was creating a diversion. Niall. They drew closer to Forseti, the superstructure rising like a goliath out of the sea, steel gray against the churning clouds. Erik guided the craft to the left, away from the boat deck, and when Finn looked up he could see the Puma wheeling above them. They would take the main fire, allow the boat to get a foothold somewhere on the metal rising from the sea. Under the platform, the sea settled in a couple of places, and the two men managed to get themselves off the boat and onto the structure itself. They were on unmoving land when an explosion from the boat deck had Finn scrambling the rest of the way up to the deck.

Niall was up there.

When they reached the deck, it was empty, a great pipe split at a valve, and metal peeled back like it was nothing more than paper. There was no sign of a hijacker and Finn signaled for Erik to cover him. If Niall was anywhere up there, then Finn was finding him.

He followed close to the gray walls and, staring through the rain, he attempted to make out anything except crooked pipes and chaos. Then he spotted what he assumed was one of the hijackers. It was difficult to tell because metal had sliced into his face and cut into skin. There was no blood, the sea had washed him clean, but he hung like a grotesque scarecrow and Finn couldn't even think that Niall was there somewhere just as dead.

Above them, the Puma was backing off from fire. He could hear at least two weapons firing, and Delta returning fire. That would pull the focus from him and Erik; they had a chance of getting people off this place. Including Niall.

White material caught his eye and he realized it was a sweater. In seconds, he was there, yanking at an unconscious Niall, cutting away the wool that had him caught and freeing him. He felt for a pulse. There was one, and just as Finn contemplated where he would be hiding Niall until this was all over, Niall opened his eyes.

"Finn," he choked.

Finn didn't have time to feel relieved. The rest of Delta was taking the heat, and he and Erik had a mission. He glanced around at the mess of metal; something that Niall had done there had made things right for him and Erik.

"You did good," he said as he assisted Niall in getting up. "Can you stand?"

Niall groaned and pushed himself to stand, taking a lot of his weight by himself. "I'm okay." The crunch of glass had them both looking down. On the ground lay Niall's glasses, twisted with one lens shattered. He couldn't look. What if that had been Niall?

"You said one crew dead," Finn repeated.

"Jeff." Niall nodded as he blinked water from his hazel eyes.

Finn spoke into his comm. "I have one hostage alive. Confirmed one dead hijacker, one dead crew."

Niall is alive.

Erik moved out, Niall behind him, Finn bringing up the rear. Niall appeared to get with the plan and didn't for one minute drop behind. They made it as close to the accommodation module as they could then regrouped in silence. Erik gestured to indicate that there was a hijacker in sight and silently pulled out his knife.

Finn held out a hand to stop Niall moving and counted down with Erik. When Erik moved, it was stealthy, but somehow the hijacker must have sensed something as he turned at the exact moment Erik was on top of him. A short scuffle later and the second hijacker was dead, sprawled with his throat cut.

Erik held up two fingers. Two dead hijackers. Two to go.

Finn faced Niall. "I need you to get inside the accommodation module, okay?" Niall looked like he was in shock and Finn stepped a little closer. "Can you do that? I need you inside where you can lock yourself in."

"What about the hijackers?"

"The two left are occupied with the rest of Delta, you have to trust me. Can you do that?"

Niall looked at him, shivering, his skin so pale, his eyes bloodshot and his glasses gone. He looked like death.

"I can," he finally said.

"Then I need you to go find the rest of the crew and stay with them." Finn kept his tone level, even when Niall gripped his jacket and opened his mouth to talk.

"Find me, okay?" Niall said firmly. "Come find me."

Then, before Finn could say a word, Niall turned on his heel and hobbled in the opposite direction. He was cradling his arm, limping, but Finn hadn't seen blood.

"We're taking fire," Cap's voice echoed in his head, and he pulled himself out of the need to grab Niall and just leaving this place. *Break the firing.* Then memories of what he's seen Svein do, of the bodies in Alta of fellow ERU members, of the laughter as he'd thrown himself off the dam like some kind of action movie cliché, assailed him. The guy was a killer and Delta needed to take him down.

Finn and Erik continued onward and upward, covering each other as they took flight after flight toward the helideck. The ascension felt like it took an eternity. The other members of the Delta team were putting themselves in harm's way in the Puma, drawing fire. Finn and Erik had to get up there and neutralize it so the Puma could land. An explosion sent shockwaves hard enough to have Finn stumbling back downstairs, and a crash of twisted metal blocked his way.

"Fuck, we're blocked," Erik shouted.

They turned on their heels and went back the way they came. The only way up was to find the next corridor and approach the deck from another angle. Fire chased them, and they ran in the opposite direction to where they'd been heading. They reached the last area before the alternative exit and skidded to a halt. Svein stood at the door facing them. And immobile, gripped by his throat, was Niall, a pistol at his temple. Svein had utter focus and determination on his face, and there was an evil light in his eyes.

Chapter Seven

Finn stopped in horror. In his head, Niall was safe and wasn't held by a madman intent on killing. This was wrong.

Erik had the presence of mind to make connections in his head that Finn couldn't make. He cursed but didn't stop and stare in shock. Instead, he scrambled back and away until only Finn stood in the face off. They had to get the focus off the Puma and the rest of the team, and that was Erik's job now. Because Finn had to deal with Svein.

"Put the guns down," Svein said. If anything, that made Finn grip the barrel of his Sig harder, and angle his rifle just that little bit higher. Svein pressed the barrel of the pistol harder, and Niall closed his eyes.

Finn stepped closer, his gun still raised. He could take Svein in one shot, but from that angle, Niall would be collateral damage. *Niall would be dead.* Deltas didn't let hostages die if they could stop it. But he wasn't dropping his gun. In all the scenarios where he dropped his weapon, he was dead in seconds and Niall would be as well.

"You think I won't kill him?" Svein said. His tone wasn't threatening, more questioning. "Drop your weapons."

"What do you want?" Hijackers had agendas: the release of political prisoners or money being two of them. There had to be some kind of ground that Finn could give way on without Niall dying. Niall still had his eyes closed, his right arm cradled, and now Finn could see blood darkening the sleeve of his shirt and staining the skin at his wrist.

Why didn't he say he was bleeding?

As if Niall had heard his thoughts he opened his hazel eyes and stared directly at Finn. There was fear in them, but also utter trust in the way he wasn't panicking.

Svein huffed a laugh. "I don't want a thing. I want you. Simple. You and your team for killing me, but you most of all for missing my heart and leaving me for dead."

"Let the hostage go." *Don't personalize the hostage, don't show you love that man more than life itself.*

All the time they talked, Finn calculated trajectories. He could shoot through Niall, but that would just catch Svein in the shoulder. He had to be calm and focused about this but seeing Niall gripped so tightly was messing with his focus. If he was going to shoot, then he needed to be ready. He hoped to God whatever happened that Erik had somehow removed the last shooter from the platform so that the rest of the ERU could land and give backup. That was one less thing to have on his conscience.

"I wasn't aiming for your heart," Finn said clearly. He wanted to engage Svein, try and explain something enough so that this all slowed down. "Wasn't even trying to kill you. Let the hostage go."

Svein's lips peeled back in a parody of a smile. "Fuck you," Svein said, and Finn looked into pale silver eyes that held madness. "You think I don't know who Niall Faulkner is? Warming your bed and making you slow. I've been watching you, and it was just a matter of time until Forseti was going to be your grave."

"I don't know the hostage," Finn lied. Then, like the decision was made for him, Niall slumped in Svein's hold. Finn reacted on instinct, and the bullet left his gun even as he moved. It carved through Niall's arm, caught Svein low on his side, enough for Niall to fall, enough for Svein to curse and twist away. Finn was on Svein before he had a chance to regroup, using his bodyweight as a pivot and landing a punch to Svein's face as he fell to a stop. They grappled, and neither had the upper hand, but Finn knew this was a fight of attrition. Sooner or later Svein would tire as he lost blood and Finn would take his advantage.

He couldn't see Niall, couldn't even take a moment to worry where Niall was as Svein gained the upper hand, his arm around Finn's throat.

It can't end like this. With preternatural strength, he twisted and threw until Svein hit the solid wall and for a split-second Finn had the upper hand. Then everything went to hell, the whole platform shifting with another explosion. Svein and Finn were thrown to the floor and fuck, Svein laughed, even as he relaxed his hold of Finn and grabbed at a knife of his own. They jumped back and apart. Svein was just as trained as Finn; they were a pretty even match. Up that close Finn could see scarring on Svein's face, and a cloudiness in his left eye. He quickly filed everything for reference even as he caught sight of Niall grabbing at Finn's fallen Sig.

No. Don't use the gun. Don't do it.

He couldn't have Niall killing. Niall wasn't the killer here.

Finn held out his knife, and he and Svein circled each other, Finn balancing on the balls of his feet, curving back and away as Svein stabbed at him. He moved the balance and swiped down, his sharp blade passing easily through Svein's thin jacket. Svein didn't falter and when Finn moved in he sensed Niall moving behind him. He realized he'd taken his eye off the ball as Svein's knife sliced across his chest, upward, to his throat.

Finn jumped back, but Svein pressed the advantage and forced Finn up against the wall, both men fighting for control with the knives. Svein was winning the battle of strength with madness in his expression and hate in his eyes. Finn relaxed his stance, waiting for Svein to press the advantage and as he did they separated and Svein held his knife in place ready to stab. Finn dropped to the floor and rolled to a crouch in seconds. His temple pounded and dizziness assailed him. Svein saw the crouch, leaned over him, knife high, and in a desperate lunge, Finn stabbed up and into Svein's throat.

"Doesn't matter," Svein choked. Finn twisted the knife as Svein weakly batted his hand, blood spilling from the wound then life leaving his eyes in an instant.

Finn shoved him away and pulled out his knife at the same time, the arc of arterial blood splattering his jacket. *This time, fucking stay dead.* He glanced at Niall, who stared at him with horror in his expression. He looked so damn pale with the Sig in his hands, the aim of it right at Svein on the floor.

Finn moved quickly, taking the pistol from Niall's hands. "He's dead," he said.

Briefly, Finn embraced Niall, but they couldn't stop.

"Tango one is down, Erik. Tango one is down."

"Copy that, Delta Seven," Erik replied. "Helideck clear, tango four down."

"Exfil in ten," Cap responded. "Let's get these hostages off Forseti."

"Why did he…?" Niall pointed at the dead Svein on the floor.

Finn didn't have time to talk about it. He had to get to the helideck and get the hostages off the platform, including Niall. Finn checked Svein's pulse one last time, there was nothing. Then he considered direction and with Niall right behind him they headed upward.

"I was going to the others," Niall said as they climbed. "He was just there. I tried to…"

Niall stopped walking, leaning on the metal banister and bowing his head. This was inevitable; he'd been running on adrenalin and abruptly that had left.

"Keep going," Finn encouraged.

"Why did he…"

"I have a bad feeling about this," Finn said hurriedly. "I need you topside."

Niall nodded, visibly pulling himself together and straightening. "Let's go."

About two flights from open air, Finn was pulled up short by shouting, Erik's voice loud over the headset. "Abort. Abort. Helipad is wired."

Finn heard cursing from Cap and held his breath. When an explosion didn't happen, he assumed they had managed to abort the Puma landing.

"Jesus Christ Finn, you need to get your ass up here and see this."

Finn considered everything. Svein hadn't given them a way off of Forseti. "Is there a timer?"

"I can't fucking see shit up here past explosives," Erik snapped.

Finn made a decision. "Get down here, Erik. We have to move the crew to the boat to get off this thing." Glancing at Niall, he considered whether his lover would be able to get down to the boat deck and passed to where he and Erik had left the boat. He was frighteningly pale, and his face was red with the burn of sleet and bruises.

I will keep you alive.

"Erik, get the remaining hostages to the boat deck. I'll get Niall down there."

"I can't," Niall said softly. So soft that Finn almost missed it. "I think…" He slumped against the railing and only Finn grabbing tight stopped him from falling.

"We have to get lower," Finn said. "They rigged the helideck to stop the Puma from landing. Our only way off is with the boat."

Niall looked up at him, focusing in on him, his eyes wide, then he coughed. He opened his mouth to say something but closed it just as quickly. "Let's move," he finally said.

Together, with more of a stumble than a walk they began descending back the way they'd come. Every step was exertion and Niall was becoming heavier with each one. Finn could feel the blood on his hands, the sticky wetness was an indication something was seriously fucking wrong.

"I love you," Niall murmured. "I know you don't want to hear it but if we die—"

"We're not dying." Finn hoisted more of Niall's weight and refused to think that there was a world where Niall wasn't in it.

"I love you," Niall repeated. His voice held a hint of question. Finn had spent so much of their time together calling it an easy relationship for sex that he'd held back how he felt, but could he still do that with Niall literally dying in front of him?

They stopped for a second and Finn couldn't even think about how much further they had to go down. Nor how long they had left. Who knew what kind of timing was on the damn explosives. *Fuck*.

"Delta Seven, we're at the boat," Erik confirmed the facts.

Niall cradled Finn's face, looked deep into his eyes even as he spoke to Erik. "Get the boat away."

"Waiting for you," Erik said stubborn and focused.

If the platform was rigged, then they'd all die.

"Erik, you see anything, you go…"

"Copy."

Finn pressed a kiss to Niall's cold lips, then pulled back, "I love you," he said. "Now let's move."

And with that declaration of love they began to move again. Finn was aware that the whole platform could collapse around them, or that Erik would move the boat, or that hell, he was going to die there with Niall.

They stumble-walked down to the boat deck, the burning from the knife wound in his chest getting worse then numbing in the icy cold as they moved outside.

"Not far now," he reassured a near-comatose Niall. He

could see the boat, the tethering holding, they were six feet, five feet…he could imagine the step to take to get Niall onto the boat. Two feet, Erik was there, grabbing Niall and dragging him into the boat, Finn right behind him, the boat powering away, the faces of scared hostages burned onto his retinas. They were away, twenty feet, thirty, fifty, when a huge explosion parted the storm and the heaving seas. Instinctively, Finn covered Niall.

"Down," he shouted, and the frightened crew doing as they were told. Finn looked back at the extent of the explosion, at the fire, the hell that rained down on them, and prayed they made it out. Something smacked into the boat, then another, hitting Finn on the back and forcing him lower in the boat.

A hundred feet, two hundred…

Then the terrifying noise of the platform in self-destruct was swallowed by the storm and they were far enough away for Finn to sit upright. They couldn't see Forseti now, and he had to think.

"Cap? We need exfil…" He yanked at an unconscious Niall's clothes, revealing bone cutting through the skin in his arm, and so much blood, some congealed and some free flowing. Niall's pulse was thready, thin, barely there.

"Five," Cap answered immediately.

Finn gripped his fear and refused to let it show to anyone. Five may not be enough time to save Niall.

Chapter Eight

Niall woke slowly, step by step, each a little more painful than the last. He was aware of noise around him, of pain, and the startling white of the lights in his face. People asked him questions, his name, his age, and he was sure he'd heard Ewan's voice on more than one occasion telling him he was an uncle now, and uncles didn't do things like die on oil platforms.

Although Ewan's voice was welcome, he still craved Finn's lower, huskier tones but there had been no sign of him.

The doctor told him he'd been hypothermic, that his radius had snapped out through his skin, that he'd lost blood and was actually lucky that they'd got him back to land and to a hospital before he died from shock. That had been at least an hour ago, and since then no one had even come into his room, let alone talked to him. Right then, he'd even give a smile to a nurse if it meant he wasn't stuck here with drips in the back of his hand and his head buzzing with pain.

They'd suspected a concussion from the boat deck explosion he'd rigged with the water at high pressure. They'd worried he'd been hit by pieces of Forseti self-destructing but at the end of the day seemed like his brain had come out of this fairly much intact. Go figure.

And talking of Forseti? Niall groaned at the thought of what had happened. The platform was a hazard now. The destruction hadn't been systematic and project managed. It had been rent in two from the helideck down to the lower production deck. Apparently, according to Ewan, there had been so much explosive wired up that there was no chance of anyone getting off alive. Fires had raged in the accommodation block, the comms room, and the small room where he had hidden, and there was nothing left recognizable as an oil platform apart from twisted metal rising out of the sea.

Forseti had died dramatically and horribly, and its death throes had very nearly taken him and others with it.

A nurse came in to check his vitals, and he grabbed the chance of talking. He asked the same question that he'd done every single God-damned time he'd spoken to anyone.

"The team that got us off of the platform, are they here?"

The nurse, still smiling, shook her head. "Sorry, this is my first shift this week, I don't know of another team in the hospital."

"ERU," Niall persisted. "The Deltas."

The Nurse frowned briefly, then resumed her smiling, this time with raised eyebrows. "Oh, I think I'd notice a Delta in the place," she joked. "And no, there aren't any. But you do have a friend who is waiting to visit."

Ewan was back again. This time Niall hoped he'd brought his son with him so Niall could at least see the new baby.

The nurse leaned over to add details to his chart then adjust the drip into his non-splinted arm. They'd had to operate on the bones, knitting them and holding them in place with a metal plate and it fucking hurt today.

"Although," she added thoughtfully, "the guy out there is very rugged and sexy, could easily be a Delta." She left and all of a sudden Niall had hope inside him. Ewan was a good-looking guy, as brothers go, but no one had ever described him as sexy or rugged. To be fair though, not that anyone would to Niall. Was it possible that Finn was here?

The moment they'd shared on the stairs, just before Niall lost his last connection to consciousness had been intense. But that had been three days ago now. Three. And Finn had said he loved him, but where was he now? If Finn really loved Niall, then shouldn't he be there or something?

The door opened a little, then more fully and Niall's breath hitched in his chest. Finn. His lover looked tired. No, beyond tired—exhausted. He wasn't shaved, his hair a mess of spikes, and he looked uncertain—wary to step into the room.

"Finn," Niall said with more than a little excitement in his voice.

"Hey," was all Finn said.

Niall wriggled a little to sit more upright, sickness washing over him at the pain in his arm. Finn immediately crossed to him, placing a hand on his chest. "Don't move," he said, concerned.

Niall couldn't concentrate on not moving. "Where have you been?"

Finn shrugged then glanced behind him at the closed door. "Tidying up loose ends with Svein," he explained. Niall imagined that was all he was going to get out of Finn, secrets and all that mess associated with hijackings and hostage situations. Then to Niall's amazement, Finn continued. "Svein had been tracking you," he admitted. "Had a whole wall of crazy in this place outside of Oslo. Saw a connection between the two of us."

"Why did he want to hurt you? Us?"

"Classified," Finn murmured.

"Why didn't he just shoot you on dry land if he was watching you."

This time Finn's words were louder. "Because he was fucked in the head? Who knows." He looked pale as he spoke, like the thought of Svein killing him or Niall at home hadn't even occurred to him. He scrubbed his face with his hands. "Thank fuck…"

"Finn, I love—"

Finn interrupted quickly. "We need to talk."

Niall could see where this was going. Finn was working his way up to spouting some heroic shit where he kept himself out of Niall's life in order to keep Niall safe.

"Don't do that," Niall snapped the conclusion of his internal thought process.

"What?" Finn looked confused.

"Start all that shit about how we're better apart."

Finn looked down at Niall. "What the hell are you talking about?"

"You're going to give that whole speech about how

we're better apart just so I don't get targeted by a madman intent on killing a Delta."

Niall watched as realization passed over Finn's face. Then Finn chuckled. "I wasn't going to say that at all. Hell, he wasn't after you, he was using you to get to me, different scenario."

"So, what do you want to say?" Niall couldn't help the suspicion in his voice. He was resigned to feeling thier whole relationship was a temporary thing, and had even come to terms with it in his head. But he didn't want to hear the words from Finn.

Finn moved to sit on the bed next to Niall, and somehow in that curiously graceful way he had about him for such a big guy, he was in a position to cradle Finn in his arms. Finn sunk into the strong hold and attempted to relax. Nothing could be too bad if Finn was holding him.

"My place has two rooms," Finn said. "You could move in with me and have the second bedroom as an office. I'd move in with you, but I need to be near HQ in Oslo."

Niall said nothing, the words sinking in slowly. "What?" he finally asked.

"Will you move in with me?"

"In with you?"

"Yes, in with me," Finn chuckled as he repeated the words. "I love you, Niall Faulkner, and I'm done with this self-sacrificing bullshit that has me fucking and leaving. I want forever with you. You up for it? I'm not much of a catch, my time is up with ERU in ten months or so, and I'm back in London, and you'll just be dating a cop again. And I love you—"

"Shut up and kiss me," Niall ordered.

So he did. And Niall enjoyed it so much that he even forgot he was in pain.

Well…very nearly anyway.

Epilogue

FORSETI WAS A MESS.

Three weeks on the platform and Niall was a mess as well. Not only was it one of the hardest things he had to do going back to where he'd nearly died, but he missed Finn. And that was just ridiculous. The very nature of who they were was going to mean they would spend time apart, weeks, months even, but this was all so new, and there was no way Finn would be missing him. He'd be busy, focused on the important work he did.

"You okay?" Ewan asked. He'd asked that a lot over the last three weeks, and was still asking it as the Puma landed back at base. So far Niall had managed to gloss over how he was feeling, but with his feet on solid ground, he felt like maybe now was a good time to clear the air and get his worries out there. His brother was a good listener and maybe all he needed was for Ewan to tell him everything was going to be okay, and that relationships like the kind he and Finn had, could work.

"I miss Finn."

"Yeah, I know. I miss my family as well."

Finn wasn't family. Not officially, but the way Ewan casually implied Finn was family to Niall was a nice thing. They entered the station and Niall offloaded his case and his laptop onto the first table they came to.

"How do you do it? How do you deal with time apart?" Niall immediately asked.

Ewan crossed to the coffee maker and poured two mugs, exchanging insults with the security team who had shadowed them on Forseti. Real security guys this time, not gun-toting terrorists with hidden agendas. Seemed like Niall would have to wait for his answer until caffeine was consumed. Ewan began talking as soon as he was back at the table.

"It's exciting you know. I get home, and I see Mel, and it's like we're newlyweds again. Although she's had Adam on her own and probably needs more of the baby care help than the hot monkey sex."

Niall frowned. "I don't want to hear details about what you do with Mel."

Ewan poked him. "Well I'm not a virgin you know, I'm a married man."

"I just…I'm not sure Finn will be missing me as much as I miss him, okay. He's probably out there saving the world and not giving one ounce of thought to the idiot who nearly died on his watch."

"I thought he said he loved you." Ewan looked puzzled, then his expression brightened. "I think you need to go now."

Niall picked up his coffee and sipped at it tentatively. "After debrief and coffee," he answered.

"No, I'll cover debrief. I promise you really need to

go." He nodded to indicate something behind Niall, and it made Niall turn to see Finn standing just inside the door in his heavy coat. Something inside Niall snapped into place, and in seconds he crossed to where Finn stood and pulled him into a hug.

"Glad you made it back okay," Finn said into his ear. "Want to get out of here?"

Niall made a split-second decision and returned to scoop up his laptop bag and case. "Tell them I'll debrief tomorrow," he said to Ewan. "We'll do it together. Go home to Mel." Then he turned on his heel and followed Finn outside. He wanted to kiss his lover, to hold him so close and never let him go. But he didn't, because if he started, he wouldn't stop.

"Where too?" Finn asked cautiously. He looked uncertain, his eyes wary. There was a confusion between them; they'd exchanged the words of love, and then time and careers had pulled them apart again. Maybe Finn had rethought his stance on the whole love thing?

Niall shivered. "Anywhere warm." As if to underscore that the wind blustered around them and with it came the hint of icy rain. Finn tugged Niall towards a car, and they drove in silence away from the station. They turned off the main road and pulled up outside the cluster of apartment buildings where Finn had a room. Niall had been there before once, and it was a nice enough place, although it looked like no one lived in it on a regular basis. Finn killed the engine before turning to face Niall. It seemed like he wanted to talk but didn't quite know what to say.

"Did it go okay? On Forseti?" he finally asked.

Niall nodded. "We managed to get a workable plan to salvage." He didn't want to be talking about work. He wanted to talk about him and Finn and the future. "Look, before we… go inside and do…whatever…"

"Are you okay?" Finn asked with a cautious tone.

"No." Niall didn't mean that to come out quite so forcefully and he wished he could take it back when his big-bad-Delta flinched.

"Niall—"

"I have to say something, and what I say may make you run for the hills, but I'll understand okay? I mean, I get you're this super cop who lives for the danger and keeping us all safe, and I know we connected but, when I tell you this you might not want to do that…in there." Niall failed miserably at explaining one single thing in any form of coherent fashion.

"Niall, what's wrong?"

"I missed you, okay, I thought about you every minute of the freaking day, and I need to know whether you did too."

"Whether I did what? Missed you?"

"Yeah."

"It's important to you?"

"I'm sorry."

"Jeez, don't be. Because I thought about you every minute I could. When I was on down time, when we were in Oslo, when I wasn't busy fake killing everyone on training." Finn reached out and cupped Niall's chin. "I love you. You're the other half of me, and I hope to hell that is what you need to hear because I don't have the words like you do."

"And we *can* make this work." Niall wasn't questioning, he was making a statement of fact.

"I thought it was working already. Let's finish this inside."

They made it halfway up the stairs before Finn stole a kiss, which led to more kissing, which led to them fumbling for the key when they got to the small apartment, so much so that Finn couldn't get the door open and Niall had to help him. With the door open they finally stumbled into the room, Finn pushing the door shut and pressing Niall up against the wood.

In seconds, they were undressing each other, coats, sweaters, pants, socks, boots, everything flying from them, and Niall kissed every inch that Finn uncovered on his muscled body. This was so right, this was fire and passion and Niall craved Finn with an intensity that burned in him.

Somehow, they tripped their way to the large bed and tumbled back in a tangle of arms and legs to the mattress. Niall whimpered in his throat as Finn pushed and shoved him up the bed before covering him with his body and sighing into their kisses.

"Here is where we belong."

"In bed?"

"Together." Finn answered. "So we'll be apart sometimes, and we'll miss each other, but we'll always be in love, and we'll make so many memories that you won't have space in your head for there to be any doubts."

Niall arched up into Finn and gripped hard to his lover's forearms. "Can we start now?"

Finn deepened the kisses, shifting and pulling until they were in just the right position, an arm's length from the cabinet next to the bed. Finn reached over and located lube and condoms, and Niall relaxed against the mattress, Finn would take care of him. They kissed as Finn stretched and prepared, and the kissing was endless, only interspersed with soft-spoken words of love.

"Now," Niall said, "Please."

Finn pressed inside, so slowly, all the time kissing, and groaned as he moved. Finn stopped when he was inside, and for the longest time they rocked gently until Niall couldn't handle it anymore.

"Finn…"

Finn pulled out a little, then pushed back in, staring down at Niall, complete concentration on his face. Niall loved that about him, how he took this all so seriously. Then he didn't have time for thought at all as Finn moved faster, setting a pace that robbed Niall of breath.

"So close, touch yourself," Finn pleaded. Niall gripped his hard cock and tried to establish a rhythm but it was too much, Finn pegging his prostate with a punishing accuracy, and Niall closed his eyes as his senses went into overload. He gripped his cock with one hand, Finn's bicep with another and groaned his release as he lost it between them.

"Open your eyes, Niall, please."

Niall opened his eyes, and that seemed to be what pushed Finn over the edge as with a cry of completion he was coming hard. He rested on Niall, still inside him and just a little to the side, supporting his weight on his arm.

"God, I missed you," he admitted again. "Don't ever think I don't."

Niall could never tire of hearing the words. He hadn't been expecting love with a Delta, but that is what fate had given him.

"And we'll make this work."

Finn pressed one last heated kiss before pulling out and

to one side. Laid on their backs they both looked up at the white ceiling, hands grasped tight.

"Every single day you'll know I love you," Finn promised.

Niall smiled to himself. That was all he could ask for, and it was just what he wanted.

"Every single day."

THE END

The Bodyguards Inc. Series

MM Bodyguards & Heroes Romance

FREE with your Kindle Unlimited subscription

Bodyguard To A Sex God (Bodyguards Inc, 1)

BUY NOW

Bodyguard Adam Freeman draws what everyone else thinks is the short straw at the convention for a procedural cop show - as bodyguard to TV actor Logan Brady. Or as the Internet has labelled him, Logan 'Sex God' Brady.

Logan is taking part in a convention at a London Hotel for his show 'Night Cop' and someone is threatening his life.

Adam gets more than he bargained for when his client

combines coming out of the closet with them both trying to stay alive.

A series of stories set against the backdrop of Bodyguards Inc including:

BUY NOW

Series

1. Bodyguard to a Sex God
2. The Ex Factor
3. Max and the Prince
4. Undercover Lovers
5. Love's Design
6. Kissing Alex

The Heroes Series

MM SEALS, cops, FBI, Heroes Romance

FREE with your Kindle Unlimited subscription

Heroes – Sometimes the wars you need to fight are the ones you left at home…

A Reason To Stay (Heroes 1)

When SEAL, Viktor Zavodny, left small town America for the Navy he made sure he never had a reason to return for anything other than visiting family. He wanted to see the world and fight for his country and nothing, or no one, was getting in his way. He fights hard, and plays harder, and a succession of men and women share his bed.

But a phone call from his sister has him using his thirty day down time to go home instead of enjoying his usual nights of random sex and sleep. What he finds is a mystery on the Green Mountains and the only man attempting to make sense of seemingly unrelated deaths. His childhood friend and first love… Lieutenant Aiden Coleman, Sheriff.

There were reasons Viktor left his home. Not least Aiden Coleman with his small town innocence and his dreams of forever. Now Adam and Viktor need to work together to save lives and prove there is a hero in all of us.

When it's done, if they make it out alive, can Aiden persuade

Viktor that he has a reason to stay? Maybe forever?

BUY NOW - FREE with your Kindle Unlimited subscription

Complete Series

1. A Reason To Stay
2. Last Marine Standing
3. Deacon's Law

The Texas Series

BUY NOW

FREE with your Kindle Unlimited subscription

The Heart Of Texas, Texas Book 1

Riley Hayes, the playboy of the Hayes family, is a young man who seems to have it all: money, a career he loves, and his pick of beautiful women. His father, CEO of HayesOil, passes control of the corporation to his two sons; but a stipulation is attached to Riley's portion. Concerned about Riley's lack of maturity, his father requires that Riley *'marry and stay married for one year to someone he loves'*.

Angered by the requirement, Riley seeks a means of bypassing his father's stipulation. Blackmailing Jack Campbell into marrying him "for love" suits Riley's purpose. There is no mention in his father's documents that the marriage had to be with a woman and Jack Campbell is the son of Riley Senior's arch rival. Win win.

Riley marries Jack and abruptly his entire world is turned inside out. Riley hadn't counted on the fact that Jack Campbell, quiet and unassuming rancher, is a force of nature in his own right.

This is a story of murder, deceit, the struggle for power, lust and love, the sprawling life of a rancher and the whirlwind existence of a playboy. But under and through it all, as Riley learns over the months, this is a tale about family and everything that that word means.

Complete Series

The Heart Of Texas

Texas Winter

Texas Heat

Texas Family

Texas Christmas

Texas Fall

Texas Wedding

Texas Gift

The Montana series

BUY NOW

FREE with your Kindle Unlimited subscription

Book 1 - Crooked Tree Ranch

When a cowboy, meets the guy from the city, he can't know how much things will change.

On the spur of the moment, with his life collapsing around him, Jay Sullivan answers an ad for a business manager with an expertise in marketing, on a dude ranch in Montana.

With his sister, Ashley, niece, Kirsten and nephew, Josh, in tow, he moves lock stock and barrel from New York to Montana to start a new life on Crooked Tree Ranch.

Foreman and part owner of the ranch, ex rodeo star Nathaniel 'Nate' Todd has been running the dude ranch, for five years ever since his mentor Marcus Allen became ill. His brothers convince him that he needs to get an expert in to help the business grow. He knows things have to change and but when the new guy turns up, with a troubled family in tow – he just isn't prepared for how much.

BUY NOW

Free with you Kindle Unlimited Subscription

Full series list - complete series

- Crooked Tree Ranch, Book 1
- The Rancher's Son, Book 2
- A Cowboy's Home, Book 3
- Snow in Montana, Book 4
- Second Chance Ranch, Book 5
- Montana Sky, coming soon

The Sanctuary Series

Book 1 - Guarding Morgan

MORGAN DRAKE WITNESSES A MURDER IN AN ALLEYWAY. He is the only person who can give evidence in prosecuting the cop responsible for the crime. When the FBI safe house where he's being held is compromised, he follows the instructions of his agent in charge and runs.

Nik Valentinov works for Sanctuary, a foundation that offers witness protection when FBI security is questionable.

When Morgan's handler sends him to Nik for safety, neither Morgan nor Nik could imagine that two weeks alone in a cabin in the woods could start something more. Something way more than just trying to keep Morgan alive. Something that makes their heart race more than danger. Love.

The entire completed series

- Guarding Morgan
- The Only Easy Day
- Face Value
- Still Waters
- Full Circle
- The Journal Of Sanctuary One
- Worlds Collide
- Accidental Hero
- Ghost
- By The Numbers

About RJ Scott

RJ is the author of the over one hundred published novels and discovered romance in books at a very young age. She realized that if there wasn't romance on the page, she could create it in her head, and is a lifelong writer.

She lives and works out of her home in the beautiful English countryside, spends her spare time reading, watching films, and enjoying time with her family.

The last time she had a week's break from writing she didn't like it one little bit and has yet to meet a bottle of wine she couldn't defeat.

www.rjscott.co.uk | rj@rjscott.co.uk

- facebook.com/author.rjscott
- twitter.com/Rjscott_author
- instagram.com/rjscott_author
- bookbub.com/authors/rj-scott
- pinterest.com/rjscottauthor